# Introduction to Love and Self

# INTRODUCTION TO LOVE AND SELF

A Romantic Novel

*Joan Vassar*

iUniverse, Inc.
New York Lincoln Shanghai

**Introduction to Love and Self**
**A Romantic Novel**



iUniverse books may be ordered through booksellers or by contacting:

iUniverse
2021 Pine Lake Road, Suite 100
Lincoln, NE 68512
www.iuniverse.com
1-800-Authors (1-800-288-4677)



ISBN-13: 978-0-595-39338-1 (pbk)
ISBN-13: 978-0-595-83735-9 (ebk)
ISBN-10: 0-595-39338-1 (pbk)
ISBN-10: 0-595-83735-2 (ebk)

Printed in the United States of America

# CHAPTER 1

Queens, New York
1982

The little boy stood in the tiny bathroom of the small, dingy studio apartment listening to the grunts and groans coming from the other room. He had long since gotten use to the sound of his mother and her customers. He remembered rushing in to save her only to find her bent over, bracing herself while some man he didn't know stood behind her sweating. She had yelled for him to get back in the bathroom, the man never breaking his stride had reached what Seven now understood to be his peak. The man smiled at him while reaching for the back of his mother's dress to wipe off.

"You're only getting half of the pay for this," the man said to his mother.

"He don't know no better. You still finished, I need that money," his mother said. Seven stood there frozen for what seemed an eternity before turning and running back into the bathroom.

As time went on, he came to understand the nature of his mother's business, and how the bills were paid on the one room they called home. They had come to stay in Corona after his mother's family had turned their backs on them. That was when his mother had taken to selling ass to make ends meet. In the neighborhood where they lived, the kids would tease him, saying, "Ain't your mama a ho?" causing his young temper to flare. Seven had been known as the kind of kid that hit first (and also second), never saying a word. What was there to justify his mother was "Betty the Ho"? Many a day, other mothers would come to the door with their children in tow, sporting the wounds of a fresh ass-whipping saying, "Look what your wild-ass child has done."

Betty had taken plenty of men to her bed to keep clothes on her child's back and a roof over his head. She never took to having a pimp because she could manage her own damn money. With a cigarette hanging out the corner of her mouth, Betty stood in the doorway eyeing the other woman standing in front of her, holding her child by the upper arm.

"Is there something I could help you with?" Betty would ask calmly, knowing this bitch was here because she thought her man was paying for ass, which he was. It was none of her business. Feeding her kid, now that *was* her business.

"I said, look what your kid did."

"Bitch, if you don't get away from my door with this bullshit, I'll cut you where you stand."

The other mother paled and took a step back, never letting go of her child. Turning and walking toward the staircase, she said under her breath, "Fucking ho."

Betty watched her go and sighed. The boy was always in some shit, she thought. She wasn't a good mother, and she knew it. She barely talked to him. Shit, what was there to say? He could see how they were living. She didn't blame him, and she wasn't angry; she just figured that the less she said, the less chance she had of poisoning him. She loved him—she was sure of that. That was why she called him "Seven"—she knew he would be lucky someday. Life was balanced in Betty's way of thinking. If his childhood was ruined by virtue of being born to her, then in manhood he would be a success.

There was a knock at the door, back to work. "Boy, take your ass downstairs in front of the building till I call you." Betty opened the door. Seven passed a man coming in as he went out. Betty came to the door with a cigarette in her mouth. She was a dark-skinned woman with almond-shaped eyes and a round, plump nose. Her lips were sensual, with a permanent pout that added to her sexuality, but in truth, the shape of her mouth spoke of her unhappiness. She had long black hair that she kept permed and curled. And even when she made no attempt to comb her hair, it added a deep appeal to her face. Dressed in a cheap satin robe, Betty stood tall, thin and very leggy. This ensured a steady stream of loyal customers, but there was harshness about her that bespoke of her occupation and told of an innocence that had long since gone.

At ten, Seven had seen more than his share of life's harsh realities. He was big for his age, and his mother had told him that it made the customers uneasy to have him in the bathroom while they conducted business. As he stood in front of the building on 104$^{th}$ Street in Corona, he watched the people as they passed. As he watched some of the women, who appeared to be coming from work, he wondered why his mother had chosen this instead of going to work like other people. He wanted to be normal, and he wanted not to be teased about what his mother did to pay the bills. Seven wanted a different life.

They lived across from the green and white cathedral and next to Rosenberg's funeral home. He thought about the condition of the buildings, which stood like sentinels on either side of the street. Rosenberg's was the handsomest building on the block. The funeral home was attached to the building he lived in, and when services were held, he could see the people coming and going from the one window they had. He identified with the mourners, but not because of the death, which would have been the obvious reason. Rather, Seven understood that a certain amount of pain was public. Why else would the view from the only window they had be a funeral home? It was the same in his life: his mom was a ho, and those around him witnessed his pain.

His was a brown brick building with a long cream-colored hallway and staircases on either side of the hall. Sometimes he would go to the opposite end of the corridor and sit on the stairs to wait for her guest to leave, especially when it was cold outside. Sometimes he would dream his father would come and save them. And other times he couldn't wait to grow up so he could stop being at other people's mercy.

As for his father, Betty never mentioned him, so he never asked. It had been just the two of them for as long as he could remember. Betty was all he had, and sometimes he worried that if something happened to her, he would be alone. While he loved Betty, she rarely talked, so he never saw her the way other children saw their mothers. He didn't talk much either. Rather, he tried to blend in with the walls and not make trouble or draw attention to himself so that her customers wouldn't get angry causing her to get angry. Often he failed, finding himself in fights with other children and bringing the attention he didn't want. Most upsetting was that when he looked at other children, it was painfully evident that his life was different. He understood this was the ghetto, but even though other children's living situations were not the greatest, they were still so much better than his.

Their studio had blue carpet and one sliding glass window. The kitchen and the living room occupied the same space. The bathroom was there as soon as you walked in the front door, because there was simply no other place for it. They lived on top of each other—not just he and Betty, but everyone in the area. The streets were dirty, and they could hear the noise from the overhead train day and night all the way from Junction Boulevard.

He had made some promises to himself that he intended to keep. First, he would find the right space to fill on the planet, and he would fill it to the best of his ability. Second, he would be safe, and that safety would never depend on another's whims. Third, he would be strong. And fourth, he would make money—and lots of it.

❧ ❧ ❧

Down the hall was Lisa, who lived with her mother and father. Her father was a drunk, mean to everyone who crossed his path, and since Lisa and her mother lived with him, they were constantly crossing his path. He beat them regularly, and it was because of one of those beatings that Seven noticed her. She was eight years old, with big brown eyes spaced evenly in her face. She had a little nose, perfectly shaped lips, and rich cocoa brown skin. Her dark brown hair was parted down the middle and placed in two very neat pigtails that hung down her back. Lisa was a beautiful child.

Seven had been sitting on that side of the hall when he heard her crying and pleading, "Daddy, please, you're hurting me."

"Look what you made me do, you little bitch. Just look at what you made your father do," a deep voice said in response to her pleas.

She had screamed to the top of her lungs—until it had abruptly stopped. Seven remembered thinking that she had died and was more than relieved when he saw her a few days later being walked to school by her mother. Her eye was black, and she wore a sling around one arm, but she was alive.

Lisa often wondered why her father hated her so much. Her mother couldn't have liked her much either, since she never tried to help her. Often it seemed as though her mother directed his wrath her way to keep it from herself.

"Who the fuck drank my soda?" her father asked one day when he got home from work.

"It must have been Lisa," her mother said. "I haven't eaten all day."

Lisa had been at school all day, and although she never went into the fridge to get anything, she didn't deny it. It would have only make the beating worse. When she looked at her mother, her mother looked away, not meeting Lisa's eyes. At eight, she understood dishonesty and betrayal. They seemed to be her regular companions when dealing with her mother.

"Take off your clothes," her father said. "You'll learn not to touch my shit."

When her mother looked like she might step in, her father warned her that if she opened her mouth, she would take the ass kicking instead. Lisa undressed; her body was thin and scarred from past encounters with her father. As she stood waiting to take her punishment, her mother grabbed her coat and left.

"Get your ass in the room," her father was yelling, but once she got her clothes off, she couldn't move. He beat her where she stood. The first beating was for not going into the room to be beat. The second was for drinking his soda.

The family lived on the second floor in a one-bedroom apartment. When you entered the apartment, the bathroom was to your left, and farther into the apartment was a living room and a very small rectangular kitchen. The bedroom was in the back.

Lisa slept in the living room on a pull-out couch. The family ate dinner in the living room and watched whatever her father wanted to watch on the black-and-white TV. Her mother tried to cook meals that would please Lisa's father, but her father would always find something wrong with them. Lisa was a very thin child, as dinner was always a game of roulette: even if he liked dinner, the stress of waiting to see if he did caused her to pick at her food.

They had come to live in Corona to be near the warehouse up the street, where her father worked. The only time that Lisa moved freely about the house was when he wasn't there, but when he was home, she learned to blend in and become part of the furniture, being quiet as a mouse. Sometimes he would look at her as if he had forgotten she lived there. It was during those times that her life became hell.

One day, when her mother was ushering her to school, they encountered Seven in the lobby, heading to school himself. He smiled at her and she smiled back. Her mother, in her haste, never noticed, dragging her up the block. Lisa kept looking back at him over her shoulder until they turned the corner. Later that day, when school was out, Seven was on his way home when he found Lisa in the schoolyard crying. Her mother had not come for her, and she did not know her way home.

"I'm Seven. What's the matter?"

She stopped crying and looked at him. "Seven? Ain't that a number?"

"Yeah, I guess my mother liked the number." It was the first time that he didn't feel funny when someone questioned his name.

"You want to walk home with me? I know the way."

"Don't you live in the hall?"

Seven stiffened but said nothing. If she wanted to walk home with him, then she could. If not, that was okay too. She reached out for his hand. "You know how to cross the street, too?"

"Of course I do. I do it every day."

She laughed.

She chatted all the way home, about her dolls and school and whatever else came to her mind, holding his hand whenever they came to a street. As they approached the building from the back, Lisa looked up at the window, causing Seven to do the same. There were no curtains in the windows, and the place looked bare. Lisa frowned but kept following him around to the front of the building and into the lobby.

They climbed the stairs at his end of the hall and he stood in front of his door while she continued down the hall to hers. Lisa wondered if her mother would be mad because she hadn't waited for her. When she raised her hand to knock on the door, she noticed it was open. She pushed the door open farther and walked in. At first, she didn't understand what she was looking at. All their furniture and belongings were gone. Seven, seeing the door open, walked down the hall to see what was going on. When he reached the apartment and looked in, he immediately understood what he was seeing.

"Why don't you come home with me?"

"Where is my mommy?"

"You better come home with me. I think Betty can find out what happened."

Her eyes watered up as they backed out of the apartment. She followed him down the hall to his house and waited as he knocked on the door. There was no answer, but he could hear movement, which meant he needed to sit down in front of the door and wait. Dropping his knapsack, that's what he did. Most of Betty's customers didn't take long. Watching him, Lisa did the same. She didn't look good, and Seven felt she was beginning to understand what was happening.

"Are you hungry?" he asked.

She shook her head no. He couldn't think of anything else to ask, so he remained quiet. He tried not to think about her situation, as it made him think of Betty doing that to him. While he was in thought, his door opened and a man came out. He never noticed the two children sitting beside the front door.

"What have we got here?" she asked as both the children looked at her.

"This is Lisa," he said, looking his mother in the eye. "She lives down the hall and goes to my school. Her mother didn't meet her today, so she walked home with me."

"Well, Lisa, why haven't you gone home then?" Betty asked, looking at the girl.

"You better have a look, Ma," he said, staring hard at her.

Betty was taken aback, because he never called her "Ma." She could have demanded that he show her respect and address her as Ma, but she preferred no phoniness between them. The fact that he was calling her Ma meant that he needed her help. Betty left their door cracked and followed the children down the hall. When they reached Lisa's door, she stepped around them and into the apartment. The apartment was bare. She turned and looked at her son, who was still maintaining eye contact with her. His face showed no expression, but she knew that she needed to handle this correctly—for his sake as well as the little girl's.

"Do you know my mommy?" Lisa whispered, tears brimming in her eyes.

"Well," Betty said trying to think of the appropriate way to handle this situation. "No, I don't know your mother."

"Do you know my father?" Lisa asked, hopefully, even though she really didn't care about him. She found it hard to ask the question, but she did: "Has my mother gone off and left me?"

Betty believed in being straight with a person even if that person was a kid. She would start by asking some questions. "Did you know that your mom and dad were moving? Did they say anything to you?"

"No," the little girl said.

Betty looked into her son's face and saw that it was serious; he was searching her eyes for the answer to make things right. "Why don't you two go to the house and let me look around in here. Seven, see if Lisa would like a snack."

Seven just looked at Lisa. Then he took her hand, and they went back to Betty's apartment.

When the kids left, she went into the bedroom and found clothes thrown haphazardly on the floor. They were girls' clothes. "Shit," Betty said out loud. There was no sense going back to the school to wait for them. She thought that maybe they were running late to pick the child up and that Seven had brought her home. But her clothes were the only things they had left behind. Some things just explain themselves.

She picked up what she could manage and headed for the door. Reaching for the knob, she spied a bag of trash. There was nothing but paper in it to be tossed out. While searching the trash, she came across an address book at the bottom of the bag. The pages were falling out, but the numbers were still legible. She would go through this tonight while they slept. There was a payphone on the corner; she could make use of. This she thought was better than calling the Bureau of Child Welfare.

When she got back to her apartment, Lisa was sitting in a kitchen chair staring aimlessly out the window. Betty set the clothes on the floor by the door. Seven smiled at Betty, and she was reminded of how rarely he smiled, but, hell, she didn't smile much either. Her son was so serious that he looked like a little man instead of a child. People who saw them thought that Seven looked like her, but he didn't. He was very dark skinned with huge dark brown eyes, and a sharp nose that gave his face character. She kept his hair cut very low, and although she knew he hated it, he never complained. It was what she could afford. She knew he would be handsome like his father, but in his disposition, he would be nothing like Clarence. Tonight she would have no customers—and maybe she wouldn't for the next few days until she could get this matter settled. She couldn't afford it, though; it was hard enough paying their way, and now she had another child to worry about.

"They're not coming back, are they?" Lisa asked.

"No, sweetie, it doesn't look like it. Do you have other family here or not too far away?" Betty asked.

"I have some family, but I'm not sure where they are because my father never liked company. We never visited, and no one ever visited us, although one time we went to dinner at my grandma's house. She was very nice to me, and so was the rest of my family that was there, but they didn't seem to like my mom and dad."

*That's hopeful*, Betty thought. *Things are going to turn out just fine*. The child was better off without them. She herself wasn't shit as a mother, but she could never just walk out and leave her child. Maybe she would get out of the business and find a better way to live so that she could stop hurting him too.

"They were mean to me. I was afraid of them. What's going to happen to me now?"

"We don't have to think about it right now. We can eat and get some sleep and deal with this tomorrow. I have one question, though—what are your mom and dad's names?"

"My mommy's name is Rita Harris, and my dad is Phillip Harris."

Seven and Lisa watched TV until they fell asleep. As soon as they did, Betty went out to the payphone and began making calls. The first call was to a Jenny Walker. The phone rang twice, and just as Betty saw her watch turn to 9:45 P.M., someone answered.

"Hello?"

"Hello, may I speak to Jenny Walker, please?"

"This is she. Who is calling?"

"My name is Betty Thomas, and I live in Corona. I believe I live down the hall from your Rita and your Lisa."

"Yes, how can I help you? Has something happened to them?"

"Well, there is no nice way to say this, so I'll get to the point. My son goes to school with Lisa, and he brought her home with him today. When we tried to locate her mom and dad, they seemed to have moved away and left the child here on her own. I found a phonebook in the apartment, and your number was the first that I called. I thought that would be better than turning the child over to BCW. She is well. She's upstairs in my apartment sleeping. She's a little heartbroken, but again she's well."

There was silence on the other end. "Are you still there?"

"Yes, Mrs. Thomas, I am. I just don't know what to say. Are you sure?"

"Yes, Mrs. Walker. I believe I am correct. I went to the house. They took everything except the little girl's clothing, and Lisa was not aware that they were moving."

"I believed you the first time you said it. It's just one of those things that you want to be wrong at. My husband and I can come later to pick her up."

"That won't be necessary. She is sleeping now. You can come in the morning. She is no trouble. I'm just relieved to have found you so that the child can be with family."

"Thank you. I am the second oldest of ten children, and Rita is number eight. We are a very close family, but Rita was always just different. This will hurt our mother, but she will rejoice knowing that her granddaughter is safe. How can I get to your home, Mrs. Thomas?"

Betty was happy that the matter was resolved and she gave the woman directions to her home. She was glad that they lived in Queens somewhere and that they didn't have to travel far to pick up the child. But she wondered, if Lisa's mother had family that wanted to help her, why leave the child like this?

Betty remembered living with her mother's sister, and how her uncle would make passes at her. She had thought him harmless, until the day he came home early from work and found her getting out of the shower. He threatened to tell her aunt that she wanted him. Her aunt was a homely, insecure woman who believed everything he told her. He was very handsome—tall, jet black skin without a blemish, and straight white teeth.

Betty told him that she would not be blackmailed and that she would leave. She pushed past him in the bathroom doorway. She would leave as soon as she got dressed and start making her own way. She didn't make it. He took her virginity that day and left her with Seven. Her family blamed her for seducing her uncle and forgave him, and she had been on her own ever since.

As Betty reentered the lobby, she saw some of her customers. "Not tonight, boys. Put your dicks up," she told them. Back in her apartment, she found the children asleep and buckled down with them.

The sunlight was peeking through the window when she heard whispering. Opening her eyes, she found the kids sitting on the couch eating cereal. She smiled at them, and then she sat up and headed for the bathroom. When she returned to the living room, they both looked up with eyes full of hope.

Seven's concern for his friend made him look several years older. Lisa looked anxious and confused, as if she didn't know what to expect. Betty jumped right in, explaining to the children what she'd learned.

"Yesterday, Lisa, when I was at your house, I found an address book. After the two of you went to sleep last night, I went downstairs to a payphone and made some calls."

"You found my mother?" Lisa asked.

"No, sweetie, I didn't. But I found your grandma and your aunts, uncles, and cousins. They are coming to get you today." Lisa looked like she was going to cry, so Betty hurried on to say, "They're worried about you and they want you with them while they look for your mother."

"I want to stay with Seven," she said.

Seven's expression went blank, but he didn't respond. Betty wondered if she was handling things right. "Sweetie, Seven and I live in this little place, and as much as we would like to keep you, we don't have enough money, and we really don't have any room. Going with your auntie and uncle is the best thing for you." Seeing that Betty was not going to change her mind, Lisa gave in and said no more.

Seven watched the exchange and kept his face expressionless. He was afraid, plain and simple. Afraid that his mother might think leaving him behind would be easier for her too. Afraid that since she handled this situation so quickly, she might decide to give him away just as quickly. He was afraid to speak, thinking his fear might show or, worse yet, he might cry. Showing weakness could cause other problems.

"You guys take turns using the bathroom. Get cleaned up and then we will wait downstairs for your auntie," Betty said just as he got his emotions under control.

The morning was uneventful and quiet as they got ready for Lisa's aunt and uncle. Betty collected Lisa's belongings, and the three of them went downstairs to wait. It wasn't long before they pulled up and got out of the car. Betty was relieved to find that they were genuinely happy to see her. She had already made up her mind that if they seemed the tiniest bit strange, she wouldn't let her go with them.

Lisa smiled at them, but she remained apprehensive, until her aunt pulled from the back seat of the green Volkswagen Beetle a brand-new black doll with curly hair.

"Hi, I'm Betty, and this is my son, Seven," Betty said, holding out her hand to shake Jenny's.

"I'm Jenny, and this is my husband, James," she said, smiling at Betty.

Everyone shook hands and made the proper introductions, and Betty thought to invite them upstairs, but her place was so small that she decided against it. She never had company because there was just nowhere to put one's personal belongings, and the small confines of her apartment made her feel exposed. Its size spoke volumes about her finances, and the fact that she shared it with a child betrayed that she had no man or father for her child. No phone meant no one called or cared about her or her child.

"Did you find the place okay?" Betty asked, making small talk.

"Yes…yes we did."

Smiling, Betty reached down and handed Jenny two garbage bags full of clothes. "This is what I could salvage of Lisa's belongings."

"Thank you," Jenny said, reaching for the bag. Her husband came alive then, taking the bags and placing them in the trunk.

Lisa turned to Seven and gave him a big hug. Seven hugged her back. She then turned back toward the car, climbed into the back seat, and her uncle shut the door. Jenny turned to Betty and said, "Thank you. You can't begin to know how much this means to us. We're headed to my mother's house right now. I think Lisa will be staying with my mother or me, although several have offered their home to her. You have my number. You will keep in touch, won't you? If ever you need anything, you will let us know?"

"Yes," Betty said. "I will keep in touch."

Jenny got into the car and her husband closed the door behind her. Betty and Seven stepped back from the curb and waved as Lisa waved back from the rear window. She waved until they were out of sight.

They would not keep in touch; Betty knew it when she had said it. It was back to the harsh reality of their life, and for the first time she considered the other options that might be available. Tomorrow she would get the paper and see what was in the classifieds.

Seven thought Lisa's aunt and uncle were nice people. When she hugged him, he thought he would embarrass himself, by crying. Why didn't they have nice family like that who cared if they had food and were well? Where was his father, and why had he not come to save them? Did he care? Did he love Betty? Would he care if Betty gave him away? Would Betty leave him as Lisa's mother and father had left her? If she did, who would he get in touch with? He really knew nothing about his own family.

Seven stopped at the lobby door, when his mother would have opened it. He pinned her with his eyes. She could see his fear and confusion, but he did his best to hide it from her and the world. Then he asked the question weighing most heavily on his ten-year-old mind and heart.

"Will you leave me too, Ma?"

# CHAPTER 2

Roosevelt Island
2000

Seven had a conference call at 9:30 in the morning. Even though he conducted business from his home office, he still dressed as if he were leaving the house. His housekeeper/secretary reported to work at 8:00 A.M. to ensure his day ran smoothly. It was now 7:15, and Mary would be showing up soon. He had just enough time to get in a run on the treadmill.

His condo was located on Roosevelt Island overlooking the East River. The location was ideal for two reasons: First, he could take the tram over the river and be in Manhattan in a matter of minutes. Second, Roosevelt Island stood behind Queens Bridge and Ravenswood projects, keeping him connected with the life in which he grew up. Although Seven was rich, he couldn't shake his humble beginnings, and the truth was he didn't want to.

The condo was on the top floor of the building. There was a spacious kitchen as soon as you walked in the front door. Across from the kitchen was an oversized walk-in closest. Farther in was a sunken living room with almond-colored leather furniture, and to the right was a formal dining room. The table was made of one-inch thick mahogany with a matching china cabinet. On the left, there was a long hall lined with doors on either side, leading to smaller bedrooms and a bathroom. At the end of the hall were two French doors that opened to the master suite. The king-size bed was round and built on a platform, the furniture carved from heavy oak and accentuated with lots of earth tones that added masculinity to the décor. In the bathroom was a garden tub and separate shower, the fixtures an elegant gun-metal gray. The five-bedroom condo, which overlooked the East River and the New York City skyline from a large terrace, was home for him. It was also where he conducted most of his day-to-day business.

The one eyesore was his treadmill, which stood just before the terrace doors. He opened them no matter what the weather was like and ran for miles, thinking and plotting his next business deal. He had an eye for a good deal, which had made him successful. He was an equal-opportunity investor—he did it all. He invested in real estate, vintage cars, casinos, malls, restaurants, and anything else that grabbed him. Seven recognized a good deal when he heard one. He had been known to set up not-so-by-chance meetings to get what he wanted, and he had written contracts on bar napkins and brown paper bags. Once he had raced to Atlanta and purchased a piece of property that a major chain was interested in, flown back to New York that night, and sold the same property to the company at double the profit, making a fortune.

The conference call was from some foreign diplomat who was trying to find storage space to park his vintage cars until they could be shipped back to his country. Seven had such a space, filled with cars sure to make the diplomat's head spin. He called the garage attendant with a list of all the cars he wanted strategically placed when his prospective pigeon flew in. That way, he would make money on the storage deal and likely unload one or two of his own vintage cars in the process.

Seven was jaded where women were concerned. He respected them and was a gentleman in every sense of the word, but settling down was not for him. He knew a number of women who wanted a long-lasting connection with him, but he just couldn't do it. He was careful not to mislead them, though—he said what he meant and meant what he said. If he told a woman that he was just interested in her company and he could see that she was hearing something else, he would end the relationship. He wanted someone who enjoyed the arrangement as much as he did. Women who applied pressure and gave ultimatums were sent on their way—with a nice parting gift.

The treadmill registered five miles, and the clock on the wall said 7:58 A.M. The doorbell rang. It was Mary. Seven opened the door.

"Hello beautiful," he said. Mary Humphries was a retired schoolteacher who earned extra money working for Seven three days a week. She cleaned, cooked, and took care of his laundry. She also answered the phone, took messages, and scheduled his appointments. Mary was short and plump, the motherly type. She had long gray hair that was curled nicely, the kind that was so pretty you didn't mind turning gray if you could do it like Mary. She was light skinned, with warm eyes and an even warmer heart. She worried about his well-being constantly. Seven loved her, and she knew it.

"Just finished running, did you?" Mary said, smiling at him. "I worry that you'll waste away to nothing."

Seven laughed at that. At six foot three inches and 225 lbs, he didn't think he needed to worry about that.

"Trying to stay fit is all," he said.

"What's on the agenda for today?"

❧ ❧ ❧

Lisa was headed to work at the Plaza Hotel. She had been working there for six months and felt lucky to get the front desk job. She enjoyed her work, which gave her the chance to meet interesting people. She knew it was a dead end career-wise, but mindless work was what she needed right now, especially since her grandmother's death. Her grandmother had taken her in when she was eight and raised her, after Rita and Philip had suddenly moved away and left her with a neighbor. She never saw her parents again.

Her grandmother had opened her home and her heart to the troubled little girl. She had nurtured her, and Lisa had returned her love. Her aunts and uncles were kind, and their children were just as kind. They were all close and made Lisa feel like one of the gang. Her grandmother, however, had taken ill about three years ago, suffering from kidney failure and a host of other ailments that would plague a woman in her eighties.

She had been Lisa's best friend, and Lisa had decided to take care of her until the end. This had been more for Lisa's benefit than her grandmother's, but it caused Lisa to put her life on hold nonetheless.

"This isn't something a twenty-three-year-old should be doing," her grandmother would say. "I'm going as fast as I can. It's not good when old folks suck the life out the young."

Lisa would ignore her and say, "There is no place I'd rather be."

"How would you know if you ain't gone nowhere?"

Although it had been a trying time, when her grandmother passed, she went feeling loved and blessed, surrounded by the family God had given her. Her grandmother's one regret was not seeing Rita, Lisa's mother, again before dying.

These days, Lisa just wanted to meet people and have new experiences. She had promised her grandmother that she would move on with her life. "Three years of caring for me should have prepared you for what is coming. Shed a few tears and move on with life and love," her grandmother had said. Lisa had kept her promise, and gotten right back into the swing of life. She smiled all the time and genuinely enjoyed people.

Her grandmother had left her the house, and her aunts and uncle didn't begrudge her for it. They had grown up there, and their children had spent a lot of time there, but Lisa had sacrificed for their mother, and they were pleased that she wanted the house. They all had homes in the area, and Lisa's uncles stopped by regularly to let the neighbors know that she was not alone. In all, her life was good—considering how it had started.

She made it to work on time and was just stepping behind the counter when her manager Elise, greeted her with a smile. "I recommended that you take care of the business conference scheduled for next Thursday. It's overtime. Are you interested?"

"What will I have to do? I don't want to mess things up," she asked.

"Just see that they're not disturbed and make certain everyone knows where to go. We'll be doing the catering, so all you need to do is keep the food and refreshments coming. The host of the conference will pay you at the end of the night, and then send them on their way."

"I can do that."

"My manager agreed that sending you was a good idea. You are such a people person," Elise said, smiling and picking imaginary lint off her suit jacket.

"I'll be ready," Lisa said, "and I won't let you down."

Lisa handled everything with gusto. Her great attitude seemed to be contagious, and anyone that she met ended up thinking positively too. Still, life for Lisa was routine. She went to work and came home every night, going out when only she was invited to a card game at her cousin's house. The card game, it seemed, was the highlight of her month. Every other night, she came home from work and watched TV until she fell asleep in the living room. Later she would climb the stairs to her bedroom, get ready for work, and start all over. Life was uneventful, but she wanted it that way. When her cousin would ask her about dating, she would cringe unconsciously. Men and dating were the furthest issues from her mind, and she knew why.

Phillip Harris had stunted her growth when it came to relationships and men. Her relationship with her father gave her pause when it came to dealing with the opposite sex. He had been so vicious and brutal that her reality was skewed where men were concerned. She understood that not all men were like her father, yet she shied away from any situation that possessed the possibility of a romantic connection. She didn't need the hassle or the uncertainty. She had a job that she liked and a family that she loved. What more could she want?

❧ ❧ ❧

The sun was just going down as Seven was crossing the Fifty-ninth Street bridge. He was ready for an evening on the town. He and the lovely Sahar were headed to City Island and for a night of dancing at one of Manhattan's trendier clubs. From there, it was any man's game, he thought, smiling. He liked her company; she was so into herself that she had no time to put demands on him. He bought her nice things, and that's where their relationship ended.

As they were being seated, he realized that she had not stopped talking since he picked her up at her apartment. She talked about her hair appointment, her nail appointment, the new dress she was wearing, and the trouble she had gone through to find the proper shoes. Sahar was a small beautiful honey-skinned woman. She had a small waist, orange-sized breasts, and nice shapely legs. She dressed impeccably, and never was a hair out of place. When they first started spending time together, all he could think about was how beautiful she was.

She was so petite and feminine that she made the beast inside him roar with pure male satisfaction. That feeling died a quick death when he finally got what he wanted, a mindless companion that didn't want to know what he was thinking or to talk about her feelings. He wanted to tell her about his success today on the conference call, pat himself on the back about how shrewd he had been, but he knew she would not listen. What was wrong with him? This was what he wanted?

*I must be getting old.*

What was he looking for?

*Hell no, I'm not getting old. I just need to get rid of her.*

She was sucking the life right out of him, he realized. They would have a great time tonight, and in a few days he would send her a nice parting gift. The thought made him feel better when he finally turned his mind back to her and tuned back in to her constant chatter. He smiled.

"What's so funny?" she asked. "You don't like the color of my dress?"

Lisa had been invited to a card game at her cousin Kim's house. Whenever she went, they played spades and had the best time fighting, talking shit, and eating hot wings. During the action, someone always reneged, and the team who made the mistake always tried to loud-talk the other team into thinking that they had read the cards wrong. It was usually a women's night out.

Lisa showed up in a pair of jeans and a sweatshirt with two six-packs of 7 Up. Kim opened the door. "Hey, sweetie, glad you came."

"I'm here ready to get my revenge for last month," Lisa said laughing.

"The girls are here. Aunt Ruth said that she came to show us youngsters what card playing is all about."

"Why did you invite that card shark? We're done for."

Kim laughed and put her arm around her. She loved Lisa and wanted to see her get out more. Inviting her was her way of keeping her promise to her grandmother; it was her job to make sure that Lisa got out. She smiled at the thought. Her grandmother probably had someone else in place to make sure that she was making sure that Lisa was getting out. She missed her grandmother. They didn't come like that anymore.

"Who you telling? She already got a cigarette in her mouth crooked biting the butt, while the smoke burns that left eye. Talking about who her first two victims are gonna be. She brought Hattie from church with her to be her partner."

"That's our ass," Lisa said, and she burst out laughing.

Following Kim into the kitchen, she was spied by her auntie. "Come here, girl," Aunt Ruth said. "You know, I'm 'bout to whoop your ass in some cards."

Business had been good that week. Seven had twenty acres of property in Dallas, Georgia, with just a one-room shack on it. A developer wanted to purchase the property to build a subdivision on it, and Seven had flown to Atlanta to look at the plans, wanting to see what type of homes the builder had in mind and how many he planned to build before deciding on a sale price. After reviewing the plans, instead of selling the land, Seven decided to lease the property for one hundred years. It would be a sweet deal, he thought to himself. The developer, feeling outmatched, decided to think about it before closing the deal.

He had just touched down at LaGuardia when his cell phone rang. It was Mary, notifying him of his schedule for the day. He had planned to check on a few of his investments.

"Thanks, Mary, I'm on it. Don't bother to cook for me tonight. I have a prior engagement."

"You got it. I'll finish cleaning up and schedule your appointments for tomorrow. I'm going to see my daughter and grandchildren. If you need me, call me."

"I will, beautiful."

Seven had two friends, Gary and Sean, and they were close with their families. During the holidays, he was always invited to someone's home, but he usually felt they were inviting him simply because he had nowhere else to go. In order not to feel like an intruder, he would find some woman that didn't mind taking a cruise or something during the holidays, and then he was off. To Gary and Sean, this always seemed adventurous. It was the highlight of the holidays to find out who he had taken and what they had done. Gary and Sean were his two best friends from college; the three had known one another since their freshmen year. Both were married now, and each had two children.

Seven was lonely from time to time, refusing to look past his next date. Even when his mind would venture in that direction, he would chalk it up to the fact that all these years later it was still just him and Betty. She never talked about her family or his father, and Seven didn't pry. He didn't ask questions, because he felt that it made him look weak. She was always polite when he came by to see her, but it bothered him that she always seemed relieved to see him go.

He stopped by once a month to the home he purchased for her in Laurelton. After he made his first lucrative deal, he turned his mind back to Corona, where Betty still lived in the studio. All through college, he would call and check on her. She complained when he had a phone put in, but he paid for it. During the holidays, he never went home. The place was too small, and growing into a man made it even smaller.

He upset her once again when he told her that he had bought her a house. She didn't want the house and refused to move. He smiled as she ranted and raved because he had never heard her talk so much. He gave her a week to pack, and when he returned she had done nothing. While he wanted to respect her wishes, she had gotten older, and the neighborhood was a little too rough for a woman who lived alone and received few visitors.

He contacted the rental office and bought her out of her lease. He then came over with moving men, and they had her little place packed up within two hours. After helping her with her coat and leading her to his car, Seven drove her to the red-brick house just off Francis Lewis Blvd. The lawn was cut to perfection and the concrete stairs cut right through the grass, making a long walkway to the front door. Upon entry, there were stairs to the left and a living room to the right. Straight ahead was the kitchen, and to the back were two bedrooms and a bathroom. The dining room could be accessed through the living room, and the two rooms connected in a way that made the house seem very airy and spacious. Upstairs there were two more bedrooms and another bathroom. The carpet was brown, and the living room set was beige. The master suite boasted a canopy bed. He hadn't filled the whole house, wanting to give her something to do.

She turned on him in the bedroom. "What am I supposed to do with all this space?"

"Live in it," he said. "Live in it."

He turned and left that day feeling sad that she could not see that he cared for her. This confirmed to him yet again that one should keep one's feeling to oneself. People, he thought, didn't want to be burdened with feelings.

He did not come back for a full month, and when he did it was to see if she was still there. The weather was mild that day, and he found her sitting in the backyard on a very nice patio set sipping iced tea and reading. He stood there at the gate watching her with her head down engrossed in her book. He really looked at her: His mother was still young, although she looked slightly older than her fifty years. Her hair was streaked with gray and she dressed like an old woman. She kept her own company, which was nothing new. She was wearing a boring gray dress with a knit belt, sensible black shoes, and a shawl over her shoulders. While he was taking the time to study her, a little white dog appeared at her feet and started barking. She looked up, noticed him, and smiled. It was a first.

"I thought you weren't coming back," she said.

"I see that you planted some flowers," he said, evading the statement. "Got a new roommate, do you?"

"I'm here by myself. Butch is good company. Were you busy or just mad at me?" she asked smiling.

"I was mad at you."

Betty made no comment. He *had* been angry, thinking she didn't want him around. She did, though, and she was very proud of the man he had become. She just wanted him to move on with his life. She knew that he was successful. He just needed to let go of the past—and his prostitute mother—and build a new family and life for himself. He wouldn't do it, though, and she didn't know how to make him. When she looked at him, she saw the faces of all the men that he had seen, and this embarrassed her, making it hard to look him in the eye.

"I put money in the account for you. I see that you didn't use it."

"Boy, are you checking my account?" she asked, indignant.

"Yes, I am. I put money into the same account for you that you did for me when I was in college."

"You don't owe me," she said.

"I want to help, Betty."

"I cooked," she said, changing the subject.

"You can't cook, and we both know it. Let's get some pizza."

# CHAPTER 3

*I must be getting old.*

Seven seemed to be thinking about feelings a lot more lately, and about his past. Whenever he would stop by to see his mother, these thoughts would surface. They seemed to do it more and more the older he got. The women he dated would have a field day with this shit. How many times had he just finished having sex, still wet from the juices of it, and heard the woman he was with ask, "What are you thinking?"

"Nothing," he would respond, and it was true. Now he was thinking shit all the time.

It was late afternoon as Seven headed to his mother's house, with the business of the day behind him. He wanted to check on her and make sure everything was all right. He kept biscuits in the glove compartment for Butch, so the dog seemed to love him to the person that didn't look too deeply, but really he just knew Seven had something for him. When Seven pulled up to his mother's house, there were three cars out front, and he was concerned that something was wrong, since she never had company.

Seven used his key, and Butch met him at the door, barking. There were three women inside that were about his mother's age and one very old woman sitting in the living room opposite Betty. With them were two middle-aged men, who stood on either end of the couch. Betty was looking gray and visibly upset. She looked up at him as he came through the door, and he saw her stop breathing. He looked at the people sitting in the living room, and they glanced back at him with curiosity. His mother said nothing—she just sat there—so he spoke first.

"Is everything all right, Ma?" he asked, trying to establish eye contact. She gave none, just shook her head. The women, however, gasped collectively. He didn't look at them, but he did wonder what they found so interesting. It was obvious that Betty was in shock. He tried again to gain eye contact, but to no avail, so he turned to the strangers to see what he could find out.

"I seem to be the only one in the dark," he stated to the room at large. In unison, they smiled at him.

A portly man stepped forward with his hand outstretched, "I'm your uncle Michael, your mother's oldest brother."

Taking the outstretched hand, Seven said, "I'm Seven, Betty's son."

The old woman said, "Seven?"

He turned and looked at her, really focusing on the old woman. Betty looked like her, and he found humor in their resemblance. She reached out her hand. "Grandma Bobbi," she said with a smile.

He took her hand and shook it. "Nice to meet you," he said.

*What's going on*, he thought. Maybe when Betty came around she would tell him what was happening. He didn't know she even *had* family; he thought it was just the two of them.

"I'm Evelyn, your mother's oldest sister; that is Patricia, and next to her is Brenda. That's the correct order; your mother is the baby. Over there is your Uncle Calvin, and he was born just before me. We had another brother between us, but he died at birth, which makes your mother number seven.

They all looked at him, smiled, and said hi.

"Well, Betty, do you have somewhere that we could talk?" his grandmother said.

"We could go in the back, Mama."

Her voice was so subdued that Seven turned to look at her. Her hands were clutched tightly together, and she was still looking at the floor. Putting his hand on Betty's shoulder, he asked, "Are you all right?"

She looked at him and said, "Yes, honey, I am." It was the first time she had looked at him since he arrived.

He looked at his grandmother and she said, "We didn't come here to hurt your mother, son. We have been looking for her for some time now."

Betty stood, and her mother took up her cane and followed her to the back of the house. Seven stood staring at his three aunts and two uncles. "What the hell is going on here?"

They all started talking at once, and he held up his hands. "I can't understand you if everyone talks at once."

Evelyn started explaining, “Michael was on Merrick Boulevard and spotted a woman who looked like our sister. He followed her here and did so for a couple of days, until he told me. Then we staked out the joint and when she came out with that little dog of hers, I knew it was her.

Patricia chimed in. “Your aunt watches too many cop shows. We saw her walking the dog and we knew it was her. Our mother and father have been beside themselves wondering what became of their baby. We brought Mama here, but Daddy was too ill to leave the house.”

Seven was stunned. He thought that they had all turned their backs on them. Isn’t that what he was told? He could not remember. Where had they been all this time? His head was hurting just thinking about all this. They didn’t seem threatening, but Betty looked worried that they were there. Maybe she would talk to him after they had gone, but he didn’t think so. Then, another thought entered his mind.

“Do any of you know my father?”

The three women paled, and the two men looked angry. He wasn’t going to get an answer, judging by their reaction. He also knew it was wrong to ask them. He should be man enough to ask Betty himself. So far, though, he hadn’t been—he didn’t even know that she was the youngest of seven children. He couldn’t bring himself to ask about her life, let alone his own.

Betty stood facing her mother. She had gotten old. What could she want with her now, she thought? She remembered calling her Aunt Bea just before Seven was born, feeling alone and afraid. When Bea answered and heard it was Betty, she went off, demanding to know why Betty would try to steal her husband after everything she had done for her. “Clarence isn’t perfect, but he would never leave me for you,” she had said. “Your mother is ashamed to have such a tramp for a daughter. Don’t come back here spreading no rumors about my man.”

Betty hung up and never looked back. Her mother’s voice brought her back.

“I remember when Bea met Clarence. I knew then what he was.” Betty looked at her but said nothing. “I never blamed you. I shouldn’t have sent you to stay with them. What hurt me, though, was that you never gave me a chance as your mother. But looking at that young man in there, I see why you left. He looks just like Clarence and even more handsome. He forced himself on you, didn’t he?”

Betty just shook her head again in the affirmative.

"We don't have to get into it now, or ever. I'm here to tell you that your father is dying and he wishes to see you. We love you, and that young man in there. Here is the phone number. Think about it and call. Time is running out. Don't think too long." She got up from the edge of the bed, and Betty opened the door and followed her back out to the living room.

Seven turned as they approached. Butch was up on his feet waiting for Betty to sit down.

His grandmother broke the ice. "We're leaving now," she said, handing Seven a slip of paper with all her information on it.

The women came forward first, kissing and hugging them both. The men shook his hand while patting him on the back, and then they both hugged his mother. He saw them to the door. After locking the door, he stood there for a second with his head against it. What was there to say? He would have to go home and think about this. He knew she wasn't going to talk to him, and to be honest he was in shock. Heading back into the living room, he found Betty sitting there with Butch at her feet.

"I'm going to go home," he said, looking at her.

"Oh," she replied, and a moment later she continued, "I don't really want to be here by myself. Can I come with you? I haven't seen your place yet."

He was taken aback. She had tried to live a separate life from him for so long that he didn't know what to say.

"I have a meeting in Manhattan mid-morning, so you will have to entertain yourself. Butch is welcome, too."

"I'll pack for a few days," she said, heading toward the bedroom.

As he watched her go, he was positive that life as he knew it had changed. Whether for better or worse, he couldn't say, but it had changed. He would not examine things any more deeply for now. It was late, and thinking was hurting his head.

# CHAPTER 4

Lisa had been nervous since Tuesday. The closer she got to the conference date, the more she thought that it would be best if Maxine took over this account. She had heard that the man holding the conference was the no-nonsense type—he liked what he liked and could be hard to please. When she broached the subject with her boss, Elise said, "Girl, you worry too much. This is the Plaza. This place sells itself."

The conference was this morning and there was no turning back now. Lisa gave directions as the kitchen staff set up the breakfast bar. The appetizing spread was beautifully laid out, with coffee dispensers holding steaming hot coffee for the attendees. The packets that were to be part of the conference were placed neatly in front of each seat. Lisa was ready.

Seven was out of sorts from the evening before. When he awoke and headed for the treadmill at 6:00 A.M., he found Betty sitting in the living room. He had forgotten that she had come home with him the night before. She looked out of place simply because she had never been to his house. It was yet another reminder that he clung to his mother. The truth was, as an adult, they would have parted ways. He now realized, though, that they were still together because he would not let her go. *How healthy is that?* he wondered.

He had changed his routine this morning because his mother was there—a mistake, he now realized. Running in the morning helped his thought process. Now he just felt sluggish and tired. He hated conducting business like this.

The limo pulled up in front of the Plaza at 9:45 A.M. He headed to the conference room without delay, preferring to be there first.

The conference would feature a mixed crowd of attendees—high school seniors and college students, along with seasoned businessmen—all encouraged to let their ideas fly. He found that he got a lot of lucrative ideas from this type of meeting, but his real strength was that his mind was open to possibilities—the first step to making money. The second step was understanding that there were always options that further enhanced the possibilities. He couldn't explain how he knew what to do to make a deal happen; he just did.

As the first people started filing in, he turned his mind to business and shut out thoughts of his personal life.

As Lisa stood in the corridor directing the attendees to the correct conference room, she was puzzled by how young some of them appeared. After the first part of the meeting was over and the group took a short break, she and her team refreshed the side bar, emptied the trash, and set up for lunch. All was going well, and there were no complaints so far. Maxine had told her that the head of the conference was the type to complain and that you would know if he was not pleased long before the day ended. So far, so good.

There was a nice turnout for the conference, and everything was in order, although even if it wasn't, he didn't think that he would notice. As much as he tried, he couldn't concentrate. He could hear what people were saying, but he couldn't focus. He couldn't wait for the conference to end. He stepped out into the hall for a breather. After a few minutes, he returned, and it was evident that the attendees could feel his restlessness.

On the booklets the attendees received, many wrote about the ideas they had. Once he got home, he would have to do a lot of reading to understand the ideas being presented. Three of the young adults were from Manhattan high schools, and the other five were from NYU. As for the businessmen, Seven had been in ventures with all of them before. It was a nice mix.

As the day ended and the people started leaving, he felt relieved. He shook the last hand in the line of people making their exit. Then he went back into the room and sat down, contemplating going home. Betty was still at his house, and he didn't think that he could face her. He would go have a drink to start with and see what sort of trouble he could get into. Maybe he would call Sahar. No, that wouldn't do. He needed someone that didn't talk so much.

Why couldn't he focus? Up to now, he had had no real personal business or family issues. His life had been nothing but business. Did he want to hear the truth? Could he deal with it? Well he thought, he could surmise and guess all day, but until he and Betty had a meeting of the minds, he would never be any closer to who he was.

The scariest thing about all of this was that he could be himself for twenty-eight years, only to be newly introduced to himself as if he were a stranger off the street. His mother's family held that key, and for the first time since he was ten, vulnerability saturated his life. He resented it. Gathering up his papers and grabbing his jacket, he headed for the door. The limo was waiting.

Lisa was headed for the conference room with her team to ready it for the group that would be there tomorrow. As she was talking to a busboy about what needed to be done, she placed her hand on the knob to open the door just as Seven placed his hand on the knob from the other side. He pushed she pulled, and Lisa went tumbling back into the busboy, who caught her before she could hit the floor.

Catching her balance, she righted herself, grabbing at the god-awful jacket that was part of her blue-skirted uniform, to straighten it. The day was going too well, she thought. Just then, she looked up into the most handsome face she had ever seen. His face was black—there was no other word for it—with smooth, clear skin. He had huge dark brown eyes full of expression, and his nose was sharp, adding to the angles and planes of his face. He had beautiful thick lips that were enhanced by straight white even teeth. His hair was black and cut in an old-fashioned jersey, close on the sides and with very little on top. His goatee and eyebrows were even darker, as if to highlight his perfection. And when he smiled, as he was doing right now, you felt privileged to witness it. He was tall—over six feet, if she had to guess—and his style of dress was elegant but not flashy. He wore a dark blue suit with a light blue shirt and a burgundy tie. She was embarrassed, to say the least.

He reached out his hand to steady her, and when he was able to focus again, he came face to face with an angel. Her uniform was a little on the big side, as if she tried to hide her curves. It was an awful royal blue with a white shirt and a name tag that said "Lisa." She had cocoa-brown skin and eyes the color of chestnuts that invited him into her soul. Her nose was shaped like a button; her lips were luscious and perfect, enticing him to kiss her. Her hair was parted in the middle and hanging down around her shoulders, framing her face and enhancing her femininity. "Lisa," as she must be called, was a wonder to behold.

There was something familiar about him, but Lisa was certain that she had never seen this man before. She would have remembered him, or any interaction with him. Why did she feel this connection with him, as if she had known him in a past life? When he reached out his hand, gripping her upper arm to anchor her, she felt the current flow from him through her.

He felt it too, that powerful current, as it passed from her to him. Why had he touched her? The busboy had already prevented her fall. He felt an acquaintance with her that he could not explain. Seven decided by way of clarification that his weird mood had to do with the events of last evening and her attractiveness.

He spoke first: "I'm Seven."

# CHAPTER 5

She gasped and just stared at him.

*It can't be*, she thought.

For many years, she had wondered what happened to him, the little boy who saved her life. Her aunt had taken ill shortly after she had gone to stay with her mother's family and passed away. Anything she could learn about the boy Seven and his mother had passed with her.

"Lisa…Lisa Harris. It was you that brought me home from school that day, wasn't it?" she asked, reaching out to take his hand.

The witty line of how women fell for him all the time got stuck in his throat. The smile was wiped from his face as he reassessed the woman standing before him. It couldn't be, he thought. For many years, he had wondered if she was all right and if life had gone well for her. The walls of the elegant hotel fell away, and they once again stood in the schoolyard of PS 92, staring at each other, each seeing only the other's vulnerable inner child.

His smile returned—it was good to see her. How fitting that he saw her here today, when he was feeling so lost, unable to find his way. Still clutching his hand, she led him down to the lounge, and he followed.

"Well," he said, "can we really catch up on eighteen years in one sitting?"

"We could try," she said, laughing as they entered the lounge. "I thought about you many times over the years. I've wondered what you were doing."

When she pulled away that day in her uncle's car, he was sad. It was nice to see a friend, one who didn't judge him or his mother. That evening he cried when he thought Betty was asleep, and they never discussed her again.

"I did too," he responded, just as the waiter was approaching.

"Club soda for me," she said. "I still have an hour to go."

"I'll have the same," he said.

They had taken a table in the back of the lounge. The lighting was dim, and there were only two other patrons. The room was dotted with tables, and every other track light was out, lending to the room's ambiance. The atmosphere pushed them further into their own world.

"Your aunt and uncle, how are they. Was it all right living with them?" he asked, not knowing where to start.

"Oh yes, they were wonderful, but after the first year my aunt got sick and died shortly after. My uncle followed, drinking himself to death in grief. I ended up with my grandmother. And you? How is your mother?"

He didn't want to talk about himself. Shit, he didn't even *know* his mother—or himself, for that matter. For the sake of simplicity, he stuck to the facts.

"My mother is well. Did you ever see your mother or father again?"

She smiled. "No, I haven't seen them since the day she dropped me off at school and you brought me home."

Why would she be smiling about being abandoned by people who should have cared about her? "You're smiling. May I ask why?"

"I'm smiling because leaving me behind was the best thing they ever did for me. For about a year after they left, my biggest fear was that they would come back and I would have to go with them. Can you understand that? Living with my mother's family has been wonderful. My father beat us just about every day, and I realized as an adult that had I continued living with them, I would probably be dead. He was getting worse every day. I couldn't take it."

Seven could remember clearly hearing her scream and plead. He guessed there was a brighter side. The waiter came, placing two napkins on the table followed by the drinks.

"Yeah," he said, "I can understand that."

"I remember the first time I broke something at my aunt's house. She turned and looked at me and asked me if I cut myself. 'Be careful,' she said. I didn't know what to think. My grandmother turned out to be my best friend; she missed my mother up until the day she died. Not even for my grandmother could I wish her back, though."

She was animated when she talked, even about something so serious, and he was enjoying himself. "What about you?" she said. "How has life been treating you?"

"Me?" he said, smiling. "We continued to stay there until I left for college, and then it was just my mother. I went to University of North Carolina, and when I came back, my mother moved. I'm not nearly as interesting as you."

"I suspect that you're just being polite," she said.

He wanted to know other things about her, like was she married and did she have children. The fact that she used her maiden name meant nothing. Did she have someone that she thought was special? Did she live with someone that might object to his seeing her again? Those were the questions that for the first time he didn't know how to approach.

"You work here. Do you live far?"

"I live in Queens, just off Linden, and you?"

"I live on Roosevelt Island. I do a lot of business in Manhattan; the tram gives me easy access."

"Are you married? Do you have children?"

She laughed, thinking, *I haven't even had a real relationship yet.* "No and no. What about you?" she asked, turning the tables.

"No and no," he said feeling relieved, though he hated to admit it. He was enjoying himself immensely, and it had been a long time since he'd done so. She had taken his mind off his problems, and for that he was thankful.

"Well, I have to be going. I have to tie up a few loose ends before I clock out," she said. Lisa knew that she had a bad habit of talking too much. He hadn't really said anything. Maybe his good deed didn't carry the weight for him that it did for her all those years. She was disappointed, but she wouldn't push herself on anybody.

"When can I see you again?' he asked.

Lisa was startled by his question. "See me again?" she repeated.

"Yes, see you again." He smiled. "You couldn't possibly think I would let you go again, now could you?"

Lisa laughed mostly because she couldn't think of anything to say. Her interaction with men was limited to say the least, to be honest her father made her fearful of relationships. She didn't think she could handle being bullied, although her uncles were very kind to their wives and children, nieces and nephews, still she shied away from intimacy.

"Here is my number," she said. She took a napkin and wrote her number on it.

He reached for the napkin without breaking eye contact. "The question is when will I see you again?"

No, she thought, she couldn't handle him. She felt almost remorseful that she had not tried her hand at dating. He was intense, and his deep brown eyes bore through her, making her jumpy inside.

"When would you like to see me again?" That was safe, and it put the ball back in his court. Her palms were becoming sweaty.

"I'll wait for you to get off," he said. "We'll have dinner and I'll take you home."

"I'll meet you in the lobby," she said a little woodenly. This was the last thing she saw coming.

"Relax," he said. "I don't bite."

She turned and walked away. He watched her go, and when she was out of sight, he signaled the waiter. "Hennessy neat."

*He has teeth, doesn't he,* Lisa thought as she made her way to the locker room. She was nervous, and her thoughts were racing. How could she eat with him? What if she choked or food flew out her mouth while she was talking? *Let's face it,* she thought, *I can't stop talking.* After closing up her locker and placing her purse on her shoulder, she headed for the lobby.

Seven stood in the lobby of the hotel, the businessman from earlier gone. He had removed his jacket and his tie and loosened his collar. He smiled as she came hurrying toward him. They met in the middle of the lobby. "Are you ready?" he asked.

"Yes."

Taking her by the hand, he led her out to the curb and to the waiting limo. The driver held the door for them. As they pulled away from the curb, she was overwhelmed. Where would they go? She still had her work uniform on, and she felt out of place with him.

He reached for his buttons and unbuttoned his shirt all the way, showing his white t-shirt underneath and pulling the flaps out of his pants.

*What now?* she thought nervously. After he loosened his shirt and relaxed, he looked even more devastatingly handsome. She focused her eyes on the window and the passing scenery. As always in New York, there were many people about in a mad dash to get home after a hard day's work. They rode through Times Square and the limo stopped to let the pedestrians cross. There were tables set up along the sidewalks with people selling movies, music, and even jewelry. At another light, she saw a man with three cards moving his hands quickly while onlookers tried to find the ace. As they continued on, she could feel his presence; it was tangible. Why could she not get herself under control? She could feel his eyes on her, which made her focus on the window even more.

*She has a beautiful profile*, he thought. He knew she was nervous. This was a first for him, being with a woman who wasn't as jaded as he was. The limo came to a stop and he broke the silence. "Wait here. I'll be right back."

He opened the door and headed up the block. She watched him go, trying to keep an eye on him, but he disappeared very quickly into the crowd, so she sat back and waited. About fifteen minutes passed, and then the limo began moving slowly and came to a stop.

He opened the door and leaned in. "Here, take this," he said.

Reaching out, Lisa grabbed the package he handed her and waited for him to climb back in.

*Pizza.*

She smiled and began to feel more at ease. Maybe she would be all right tonight. She was so focused on the pizza and her own thoughts that she did not see the bottle of wine or the plastic wine glasses. She was no drinker but she liked wine. As the conversation flowed and became more relaxed, the evening took on a life of its own. They ate pizza and drank wine while the limo took them on a drive to nowhere. They drove through influential areas and neighborhoods as well as the neighborhood they had lived in together when they were children. They looked around but decided that nothing needed to be said.

He told her funny stories about college life and the people he had met. He spoke about Gary and Sean and their families—how funny their children were, how Gary was balding at a young age, and how whenever he went to his house to watch the game, his wife always kissed him on the bald spot whenever she ventured into the den.

She told him about her cousins with whom she played cards once a week. They laughed about her old Aunt Ruth and her church friend Hattie; they were a couple of card sharks.

"They curse worse than sailors when they have a deck of cards in their hands. They smoke, drink, and cheat. When Aunt Ruth gets to adjusting that wig at the table for all to see, it's on," she said while adjusting her imaginary wig. The night continued on that note—easy and laid back—yet it was different, and exciting.

Lisa looked at her watch. It was midnight, and they had been together since 5:00 P.M. It was time for her to go. She hated to end the evening. It had been so entertaining to just sit and enjoy the company of another.

*When can I see him again?* she wondered, although she would not ask. They got a chance to reconnect and see that the other was doing well. What more could she want?

Seven saw her look at her watch and hated that the evening was ending. It was late, but if he chose to, he could sleep in. No, he was being inconsiderate—it was time to take her home.

"What's your address? Write it down here and I'll pass it to the driver."

Lisa wrote it down and handed it to him. While he talked with the driver, she allowed herself to admit that she wanted him to ask her out again. They talked less as they approached her home. When they hit Guy R. Brewer, she knew she was close. *Damn*, she thought, *the night has truly ended.*

They turned on Linden, and he could see the young black men on the corner with their entrepreneurial spirit being led like lambs to the slaughterhouse. It was the way of things all over New York—on one block you would encounter drugs; on the next would be mama's house. His attention turned back to Lisa, and as they began to slow down, he wondered when he would see her again. He had to see her again, and he wasted no time letting her know.

"Tomorrow," he said. "You pick."

She smiled. Well, she *was* going to see him again after all, and she was more than elated, but pick where they were going? No thoughts came to her mind. "You can pick me up from home…I have no idea where to take you."

"You have until tomorrow. I trust you. I'm in your capable hands."

They pulled up in front of her house and the driver opened the door for them. She lived on a quiet street with houses that all looked nearly the same. There was a silver gate that enclosed the surrounding yard. There was a stoop in front of the house with about five steps that lead a to sun porch. At the door, she felt awkward and confused, so she fumbled with her keys.

He placed his hands over her unstill hands and pulled her forward, placing a kiss on her forehead. He lingered there with his eyes closed, just losing himself in her inexperience. He was hiding he knew from his life, his mother, his failures, the women he had chosen, and even his successes. The kiss wasn't sexual, but it was intimate.

Abruptly, he stepped back, releasing her hands and looking down at her. "Tomorrow."

"Yes, tomorrow," she said, inserting her key in the lock and letting herself in.

Back in the limo, he instructed the driver to take the long way back to his house, but as always in the case of hiding, our problems come to find us. As the limo approached the bridge to Roosevelt Island, he readied himself for a night of sleeplessness and troubled thoughts. Looking out the window, he spied the Fifty-ninth Street Bridge. Looming in the distance, it was all lit up, yet it appeared friendless at this hour in the absence of traffic. He had been lonely today—that was all he was willing to admit for the moment.

As he got out in front of his building, he decided he would use that company again, as the driver had been invisible. He stepped off the elevator at the twelfth floor and made his way to his door. As he stepped inside, it was dark, except for the moonlight that shone through the open terrace doors. The weather was mild for March. Placing his things down on a chair, he knew that he could no longer avoid her. He appeared at the terrace door, but she did not acknowledge his presence right away, and he did not expect her to. It was the way of things between them—he looking to be someone's son and she sowing seeds of deception. They both stared off across the river, really seeing nothing in the darkness. Should he say something? The burden was on him to break the silence, but he would not. In his home, she would recognize him—he would not tolerate less—so he waited.

"I have been waiting for you," she said. It was not accusatory, but he was looking for a fight.

"I've been waiting for you my whole life," he said, his voice masking the emotional turmoil he felt.

Occasionally, he would let slip what he really thought. What could she say? She had pushed him away to make him see his potential? What other chance did he have? She was trying to raise a man, and she herself was unsure about being a woman. In her naiveté, she believed that since her parents were married, that she too would follow that path. Never would she have believed that her virginity would be ripped from her by someone who would not see its worth. She smiled, remembering her shock and hurt about being pregnant. She remembered a group of her girlfriends talking about sex at the lunch table in school. The knowledge imparted that day broke her down.

"You can't get pregnant if you fuck and it doesn't feel good," Shirley had said, and the rest of the younger girls giggled, Betty included. What a way to find out that your friends don't know shit.

It was safer to ignore that statement, she thought, but not wise. "Do you remember where I was while you were waiting for me?"

"I'm still waiting for you," he said none too gently.

"Do you have questions, Seven, that you want to ask me? Be a man. Ask and deal with the answers you get. If you don't get answers, deal with that too."

"I knew you were an expert on the needs of men, but not on what it takes to be one. Is that your disclosure, that if you don't answer I should be a man and accept it?"

Outwardly, she continued to stare out into the darkness, showing no emotion, but inwardly his hostility was killing part of her. He was trying to antagonize her into showing her feelings.

"Do you think I like the life we led?" she asked.

"I have no idea what you liked; you have worked hard to keep yourself from me. You were not a mother to me—or a friend. I think our problem is that you are a mother, and I am a son, but we are not connected. Who are you?"

"You are your own man now, successful and brilliant. I tried to get you to move on with your life. You don't need to associate with a prostitute. I tried to distance myself from you so you would have a chance to live a different life. I tried not to taint your adult life the way that I did your childhood. Realize how we lived. Do you even know what it cost me physically to pay the bills at twenty dollars a john?"

"Do you know what it cost me? Did you punish yourself, Betty, and me in the process?" He didn't expect an answer, so he continued. "Why didn't you tell me we had family, that you were the youngest of seven children? You obviously cut them off like you did me."

"Seven, it's more complicated than that. As much as I push you away, you come the same time every month to see me. I want better than me for you, and when the middle of the month draws near, I'm afraid you won't come. I love you. You are more than a combination of me and your father. You are my only perfection."

He listened to her feelings and resented that she could touch him. Here she was at his home, hiding from her past, unable to face it. Revealing her emotions to him was freeing for her but caging for him. By not admitting to the role that she and his *father* played in his existence, she further detached him from the truth. How could he be an effective husband and father when he couldn't offer the one thing that a man is always in search of—*identity*?

"Good night, Ms. Thomas," he said as he turned to walk away, tears threatening to unman him. There was really no more to say.

*Ms. Thomas.* That remark told Betty that they had stepped down a rung. His retreating footfalls signaled the return of solitude, which she did not want. She placed Butch at her feet and he followed her into the living room. After locking the door, she made her way to one of the smaller bedrooms and dressed for bed in the dark. The clock on the night table read 2:00 A.M. as she laid her head on the pillow.

When she woke at 8:00 A.M., he was already gone. He was avoiding her, and it was time to go, to leave him to the life that she thought that she wanted for him. As she made her way down to the cab with her bags and Butch, she realized that she had come to his house because she was afraid of losing the one person who loved her unconditionally. He believed she had come because she was hiding from her family, but that wasn't so. They wouldn't know the person she was now, even if she showed them who she was. But she knew they would be back. She would go home and face her family, and the lonely life that she had created.

He left her on the terrace and went to his room. He didn't sleep; he couldn't. There was plenty said between them and yet nothing at all. Betty had always been intangible and unattainable, and he had finally decided that he would take her advice and move on. He would no longer force himself into where he wasn't wanted. As he came to this conclusion, he felt a physical pain in his chest. She was right about one thing—he was a man, and he would not allow himself to suffer because of Betty again.

He had given his secretary the day off because his mother was there, but he knew Betty would read between the lines and would be gone when he got home. Seven had two meetings today about some vacant property in Ocala, Florida, that he owned. The first meeting was with a developer who wanted to test the land to make sure it could be built upon. The second meeting was with an appraiser to determine its value. There was money to be made, but he was distracted. He told himself that it was because he was seeing Lisa that night. It was his first step in denial and the abandonment of himself.

# CHAPTER 6

The day was ending, and Lisa was heading home to wait for Seven. She had two concerns now: what to wear and where to go. Her wardrobe—if you could call it that—left much to be desired. Kim complained about it all the time, but Lisa wasn't a shopper. Money was part of the problem—she just could not afford flashy clothes. When she would say this, Kim would offer to buy something for her, but Lisa would refuse. The death of her grandmother had taken a toll on her finances. She thought she had nice clothing, but Kim claimed they were boring.

As for where to go, she didn't want to pick somewhere that was too intimate, because she was sure that Seven saw her as a friend. She settled on a black one-piece dress with an elastic middle, and she accessorized with a cheap matching belt that was supposed to go over the elastic middle, making it invisible. Her shoes were black, the kind people wear to work when they're on their feet all day. She polished her own nails, and as for her hair, it was parted in the middle again and hanging down around her shoulders. She wore just a touch of lipstick and eyeliner.

When she finished dressing, she began pacing the house, trying to get her nerves under control. Lisa couldn't wait to see him; it was all she could think about. What if he didn't come? The thought caused her anxiety to deepen. If he didn't come, then she would take herself to the movies. *You did fine before dating him,* she told herself.

*Dating.* Was this a date? Could she call it that? Just as her thoughts were spiraling out of control, the doorbell rang.

"Who is it?" she asked, knowing it was him.

"Seven," he answered.

As she opened the door to face him, her stomach did a flip. Seven was taller than she remembered, he had been standing on the second step from the top and they were looking each other in the eye. Smiling, she stepped back and let him into her home.

It was dark as he stepped onto the porch; he could see the outline of the furniture but that was all. The living room was something straight out of another time—the sofa was dark brown with little wooden legs and a matching chair, and the carpet was beige. There was a picture of a young couple on the wall, taken years before they were even born. Across from the sofa was an old-fashioned radio, the kind that people listened to before they had television. Just beyond the living room was a formal dining room that he could see from his position standing in the doorway. There was a matching cabinet and table, made of heavy maple. On the right were stairs leading to the bedrooms. The house was immaculate and made him feel like he stepped into another era.

"Come in and make yourself at home," Lisa said, smiling and happy to see him.

She was so genuine in her welcome that he felt warm and happy to be there. Seven responded in kind, "So, where will you be taking me?" he asked, smiling.

"There's a nice Japanese restaurant in Flushing where we can watch them cook our food," she answered while motioning for him to sit. "Can I get you anything?" she asked.

He was wearing a cream-colored linen shirt with brown slacks and a brown leather blazer. When he sat, she noticed that his shoes were also brown leather and looked too expensive to touch the ground. Again, he was elegantly dressed but not flashy.

Lisa reassessed him; his very presence was commanding as well. Seven was so tall that when he stood, she had to step back a little to look into his face.

"No, thank you. I'm ready whenever you are," he said.

"I'll go get my things."

As she turned and made her way up the stairs, he took in her clothes. Her dress and shoes were modest and very plain. Although he searched, he could find nothing calculated in her appearance. The women he dated were cunning in their allure and as jaded as he was. That wasn't a judgment, just an assessment. The power struggle started before they got into bed, but from the way Lisa dressed, he somehow got the feeling that she was looking to enjoy his company. She was shorter than he remembered, and her body was very well formed, although the dress accentuated nothing. Her hair was deep brown and layered, with a healthy bounce to it. She wore no makeup other than lipstick, as far as he could see. She was physically beautiful, but she exuded an inner beauty as well—virtue. Lisa's background was no different from his, which meant it was harsh, to say the least. Where did she come by such a commodity?

"I'm ready," she said, breaking his train of thought.

Helping her with her coat, he said, "So am I."

She went out first and stood on the stoop, and he continued down to his truck while Lisa locked the door. He had a black Pathfinder with tan leather interior. She climbed in, gave him directions, and they were off.

"Who do you live with?" he couldn't help but ask.

The question made her feel vulnerable. She had told him that her grandmother died, but she had been evasive about her living situation. When they were children, he hadn't been a threat, but as a man he was, even if he didn't intend to be. The way he was making her feel was scary enough. She wracked her brain for an answer and decided on the truth.

"When my grandmother died, she left me the house. I live alone."

He kept his eyes on the road. The atmosphere in the truck was cozy, with jazz playing in the background. He felt relieved when she answered, not knowing what to expect. "You thought about whether to tell me the truth. Why?"

Lisa decided on the truth again. "As a single woman living alone, it's not something that I just tell everyone. I guess for my own safety."

The conversation flowed freely from there. They talked about anything and everything that came to mind. The only lull in conversation came when he was parking and they were entering the restaurant. They were shown to a secluded table, and their chatting started up again in earnest. She ordered a shrimp fried rice dish, and he ordered a beef fried rice dish. As for drinks, he ordered red wine. A bottle was placed on the table, and Lisa was careful not to consume too much because she had not eaten all day and the one glass she had went straight to her head. The chef appeared and entertained them with his culinary skills, and then it was just them.

"How did you come to work at the Plaza?" he asked. He couldn't seem to learn enough about her.

"My cousin has a friend that works there named Elise. I came in for an interview and the job was mine. What do you do besides terrorize the staff at the hotel?" she countered.

He told her about his first deal back in college, when he and some friends bought a run-down apartment complex in South Carolina, fixed it up, and sold it. From there, it was on to his next venture, and so on. She noticed that when the conversation was directed at him, he turned it back toward her, but she wasn't one to pry. He kept the chatter about himself superficial, and that caused her to feel their conversation was a bit one sided. "When can I see your mother?" she asked.

He stiffened noticeably. Of course she would want to see Betty. She probably wanted to thank her. He hadn't thought about that.

"I'll make arrangements to bring you by her house one of these days. My grandfather is sick, and she is busy dealing with that."

He was lying, creating an illusion of closeness within his family that did not exist. What was worse was that she had shown concern for him and Betty because of it.

"Oh, I'm sorry to hear that. I know what that's like."

He shook his head in acknowledgement and changed the subject again. They were so engrossed in each other that they were among the last to leave. When she laughed at something he said, she threw her head back and hooted with enjoyment, showing all her pretty white teeth and bouncing her hair. He found this so attractive that he wanted to keep her smiling.

There was a wind as they walked through the parking lot, and a full moon shone down on them. Seven opened Lisa's door first, helping her in. When they were moving along, he thought about how he didn't want the evening to end. But he wouldn't rush things or force it, he would take her home. The combination of excitement, good food, wine, and the warmth of the truck caused her to fall asleep. Her quietness drew his attention, and at a stoplight he studied her. She looked even younger in her sleep. He smiled, feeling happy that she was secure enough with him to fall asleep. As he turned on to her street, he nudged her shoulder, and she opened her eyes. As she looked at him, she was a little disoriented.

"You fell asleep," he said.

She sat up, mortified. "I'm sorry," she said. "This is my second late night out in a row, and I was so excited about seeing you tonight, I think it took a toll on me." She just talked too much, she thought.

"No need to apologize, and it's a good thing that tomorrow is Saturday—you can sleep late," he said. "I'll pick you up around 2:00. I have a few errands to run, and then I'll come get you afterwards."

"What are we doing?" she asked, unable to believe that he wanted to see her again.

"Don't bother to dress up; jeans will do. We'll just hang out, and I'll show you where I live," he answered.

"I'll be ready."

Seven got out of the truck and opened her door for her. He walked her to the house, and, taking her keys, unlocked the front door. As the door opened, they stood facing each other. She smiled at him, and he could see the shyness in her eyes, but she didn't look away. Her honesty allowed him to look into her core. He leaned down and kissed her. The kiss was a soft touching of his lips to hers, and when she was about to pull away, he caught her bottom lip between his teeth and kissed her again. It was the only place they touched.

Finally, he whispered against her lips, "Tonight was perfect."

Turning abruptly, he walked away. As he pulled away from her house, he was deep in thought. He could still taste her sweetness, and the artlessness of her kiss filled him with hunger that he had to fight to control. She smelled of some heady fragrance unique to her, and every breath he took while in her presence submerged him deeper into a sensual awareness of her. He didn't want to frighten her with his need and more importantly he wanted to be a part of her serenity. In his dealings with the opposite sex, he knew that he had never experienced sex with such an undertow of sincerity. In fact, he had never felt such intimacy as when he kissed her tonight.

She stood there with her fingers on her lips, still feeling the pressure of his lips as she watched him drive off. She then entered the house and sat in the living room, reliving the kiss and what he had said to her.

She sat and thought about her situation: She was twenty-six with no real understanding of men. In everything she did in life, she would always think before leaping. She was cautious to a fault, and as a result she never really lived. Seven was more sophisticated than she was, but Lisa decided that she would ride this wave until he was tired of dealing with her. When that day came, she would just consider herself happier for having experienced him…them.

Seven and Lisa made plans regularly to spend time together. They went for walks in Central Park and took the Circle Line around Manhattan, enjoying each other's company. They ate at the finest restaurants and the cheapest too. They talked and laughed about everything. The days turned into weeks, and it seemed that neither could concentrate on work. They were like children watching the clock.

One day at work, Lisa fell asleep during a meeting and started to snore lightly. Elise nudged her, but not before the director noticed. She was embarrassed, but she was a good sport, and that evening at his house she told Seven about it. He laughed and felt bad for her. He was keeping her up later each night as they spent time together, but no matter how late they hung out, she always asked to go home, and he would take her.

When he came to her house to spend time with her, they would sit up and watch television and make a big deal out of cooking for each other. Sometimes they would cook two separate meals and compare their culinary skills—hers were always far superior. She fried whiting fish filets with fries and a Greek salad. He made scrambled eggs and burnt toast. Lisa made a rack of lamb and baby thin-skinned potatoes with fresh peas and baby carrots. Seven made Hamburger Helper, and most of it stuck to the pot. Finally, she was onto him. The worse he cooked, the more intricate her meals became with him as the benefactor.

"You're not really trying to cook, are you?" she asked indignant.

Seven could hardly keep a straight face. "Yes, I am," he said.

Yes, she was definitely being tricked into cooking for him, and he was living high on the hog. He would eat, praise her, and the next thing she knew, she was cooking again. The occasions when he would cook were growing further and further apart.

"Well, I won't be cooking next week—it's your turn. I really want to see the new recipes you came up with."

"Oh, next week I had planned on taking you out."

"Just as I thought. You don't plan on cooking at all. Ya bum," she exclaimed, turning and spraying him with the cold water from the sprayer by the faucet.

"Oh, hell no," he said as she sprinted past him through the dining room, across the living room, and up the stairs.

He was hot on her heels, taking the steps two at a time. When she made it to her room, she tried to close the door, but he jammed his foot in the doorway. She was screaming that she was sorry, and he yelled, "Wait till I get you." So engrossed were they in their teasing and playing that they failed to realize that they had ventured into no-man's land, the bedroom.

When he shoved the door, Lisa turned to flee and found there was nowhere to run. Leaping for the closet, he caught her by the arm and yanked her toward him. Pulling in the opposite direction, Lisa screamed that she was sorry. He was laughing in a sinister way, which let her know that she was in for it. Facing him, she could see that his shirt was wet, along with his face and hair.

When he had her pinned against door, the look in his eyes changed. Seven placed his hands on either side of her head, trapping her. His nostrils flared like any male catching the sent of a female drenched in sexuality. Leaning down he kissed her throat, tasting the sugar of her cocoa-brown skin. She drew in a sharp breath, drawing his attention back to her eyes, and she didn't look away. It was part of the honesty that was her, to allow him to peer into her thoughts. He placed his lips against hers and kissed her with innocence at first. When she responded by permitting her lips to part slightly, he pushed his tongue into her mouth, tasting her intense sensuality. Lowering his hands to her shirt, he unbuttoned it, and when it parted, he cupped her breasts through her bra, running the pads of his thumbs over her nipples through the fabric.

Lisa moaned into his mouth, sending a powerful jolt straight to his dick, causing it to stiffen. Breaking the kiss, he pulled his shirt over his head and tossed it, and then he pulled her to him to feel her skin on his. The contact was intense. Hungrily, he kissed her again—rough and demanding—his tongue unrelenting in its mating with hers. Need pushed him to the brink and caused him to reach for the button on her jeans—and then the spell was broken.

Catching his hands and breaking the kiss, she whispered, "I'm not ready for this."

He was dazed, and had to close his eyes to gain control. Still holding her pants at the button, he just couldn't seem to let go. He wouldn't take it; it wasn't him. Leaning his forehead against hers, he continued to concentrate and breathe deeply, and when he could speak he said, "I'd better go." His voice was coarse, and gravelly even to his own ears.

Shaking her head yes was her only response. Seven then stepped back, taking in her appearance. Her shirt hung open, and he could see her firm breasts and hardened nipples. Her hair was tussled, and her lips were swollen from his kisses. She was stunning in her awareness of herself and him. He reached out to touch her cheek with the back of his hand, and she pulled away.

"No, baby, don't be afraid." He noticed that she wasn't breathing and was looking at the floor. Seven loved it when she looked him in the eye. She had a welcoming, embracing look. Turning, he headed for the door without his shirt and was gone. Down in the living room he paced, giving her a moment to collect herself. Fifteen minutes passed, and she did not come down, so he turned and headed for the stairs. As he placed his foot on the first step, he heard her door open and she appeared at the top of the landing.

He had his coat on. She looked at him standing there with no shirt, and he was beautiful. He radiated masculinity, his muscles rippling as he removed his foot from the step. This was maleness at its best, she thought as his abdominal muscles tightened and loosened with his tension. His chest jumped as he placed his hand on the banister. She could not handle him—he was too much.

"Come lock the door," he said, speaking as if he was leaving, but he made no move toward the door. She just wanted tonight to end.

They were at a standoff, plain and simple—he would not leave until she came down, and she would not come down until he left.

*I'm an adult*, she thought. *This is silly*. So, taking a deep breath, she headed down the steps. She expected him to step aside, but he didn't, so she stopped at the second step from the bottom and came face to face with him. Lisa didn't know where to look—down meant seeing his chest and up meant looking him in the eye—so she settled on just past his shoulder.

"Look at me," he said, his voice sounding more natural again. "I thought you felt safe with me," he continued, feeling tainted by his past and hers.

"I felt a little shaken is all," she whispered. "We were moving too fast, and I needed it to stop before it got out of control."

He felt rejected, not because of the sex—this was not his first time by any means—but by her lack of trust for him. The familiarity they experienced seemed stained by things that he couldn't see. He wanted to feel welcome, as he had just an hour earlier, but he didn't force it. He smirked, stepped back, and headed for the door. His name was on her lips as he walked away, but she didn't call him; she wouldn't be able to handle it if he stayed.

Outside it was freezing, typical for late March in New York, and his emotions were all jumbled up. Seven didn't even notice that he was wearing his coat opened with no shirt. After starting his truck, he pulled away from her house and headed home. He was hurt—there was no other word for it—and unrealistically he blamed her, for pushing him away. He could not see that he was shadowboxing with Betty; all he could understand was that he had decided not to allow himself to be hurt by anyone again, and it was happening *again*. It crossed his mind to see Margarita, to immerse himself in her body and mind, showing her where he hurt and having her lick his wounds. It would not do, though. He knew he wanted Lisa and no one else. He would wait for her.

# CHAPTER 7

When Mary showed up at 8:00 the next morning, he was in a bad mood. He had a phone conference at 9:00 A.M. and a meeting in lower Manhattan at 1:00. She was bringing him abreast of his schedule, but he wasn't listening.

"Is there something wrong?" she asked.

"No, nothing is wrong. I have to be on my way. If you need me, call me," he said, and he headed for the elevator, leaving Mary to wonder after him.

He didn't want to talk about mundane things. He felt like ditching his meetings and going to the hotel to speak with her. There was a limo waiting for him, and he took care of his conference call while he rode to his lawyer's office. When his cell rang, he was disappointed to see that it was Gary.

"I'm just going to ask: Who is she? That can be the only reason why we haven't heard from you."

Seven laughed and feigned ignorance. "I have no idea what you're talking about."

"What's up, old man? If it isn't one of your many women, why haven't I heard from you in weeks?"

"I've been busy working trying to make a living. How're the kids and Valerie?"

"Fine. They asked about you. When are you coming by for dinner?"

"Soon. I'll call you and let you know in about a week," Seven said.

"I'm going to hold you to it. We guys should have a night out. Talk to you later. I have to get back to the grind."

"All right man."

Seven spent the rest of the day in a fog, and when his afternoon meeting finished early, he decided he would call her at work. Lisa was so behind the times she didn't own a cell phone.

"Plaza Hotel, how may I direct your call?" the answering voice said.

"Hello, may I speak with Lisa Harris?"

"Ms. Harris is not in today."

His inner voice told him to go home and give her time, but he didn't listen. He went home, but stayed only long enough to change clothes and get his truck. Then he headed for the expressway. Soon after, changing his mind, he decided upon Queens Blvd. It would be faster, since rush hour traffic was getting thick. Stopping, he picked up some flowers and two frozen TV dinners from a bodega on one of the side streets. She was right—he really didn't want to cook.

Lisa was just stepping out of a car, and the young man with her was closing the car door for her. She was smiling at him. Seven parked his truck in front of another house on her street, watching the scene unfold. His rage heightened as the guy with her opened the back door and pulled out groceries. He guessed that she was going to cook for him—maybe, Seven thought, the guy didn't mind cooking for her. Clutching the steering wheel, he tried to get his feelings under control, enough so he could drive away. However, as soon as he thought it he knew *he couldn't leave?* He wouldn't wait on the street like some pussy. The thought of another man touching her was more than he could take.

As the front door shut behind them, he got out of his truck and made his way to the house. As he stood there contemplating what to do, again, something told him to go home. They had not decided to date exclusively; in truth, they had not labeled their relationship at all. He was out of control—and over a piece of ass he wasn't even getting. However, as soon as thought entered his head, the idea of degrading her to make himself feel better made the pain sit heavier on his chest.

He was hypersensitive, and everything seemed louder that normal. Seven knocked on the door and waited, and when there was no answer, he banged, although he thought he was still knocking. He heard footsteps approaching the door, and then…

"Who is it?" Thankfully—for all involved—it was Lisa who answered.

"Seven," he said, and he could hear the aggression in his own voice.

She opened the door apprehensively. Lisa was happy to see him, even though it didn't show on her face, as she still felt awkward from the previous night. She had never been naked—or almost naked—in front of a man before. He was back, and the sight of him made her weak with relief. All night, she worried that he might not come again. What would she have done then? In the morning, her eyes were swollen from crying, and she couldn't show up at work like that. Lisa loved him. How could she not? He was funny, successful, and beautifully handsome. But sex for her meant commitment, and the act was so causally done nowadays that she felt it unsophisticated of her to expect him to love her because she gave herself to him. Two issues weighed heavily on her mind. One was her father, and his treatment of her mother and her. The other issue was Seven's ability to steal her heart without sharing anything that was truly him. Seven was evasive on all fronts, and this made her feel clingy.

Seven totally misread her body language, mistaking her shyness for guilt, but when she looked him in the eye, he felt her acceptance melt the ice from his heart. *Go home*, he thought, *and don't look back*. She had him tied in knots—and very seriously, he thought she could get the other man hurt. Her hair was pulled back in a ponytail. She wore jeans, a white t-shirt, and some footsies. She was adorable.

"I was afraid that you wouldn't come back after last night," she whispered. "I was miserable all day—I missed you so bad."

Forgetting about the man inside, he opened his arms to her and she flung herself into them. "Baby," he said. His voice was gravelly with emotion.

Just then, from behind her, they heard the man say, "Lisa, what's taking you so long?"

Seven's body went taut, and she felt it. Lisa smiled and took his hand and led him into the house. Seven assessed the younger man. He was tall, although not as tall as he was, with light skin, a big nose, and light brown eyes. There was no aggression in him.

Seven felt like pissing on sticks. She was his. *You might as well get your coat*, he thought, *because you're leaving here, my brother*.

"Seven, this is my cousin, Alex," she said. "Alex, this is my honey, Seven."

It took a moment for the information to register, but when it did he relaxed visibly. Lisa was relieved when she saw him calming down and was happy she hadn't delayed in making the introductions. Alex stepped forward, extending his hand,

"I've heard a lot about you," he said, shaking Seven's hand.

*Wow*, he thought to himself. *Now she tells me*. He smiled and said, "I deny it all."

They all laughed together, and the tension surrounding them dissipated. Alex, it turned out, was her younger cousin. Apparently, the males in her family came by periodically to check on her and to let the neighbors know that she wasn't alone. As for Seven, he was still jealous, although he didn't let on. This knowledge put them on uneven ground. She really didn't need him to take care of her. Lisa's family looked after her, and he felt alone again.

They had dinner together—fried chicken, corn on the cob, biscuits, and a nice tossed salad. They talked about the card game that was being held at Kim's house, and Alex wanted to know if they were coming.

"No," Lisa said, thinking that Seven wouldn't enjoy that.

"Scared of Aunt Ruth are you?" her cousin asked.

Seven thought that was funny but said nothing. He knew she had refused the invitation because of him. He wanted her to himself a little longer, and she was just as in tune with him. He was acting like a selfish prick, and he knew it. They moved to the living room to watch TV. Alex made his excuses—saying that he was going to meet up with some friends—then they said their good nights.

Lisa walked him to the door, and they talked for a few more moments before he left, Lisa locking the door behind him. When she came back to the living room, the tension was so thick it could be cut with a knife. She sat down next to him and started watching TV as if he weren't there. He smiled.

"You're nervous of me again," he stated, placing his mouth to her ear. Damn, he was glad that her cousin had left.

His voice tickled her ear, and she moved her shoulder to protect it, but she didn't answer. Talking to him before Alex left had been easier. Seven kept his mouth to her ear and she started laughing. Then he put his arm around her and whispered, "You're not going to answer me, are you?"

When she turned to answer him he kissed her, pushing his tongue into her mouth. Keeping himself under careful control, he tasted her, and she was sweet. At first, she was stiff, but when she became pliant he pulled back, and heaven help them both she whimpered. Seven, however, was not taken in by her slight eagerness, and ended the kiss. He wanted to build her trust in him, because he felt low when she didn't no matter how misplaced her fears were.

"I am nervous," she said, "but it's not your fault."

"I will not hurt you, baby. Trust me. I am ready whenever you are," he said between kisses.

They watched TV and cuddled, and when the hour grew late, he knew that he had to begin the long trek home. Lisa had fallen asleep in his arms on the couch, and it felt right—he didn't want to disturb her. He adjusted himself and she awoke. She looked at him, smiled and stretched. It was toasty in the living room, but nevertheless the evening was over.

"I got to go, baby."

"I know," she said.

Seven stood, helping her up, and then grabbed his coat off the chair. Walking to the door, they kissed, and he stepped out into the night air. When the door closed behind him, he said to himself.

"Damn, it's cold out this bitch."

Lisa stood on the opposite side of the door, hating to see him go. She ran upstairs to her grandmother's room, which was in front of the house. Moving the curtain slightly, she watched him get into his truck and pull away. That night, back in her own room, she prayed that this was not a mistake, that her heart wouldn't be too broken when this was over. She loved him, and there was no turning back.

# CHAPTER 8

As the weeks became months, their feelings for each other grew. They spent a lot of time together, doing things that lovers do. Lisa invited him roller-skating, while Seven invited her to a horror movie so he could get close and cop a few feels. He was worse than an adolescent. She cooked for him, and he stopped pretending that he liked to cook.

He bought them bikes and they went bike riding in Prospect Park. They took an exercise class together and it was then that he realized that she cursed. The young couple still had not labeled their relationship, but without question, they were on the same page. Seven and Lisa were in their own world.

Work suffered for both of them, as they could never wait to see each other. At 5:30, he was always there to pick her up. He scheduled his meetings in the morning to make sure that he could pick her up in the evenings. Lisa got a cell phone so that he could call her any time of the day. When they were not together they talked on the phone. Lisa sometimes got back and neck pains from holding it there so long. *There are just times when you need to put the phone down*, she thought. As with all newly dating couples, no one else existed.

When the middle of the month came and went with no visit from Seven, Betty was hurt. Why, she didn't know—he had done what she had asked of him and moved on with his life. She missed him terribly. It had been two months since she had seen him.

Then, one day, the doorbell rang. She raced to the door, only to find her mother, along with her sister Brenda. They had come by for a visit.

"You had to be expecting someone else, because if you knew it was us you probably wouldn't have answered," said her mother bluntly.

"Come in," Betty said.

"I'll get right to the point," Bobbi said. "Your father is dying. Aren't you going to come and say good-bye?"

"It's hard," Betty said. "I'm not who I used to be."

"None of us are. I'm not judging you. I love you. Why do you continue to cut us off? Have you poisoned my grandson against us, too?"

At the mention of Seven, Betty broke down and began to cry. Her sister and mother both rushed to her side and began hugging her. "What is it?" her sister asked.

"My son hasn't come to see me in two months, and I miss him. I pushed him away because I wanted better for him, but now it just appears that I cut off my nose to spite my face." She hiccupped.

"You haven't learned anything. Look at what you're doing to your father, pushing him and us away. You have always been my most independent and complicated child. Open yourself up to those that love you—it's all we have in this life."

"We don't care who his father is—we love you both," Brenda said, squeezing her lovingly.

Betty was glad they had come. She felt so alone. Brenda was the sister right before her and they had been close growing up. They had argued about her going to live with her aunt and uncle, Brenda not wanting to be separated from Betty. The move had resulted in twenty-eight years of estrangement—not only between Betty and Brenda but between Betty and her whole family. Now, when Betty thought there was nothing else to lose, she had lost her son.

Betty was up front with her mother about what had happened to her at her aunt's house. Although she really didn't want to know what had become of her aunt and uncle, she asked to better prepare herself to face the situation. It wasn't just her feelings that she needed to consider, but also her son's, and those of any of her future grandchildren. She wanted her son to value himself and understand that even though he had been conceived through rape, he was still her love child. Betty realized that she had handled their lives poorly, but she had made the change from prostitute to working woman. She could become, if not a mother to him, at least a friend.

Brenda told her about how she too had gone to stay with their aunt, how her aunt's husband had made passes at her as well. She told Betty about her suspicion that her disappearance had something to do with them. Her mother then chimed in, telling her that they lived on Hook Creek Boulevard, in a house that her sister had spent her life paying for while her sorry-ass husband did nothing.

"The family doesn't see them. They're old, and they barely come out. The last we heard, he had a stroke. You know my sister was never able to give him children, and it turned her into a bitter old bitch. As far as I'm concerned, Seven belongs to us."

Betty wondered if her mother understood that Seven was his own man and belonged to no one. He was not their baby to protect, but a man. Time, it seemed, had stood still for all of them.

The three women talked for hours, clearing the air on a number of matters. Betty had decided that she needed her family, and she would start by dealing with her siblings along with her mother and father first. She hoped that, in time, Seven would come around, but she worried that he might never understand what had driven her. Shit, in all honesty, Betty didn't understand what had driven her. Somewhere along the line in her quest to be more than just a victim, she had victimized the people that she loved instead of finding ways to empower herself.

Over the next few days, Betty went to see her father. The first meeting was emotional. Walter cried when he saw his daughter, and she cried with him. She learned that, beyond his health problems, he had lost the will to live. He was old, eighty-seven. Looking at him sitting on the couch in the den, she thought about how time played tricks on you. When you see a person every day the aging process is almost invisible—they get older, but you can't see it, because life affords us a small amount of compassion on what will be the inevitable. But go away for any length of time, and that which makes the aging of a loved one bearable disappears, and in its place is life—uncut.

Walter and Bobbi Thomas still lived in the same house just off Atlantic Avenue at the borderline of Queens and Brooklyn. In her youth, the house seemed larger. Now it appeared to have shrunk. The girl's room was now the den, and it was there that she now saw her father again, sitting in front of the TV, asleep. In his prime, her father had been a big bruising man of six feet two inches tall. Thirty years he worked for the Mass Transit Authority, he supported his wife and children—financially and with love. When he came home from work, Betty could remember them lining up for him to throw them in the air, her mother at the end of the line waiting to be kissed. Sometimes he would threaten to toss her up in the air and catch her, and as children they would get so excited, begging, "Please do us again before you do Mama." On weekends, he would do yard work, and his muscles would bulge with the strain. In contrast to the memories, her father sat before her, age weary. Where his shoulders had been erect, they were now slumped. His posture, once tall and straight with strength, was now hunched. Where he had sported a full head of thick black hair, it was now all white and bald in the middle.

Betty felt regret, not because he had aged—that was part of life, and it was fair. Her regret came from the gap of twenty-eight years that could not be filled with memories that would make his appearance acceptable to her brain. She had two memories now—one of him as a young man and one of him as an old man and nothing to bridge the gap.

She thought of Seven and the bridge that had been burned between them, and she realized that she did not want this for them. The only cure for regret was to learn from one's experience and, most importantly, to be willing to change.

The doorbell rang, and her mother answered it. In piled her brothers, her sisters, and their families. Today, Betty thought, will be my first step toward building new memories.

❧ ❧ ❧

Gary's wife, Valerie, had decided to throw him a surprise birthday party. Seven had received his invitation, and he knew he could not miss the party. He had been spending so much time with Lisa that he hadn't seen Sean or Gary. They would make an appearance, meet everyone, dance a little, and be on their way, he decided, but when he told Lisa, she didn't look pleased.

"What's the matter?" he asked.

"I don't have anything to wear." She said, sounding concerned.

"We'll go shopping," he said, thinking that he had solved the problem.

"No, I'll take my cousin. I need a woman's help. What day is it?"

"The party is this Saturday."

"This Saturday! How long have you known?" she yelled.

"I had the invitation for a while, but I wasn't sure I wanted to go. Whatever you have already to wear is good enough."

Lisa decided not to waste time—she had shit to do. "I'm going home early tonight. I'm playing hooky from work and going shopping tomorrow," she said, standing up.

Seven was on his feet since he was the one driving her home. He hated when things happened to break their stride. "I'll get my keys."

Lisa was on the phone to Kim before he could pull away. "Kim, it's me, Lisa. Wake up."

"Is something wrong?" Kim asked with urgency in her voice.

"No, honey, everything is fine. I have a different emergency. I've been invited to a party and I have nothing to wear."

"That is a crisis," she said, coming to life again. "So, has this got anything to do with *Seven*? You know you're wrong, leaving me to hear about him from Alex. Then I have to sit around waiting to hear from you and pretend I don't know anything. This is bullshit."

Lisa laughed. She knew it was coming, but she was glad Kim was being a good sport about it. "Ok, girl, you only get the scoop if you help me."

Kim began coughing. "I'm already getting sick. I'm going to have to call in." They both laughed.

They talked about Seven, the nice things he did and said. She told her cousin about her feelings for him and about how he seemed to feel the same way. Lisa made Kim aware that he was the little boy that found her in the schoolyard that dreadful day. They talked about Aunt Jenny and Uncle James and the first time they had seen each other. Sometimes it was good remembering painful situations from the past—it made the present and the future that much more sweet.

Kim picked her up by cab and they rode to the subway over on Archer Avenue. Once on the train, they planned their shopping strategy. On Fifth Avenue, they shopped until they dropped, visiting store after store. Lisa thought her skin might be chaffed from putting on and taking off so many clothes. When lunchtime came and she still hadn't bought anything, they decided on pizza. They sat at the window of the pizza parlor, people watching. The weather was mild, which was often the case in late May in New York.

With their bellies somewhat full, they rested awhile and then headed back out into the mean streets. Lisa could have eaten two slices with a large soda, or maybe a chicken parmesan sandwich, but Kim wasn't having it.

"Eating and shopping can get you in trouble. We want the dress to look nice. We don't want to have to imagine away the pouch caused by a heavy lunch."

Then, the first bit of magic happened: as they passed a shoe store, Kim started screaming, "Those are our shoes!"

They went in and exclaimed to the sales lady, "That shoe, size eight."

They left the store a few minutes later with half of their mission completed. While passing a little boutique, Lisa spied a dress that put the "E" in elegant.

When she tried it on, they both knew. Kim, being her big cousin, bought her two other really nice dresses, and when Lisa would have refused, she said,

"I love you, and I want to do something for you. Please don't ruin it for me. This is from me and Wayne."

On their way heading home, they laughed and talked about everything. It was then that Lisa decided to seek advice from her cousin. "How did you know that Wayne was the one?"

"I just knew. Why? Do you think that Seven is the one?"

"I never been in love before him, but I'm not stupid enough to think that just because I'm in love, he's the right guy for me. I just don't know."

"You know that a man is one hundred percent of what he shows and only fifty percent of what he says. In other words, is he keeping his word when he says that he is going to do something? Have you been to his house? Is he tender after sex—when it really counts?"

"As far as I can see, he does keep his word to me. I have spent a lot of time at his house. He answers his phone freely in front of me. As for the sex, we haven't gotten there yet."

Kim turned and looked at her. "You haven't fucked him yet? How long have you been seeing him?"

"Almost three months."

Kim just whistled. "You spend every evening with him, and it goes nowhere?" She was amazed. It was good in this day and age to be responsible, but she was still amazed. "How long do you normally wait before becoming intimate with a man you are attracted to?"

Clearing her throat, Lisa just stared at her. What could she say? She hadn't expected the conversation to take this turn. Further illustrating her point about, how green she really was.

Kim, being no dummy, sat there with her mouth open. "You never had sex?" she asked incredulously.

"No," Lisa said wanting to change the subject.

"Oh shit," Kim said, staring at her as if she had a chicken growing out of her head.

Lisa thought Kim was going to stand up on the "F" train and announce that her cousin was a virgin. Then, once she had everyone's attention, maybe she'd charge the other riders admission to take a look at her. "Does he know?" she asked.

"No, we haven't—"

Kim cut her off. "I know—you haven't gotten that far yet. Oh shit," she said again.

"Let's change the subject," Lisa said.

"I'm sorry," Kim said. "You are twenty-six. How—?"

Lisa cut her off, knowing her question. "Listen, when Grandma got sick, she was what was important at the time. I didn't have time to chase around guys and do the things people my age did. It wasn't an imposition, though. I loved her, and wouldn't have changed a thing."

They talked more about sex, love, AIDS, and pregnancy, and Lisa felt like a kid. Kim did advise her on one other important thing, and Lisa wholeheartedly agreed. "If you can't talk to him about sex, then you shouldn't be fucking him," she said.

When they went their separate ways that evening, Lisa realized that she could no longer continue to behave as though the sexual tension between her and Seven didn't exist.

That evening, after he showed up with two frozen TV dinners and some flowers, they sat in the living room eating. He talked about his day. He was having problems with the developer in Georgia, and it was pissing him off. He then asked her a question, and he realized she wasn't listening to a thing he said.

"Are you worried about the party? I'm sure whatever you picked will be all right," he said.

"How many women have you slept with?" she asked out of the blue.

He didn't mind being asked, but tell him the game and the rules and he would play fair. Being blindsided with this question made him want to…What, laugh?

"Okay, we're talking about my sex partners now. I just want to be in the same conversation," he said evasively. Shit, he didn't know. What he did know from recent tests was that he didn't have HIV, and he was consistent with the condom. After living with Betty, how could he not be?

"Do you plan on avoiding this conversation like every other conversation about you?" she asked.

"Let's make this conversation as healthy as possible," he said. "I'm not going to go back and bring up every woman that I ever slept with. I have had my share of women. I have been tested. I'm healthy, and I am consistent with condoms. I am also willing to get tested again—with you."

She kept eye contact with him, but he was a man, and he didn't squirm under her scrutiny. He wanted her intimacy, her trust, and her love. "I will not ask you about your past relationships or judge you by them. I'm only concerned about now and what it will take to make it work with us."

Lisa smiled, leaned forward on the couch, and kissed him, biting his lip and then suckling it to counteract the pain she had just caused him. She snuggled close to him, the dinners forgotten, and gave him just a taste of what intimacy and trust would be like for them.

# CHAPTER 9

Kim showed up at 9:00 A.M. on the Saturday of the party to help Lisa get ready.

"He's not picking me up until 8:30 P.M. Why are we getting ready now when we have eleven hours?" She laughed.

"That's barely enough time," Kim said.

The women started out by getting a pedicure and manicure. Lisa decided upon a French manicure for both her toes and her hands. Next, they went to eat a hearty breakfast so that there would be enough time to digest her food; anything after that, Kim told her, would be water and salad. Kim drove them to a cosmetics store on Jamaica Avenue, where they bought a lipstick that complemented Lisa's complexion perfectly.

On their way back to her house, Kim let her know what the agenda would be. "We'll wash your hair, and then you'll rest for about an hour. Later, you'll soak in a nice hot fragrant bath and then get dressed and greet him at the door." Lisa thought it was overkill, but Kim was enjoying herself, so she allowed herself to enjoy the day too.

While Kim was styling her hair and showing her a few tricks with the hot curlers, Lisa told her about her talk with Seven the night before. Kim smiled, but she would reserve judgment until she got her own first impression. She was still a little worried about Lisa, though, and wanted to make sure her cousin was all right.

Before long, 7:00 P.M. came—time to get the show on the road.

✤ ✤ ✤

Seven hadn't seen her all day, and he was feeling irritated. They usually spent all of Saturday together, but Lisa had called to tell him that her cousin had shown up this morning and that she would see him this evening when he picked her up. To keep himself busy, he ran on his treadmill, went to the barber, and picked up some clothes from the dry cleaners. When those few errands were done he still had time to kill, and he was restless.

Part of the reason he was agitated was that he wanted to buy something nice for Lisa, but he didn't know what would be appropriate considering their relationship. He had never dated a woman who wanted him just for him. He had wanted sex and a showpiece for certain business functions, while they had wanted fancy clothes, jewelry, and money. This had never upset him, because fair exchange was not robbery. But with Lisa it was different; he wanted her to understand that his feelings were running deep, although it had never occurred to him to tell her how he felt.

He drove to the jeweler in Downtown Brooklyn that he visited whenever he needed to purchase parting gifts for the women in his life. Old Mr. Kriesberg had owned his shop for over thirty years, and he was now in business with his son and grandson. As Seven pushed in the door to the shop, the bell rang overhead, and from the back of the store, old man Kriesberg appeared with his grandson in tow. Kriesberg was a short old white man with thick, bushy gray eyebrows and long gray bread. His eyes were black as coal, and there was a gleam to them that Seven understood. The old man had a love for making money and transacting a good deal, just like Seven did. The younger man was still learning the ropes, and his blues eyes were closed to opportunity and a good prospect. The old man, however, was still working to make certain that no great opportunities went ignored.

"Seven," he said, "good to see you, my man. More lady trouble?"

Seven smiled. "No, sir. I was looking for something for a special young lady."

"Come to the back; I have some new pieces I think you might like," he said, gesturing.

Seven followed him into the back. He and the old man then sat at a table and waited until his grandson brought in a little glass case from the safe. The old man opened it and Seven was awed by the beauty it contained. It was awkward to say the least for Seven, as he had only bought jewelry for women when he decided he no longer wanted to see them. The pieces were exquisite—necklaces, studded earrings, bracelets for the arm and ankle. He had a difficult time choosing the right piece.

He settled on a studded pair of earrings and a gold necklace with a matching diamond pendant. The pieces were elegant and not at all flashy—they would enhance her beauty rather than take away from it. Though Lisa was an unusually beautiful woman, she remained plain in her dress. Still, her beauty could not be pushed into the shadows. He had been places with her, like the supermarket, the video store, and more, and noticed men noticing her no matter how plain her dress was. Her appearance did not provoke disrespect or lust but rather inspired that trait that God placed in men—to guard and protect the female. She was so untainted and natural in her beauty that she reduced even the most sophisticated of men to their most primitive selves.

He could see the lights on throughout the house as he pulled up to pick her up. He made his way to the door at ten after eight. Seven had made reservations at a swank French restaurant on the lower east side, and afterward he planned to carry her off for an evening of dancing and socializing. It would be the first time she would meet his friends, and he didn't want her to feel pressure. His friends were a laid back group, and they would love her.

He knocked on the door and her cousin, if his guess was right, answered. She was short, with pretty brown skin that had a reddish hue. Her teeth were pretty, white and even, and her smile was welcoming and very friendly.

"You must be Seven. Come in."

"And you must be Kim," he stated, smiling.

"Yes, I'm Lisa's older cousin. It's so nice to finally meet you."

"Same here," he answered, finding her very pleasant.

"Lisa is upstairs getting ready. Can I get you anything?"

"No, thank you. We have dinner reservations first."

"Oh, that's romantic," Kim said sighing.

He chuckled, thinking that she resembled Lisa in many ways. After meeting Kim, he guessed it wasn't so bad sharing Lisa today. As with Alex, he noticed that there was something about them and this house. Even though Lisa lived here alone, they all seemed to consider this home. Lisa, it seemed, treated them like they lived there too. They must have spent a lot of time here when they were growing up. The feeling he got about her family was that they were warm toward one another.

Kim interrupted his thoughts. "I'm going to see if Lisa needs anything. You'll be all right?"

"Yes, of course. I'll be fine."

Kim went racing up the stairs and burst into Lisa's room. "Lisa, he is so handsome." It was an understatement. Seven had taken her breath away.

Lisa laughed. "You met him? He is here, then?"

"Yes, he is," she said, sighing again.

Helping Lisa with the finishing touches, Kim couldn't wait to see what they looked like together. Stepping back from her, she looked at Lisa and said, "This is going to be a beautiful night for you."

"I hope so. This is my first time meeting his friends, and I want everything to go well."

"Okay, stay here and count to thirty and then come down."

"All right," Lisa said, laughing, Kim watched too many soaps, she thought.

Downstairs, Seven was checking his watch when Kim appeared. "She'll be right down," she said before he could ask if everything was all right.

He was about to respond to Kim when Lisa came into sight on the stairs. She made her way down very carefully, giving him the eye contact he appreciated. When she reached the bottom step, he stood dumbfounded. Her loveliness strangled the words in his throat. She wore an off-the-shoulder black dress with a thin strap that went around her neck and attached in a knot at her breast, accentuating her cleavage. The dress itself was nothing more than a piece of material that covered her from her breast to just above her knee, with style. Her shoulders were a smooth honey brown, that made him want to touch her. Lisa's hair was swept up in a French roll with little wisps of curls framing her face. The shoes she wore were sexy and very feminine (black with three pieces of leather crossing her foot in sections and a thin strap making it a very classy sling back), and to finish off the ensemble, she wore a sheer wrap with tassels that dangled around the edges. There were black flowers embroidered in the wrap. As for accessories, she wore a pair of her grandmother's gold earrings.

Kim felt like an intruder as she watched the exchange. Lisa might not have known for sure, but judging by his eyes, Seven was in love. He stood there just staring at her as if he had not ever seen her before. Kim was like a proud mother, and to her, Lisa deserved happiness.

It took him a moment to regain his speech, and when he finally spoke he said, "You are lovely."

He was going to wait until they were alone, but he decided that now would be fitting. Reaching into his pocket, he produced a velvet box, and both women took in a sharp breath. He smiled, glad to be giving her a token of his affection. When he opened the box, the earrings were in the corner of the velvet bed, while the necklace lay flat.

"Oh…" was all she could say, tears sparkling in her eyes.

Kim was crying as she said, "Put them on her and I'll get the camera."

His hands shook as he stepped behind her to close the clasp, and when his fingers brushed the nape of her neck, he too breathed in sharply. When she turned to face him, he saw that the pendant had fallen to the swell of her breast, and he thought she looked magnificent. She exchanged her grandmother's earrings for his diamond studs.

He wanted to march her back upstairs and fill her with the juices of his labor, then lean back on his knees between her still-parted legs and watch his essence flow from her core. He wanted her.

Seven was dressed in a black suit with a white shirt and black tie. He was in every sense of the word striking. Lisa said. "You're beautiful." Seven didn't know how to take the compliment, as he felt *beautiful* was a word that best described a woman.

"Are we ready?" she asked shyly.

"Yeah, baby, I think we are," he answered, and Lisa knew he was talking about so much more.

Taking her hand, he led her from the house and out into the balmy night air. When Kim closed the door behind them, he spun her at the curb and kissed her thoroughly, and when she would have pulled away, he suckled her lip to keep her with him. There was a heady fragrance around her that made him hard. Reaching behind her, he clutched the roundness of her ass and pushed her ever so slightly against his length. She whimpered, and he moaned. Seven and Lisa were on the same page, and it was a beautiful thing.

The lighting in the restaurant was dim, the atmosphere sexually charged, and they both felt it. They toyed with their food and spoke about ordinary happenings, but everything seemed to have a sexual innuendo behind it, and they both caught themselves swallowing hard. Tonight, he thought, was going to be rough. He already felt as if he couldn't keep his hands off her. He kept thinking about her wearing nothing but the pendant and earrings he had bought for her. Seven laughed at himself when she excused herself to go to the rest room. He just needed to calm down, and his constant state of erection would pass. He was no green boy out with his first woman. Yet he still had to pep talk himself so that she had a good evening and didn't see him for the beast he was.

When she returned, he had already paid the check and was holding her wrap. They headed to the truck and were off to the party. On the way, he told her about Gary and Sean and what they did for a living.

"Sean is a criminal lawyer. He represents the crème de le crème of New York when they have brushes with the law. Gary is a chemist. He works for a major pharmaceutical company and hand-in-hand with FDA."

"How interesting," she said, knowing she was going to be out of place.

"Valerie is Gary's wife. She's a sweetheart. They have two girls—Kenya, age three, and Michelle, age five. Sean is married to Rhonda, and they have two boys—Bilal, age two, and Hassan, age four. They're a funny bunch, and down to earth."

As he was talking they pulled into the parking lot of a hotel just off the Van Wyck Expressway. He let Lisa out at the front door and parked. She waited for him, and they went in together. The gathering was in a reception hall at the back of the main floor. As they approached the door, they could hear the music and laughter. It was time, Lisa thought, to meet his friends and either pass or fail.

Reading her thoughts, he said, "I make my own decisions. You can't fail at this."

Inside the reception hall, lining the dance floor, there were tables with white cloths and candles. Off to the right was a large table weighed down with all types of fine fare. The caterers were on hand to serve at the guests' request. There was a bar with several bartenders serving people as they came and went. Each table had labels bearing the names of the guests who would be sitting there. It was a very classy setup.

Seven spied the gang and, squeezing her hand, headed over to them with Lisa in tow. Reaching the table, two men stood up and shook hands with Seven, slapping him on the back. They called him names and he did the same. There were three women at the table, and two of them stood. "Where have you been? You know we worry when we don't hear from you," the shorter of the two women said.

"Rhonda," he said with enthusiasm, "I don't come around because you made it plain that Sean is the only one for you."

She hit him, and they all laughed. "She's right, Seven—where have you been? The kids have been asking for you," Valerie said.

"I've been busy working trying to make a dollar."

"Seven, you remember my cousin Sherri, don't you?" Rhonda said with a twinkle in her eye.

Shit, he thought, she was trying to match-make again. He had gotten after Valerie and Rhonda about this before. Well if they were embarrassed, that was on them. Every time he came to a gathering, they did this; it was one of the reasons why he had contemplated not coming. Reaching behind him, he carefully pulled Lisa to the front. "Everybody, this is Lisa, my date. She and I have been seeing each other for months now."

Gary and Sean put their heads down. They had warned their wives and wanted nothing to do with this, but Gary, being a good sport and knowing his wife meant well said, "Well, Lisa, it's nice to finally meet you. I now see why the old dog hasn't been returning my calls."

Sean came forward second. "Welcome, Lisa. It's nice to meet you."

Valerie, following her husband's lead said. "I'm glad you could both make it."

"Hello," Lisa said, "I'm glad to be here. Everything looks so pretty, Happy birthday, Gary."

Rhonda, however, stood her ground. She was trying to help her cousin find a man, one with money. She didn't speak to Lisa but addressed Seven: "Sherri has been waiting to dance with you."

Sean's wife had always been a bitch, and Seven had never liked her. She was only interested in the money, not Sean, but that was Sean's issue, not his. Lisa was his issue, and he didn't appreciate the blatant disregard coming from Rhonda. He was annoyed with Sherri as well. They had played adult games once upon a time and had gone their separate ways—a mutual decision, or so he had thought. It seemed that anytime there was a gathering, she would end up there like a fifth wheel. She was now wearing the bracelet he had bought her when he decided to call it quits. Rhonda knew of some of his ventures, no doubt from Sean, and sought to get a pigeon for her cousin. Just as he was about to straighten the bitch out, Lisa squeezed his hand.

"Let's dance," she whispered.

"That sounds like a great idea," he responded, and he walked off without addressing Rhonda again.

Looking at Lisa, he could see that she was uncomfortable but not willing to turn tail and run. He hated that she was coming face to face with his past. He didn't think he would like meeting someone that she had been intimate with. In fact, he was sure of it.

Out on the dance floor, the crowd was doing the electric slide, and with the drama forgotten, Lisa and Seven had fun. The lighting on the dance floor was dimmer than at the sides, where the tables were. The DJ was in a booth, elevated and away from the dance floor. He was good, Lisa thought. He played everything: rap, reggae, rhythm and blues—you name it. She danced with Gary while Valerie danced with Seven, and they laughed and yelled when certain songs came on. Everything after the introduction fiasco had gone perfectly. For such a big guy, Seven was a great dancer, and when the music switched to reggae, her panties got wet with all the rubbing they were doing.

Off the floor, he got them drinks and found an empty table for just the two of them. Lisa suspected Valerie had set up the extra table so that they wouldn't have to sit with Rhonda and cousin Sherri. Seven went off to get them plates, but as soon as he walked away, a tall, very handsome man walked up and asked her to dance.

"No, thank you," she stammered. "I'm here with someone."

"Come on, it's a social event. It's just dancing," he said, looking at her cleavage.

Seven was just walking up when he heard her say, "I've danced to almost every song. I'm tired."

He smiled. He knew that she wouldn't dance with anyone else, but what he didn't like was that he didn't want her to. Stepping around the guy, he said, "Brian, you're not trying to steal my woman, are you?"

"Yes, Seven I am," he said boldly.

"Having any luck?"

"No. It would be that you have the prettiest woman in here and she won't dance with anyone but you."

Seven smiled and shook his hand. He had made some very lucrative business deals with Brian and liked how he thought—or at least he had until he saw him flirting with Lisa.

"Dance with me?" he asked again. "I'll return you to him when the song is over."

Lisa stood, placing her hand in Seven's and whispering in his ear, "I need some air."

Seven set down the plates. "We'll be back," he said to Brian.

They left Brian staring after them, wishing that he was taking care of her needs. Brian spotted Sherri sitting at a table staring after them too and asked, "Would you care to dance?"

The grounds were well manicured behind the hotel, and lamps dangled from the trees, giving the place a romantic feel. There were plenty of lovers out tonight. Some were dancing, while others were walking and talking.

"Are you having a good time?" he asked.

"The best."

He smiled and moved them to a spot where the lamp light barely touched them, and he kissed her tenderly. Then, taking her hand, he led her back into the party and onto the dance floor again. As she danced with him, he noticed that a few more wisps of her hair had fallen. Her cheeks glowed with health and excitement, and he had to admit that she was in his system.

The crowd sang "Happy Birthday" to the birthday boy, and champagne flowed freely for the rest of the night. Lisa noticed that Sherri had stopped rolling her eyes at her and started hanging around Brian. Rhonda never came around, which was good because she didn't feel like being phony.

Valerie was average height with smooth brown skin and a short haircut that became her. She had deep brown eyes and was very pretty. Her personality was warm, and she took to Lisa immediately. In the ladies' room, she apologized to Lisa for the misunderstanding, and Lisa assured her there were no hard feelings. They went back out to the party and had a wonderful time.

It was about three in the morning when they called it quits and headed for her home. Again she had fallen asleep during the ride, and he was content. Pulling in front of her house, he leaned over and kissed her nose. "We're here, sleepyhead. Wake up."

She opened her eyes and stretched a little. "Here already? That was fast."

They walked to her door holding hands. Seven took her keys from her and opened the door. They walked onto the sun porch, and before she could walk into the living room, he pushed her up against the door and began kissing her. This was the little piece of heaven that he had waited for all night. First he kissed her lips lightly and then lowered his head to her neck and shoulders, tasting her. He began grinding himself against her and she could feel the impression of his rigid length within his pants, and to his surprise, she began to respond to his movements.

He removed the strap from around her neck and pushed her dress down, revealing her breasts. The cool air caused her nipples to harden, and Seven wished the lighting was better. He cupped her breasts and ran his thumbs over her nipples, further enflaming them. Lisa's breath became shallow, and it turned into a pant when he leaned down and began sucking her nipple. He changed nipples, wanting to sample them both.

Lisa had never experienced such a feeling, and she cried out at the sensation that started at her breast and pooled down between her legs. Blindly, she clutched at his head so that he wouldn't pull away. "Seven...Seven...Oh..." she moaned.

His head was spinning, and though he knew he wasn't going to get any satisfaction tonight, he couldn't stop himself. Lifting her dress, he pulled at her underwear, ripping them on the sides. Lisa was dazed and didn't think to stop him. He stuffed her panties in his pocket and kissed her. When he reached down to touch her pleasure spot, they both moaned into each other's mouths. She was wet and ready. He rubbed his fingers on her sensitive clitoris and her knees gave way, but he held her in place. He stroked her until he was pulsing, and Lisa was sobbing. When he could take no more he pushed his finger inside her, still rubbing her button with his thumb.

"Oh," she panted, "I'm dying."

Seven was dying too. Lisa was wet and tight. He could feel her muscles clamp down on his finger, and he wanted to burst. The feeling was intense, and the only thing that saved him was knowing the outcome. She opened her legs wider and he groaned, pushing his tongue in her mouth and making the same motion with his tongue that he did with his finger. He bought her to her first climax, and as her body began to quiver from within, he knew he was in trouble. Leaning her head back, she sobbed his name over and over again.

They stood there holding each other in silence, and finally, when the world came off its tilt, she whispered, "I love you, Seven."

He hugged her desperately but said nothing for a few moments, and when he did speak, he said gruffly, "I'd better go."

She shook her head, kissed his lips, and then stepped aside. He opened the door and didn't look back as he headed to his truck. As she watched him pull away, she had a moment of clarity. She did not feel insecure because he hadn't responded in kind—she had verbalized what she'd felt, and it felt right.

On his way home, he thought about her words, and his chest constricted. He felt love surrounding them, but he had never expected it to be spoken. He tried to downplay how much it meant to him that she had said it, but he couldn't. Until that moment he really hadn't understood how lonely he was, and, God help him, he cried.

# CHAPTER 10

As he walked into the building, the sun was coming up.

*So much for going to bed.*

He went straight into his office and started checking messages. The land developer in Georgia was still hounding him—they couldn't agree upon a price or terms that would make both parties feel like they'd won. They had haggled relentlessly, and Seven was getting tired of it. He was beginning to think that it would be best to hold the land for another six months and start the process over when the developer understood that he wasn't desperate.

There were messages from Gary and Sean, who wanted him to go to a sports bar with them in Jersey. The last message was from Betty.

"Hello, I, uh…haven't seen you, and I was wondering if you were okay. Please call me."

He stared out the window at the water and the few cars that made up Sunday-morning traffic on the FDR drive. As the sun danced off New York City, he thought about Betty and the fact that she had called. What was he supposed to do with that? He was doing what she wanted him to do. He didn't feel like dealing with his mother—her secrets or even her truths—at this point. He wasn't mad at Betty; he was numb where she was concerned. When he tried to think about his childhood, his mother, or his faceless father, there was nothing, and he didn't know if that was good or bad.

Lisa was another matter. Her words and actions frightened him. He was forced to admit that she was all he had. He had friends and associates, people that he could laugh and joke with, but in a full room, he experienced loneliness quite often. He would chalk it up to his individuality—he just wasn't into what they were into, or they weren't where he was mentally—when in fact he just didn't fit in. When it came to talking about himself, he didn't; if he shared himself, people would see that they really didn't know him and, what's more, that he didn't know himself. Lisa, he thought, was the answer to his future happiness, and he would seize the moment with her by binding her to him. He didn't understand it now, but he would later: When one abandons self, one can't participate in the act of being in love, because love requires the sharing of one's self. Seven was plotting to steal what Lisa was willing to give him freely.

It was 9:00 A.M. when he decided that he needed sleep and headed back his to room. Seven barely got his suit off before he fell into bed. He was asleep as soon as his head hit the pillow. He was exhausted both mentally and physically, and he slept dreamlessly.

When Lisa woke at noon, she showered, dressed, and went downstairs to wait for him. Since he had left this morning, she could think of nothing else but the pleasure he had given her. She could still hear her panting, mindless words. Lisa felt shy but not embarrassed. Yesterday had been wonderful, and she wanted more of the same from him. When she told him that she loved him, he hadn't responded, but she could feel the love that surrounded them. The embrace that they shared was intense—his action had spoken of what he could not verbalize.

Her thoughts wandered back in time and she could see them as children standing in the schoolyard of PS 92. She could remember asking him if he knew how to cross the street and his indignation at the question. He had been very serious through the whole ordeal and never really smiled. The little boy that he was comforted her and protected her as well as any ten-year-old could have done. *There was strength within him then and there is strength within him now*, she thought as she walked into the kitchen. She smiled, not realizing that the main reason she was recalling the scene of yesteryear was to gain some insight into the man he was now, because—to put it simply—he wasn't sharing himself. As the day passed, she didn't hear anything from him, so she called him. The machine picked up.

"I was thinking about you. Call me, honey."

He was up sitting on the end of the bed, staring at the machine as her voice came through it, but he didn't reach for the phone. As he headed toward the bathroom to shower, he decided that he wouldn't see her today. It was a desperate attempt to gain control of his emotions. He wasn't rejecting her, but he needed to prevent the feeling of drowning. He thought that by depriving himself of her company, he would become stronger and his need for her would be less intense. He worried that if she took her love from him, he wouldn't be able to survive.

On the other hand, Lisa did not lie to herself about her limits and weaknesses. She embraced her new feelings of love and did not see them as a threat. She didn't have the same worries about relationships and love that he did. Her only fear was marrying a man who turned out to be an abuser like her father. But the mere act of admitting that fear robbed it of its strength.

In his office, Seven began organizing his schedule for the week to come, trying to whittle away the hours until he would see her again. He took care of the correspondence that had piled up on his desk since he had started spending so much time at her house. For Mary, he left his dry-cleaning laundry in a basket at the door, along with tickets for things that needed picking up. He would also need to go away for a few days on business, but he put that trip off for right now.

He had been working for several hours, and evening was approaching when his doorbell rang. People very rarely came to see him, except Mary. Smiling, he thought it was Lisa and headed to the door, but when he looked through the peephole, all he saw was the top of what appeared to be a wig. He opened the door, and standing there was Betty's mother, his grandmother.

"I had to come see you, because it appeared that you weren't going to call me or come by. You ought to be ashamed making an old lady trek way over here, not knowing whether you were home or not."

The whole thing threw him off, but when he recovered and noticed her leaning heavily on her cane, he invited her in.

"Oh, your home is beautiful," she said, reaching out and grabbing his arm to steady herself as they headed into the living room.

He smiled. "Thank you. How did you get here?"

"Your Uncle Calvin came by to see your grandpa and me. I talked him into driving me over here. Your Aunt Brenda is with your grandpa."

"Well, where is Calvin then?"

"I told him that if I didn't come back down within ten minutes, he could leave and you would take me home."

His eyebrows shot up. He had been manipulated. Maybe, he thought, he should allow her to handle the deal with the Georgia developer. She would get the terms he wanted *and* at a better price than he was asking for.

"How did you know I would let you in...or that I will take you home?"

"You're my grandson, and even though you don't know it, I know you wouldn't do anything to hurt me on purpose. Also, you love your mother—I saw that when we met the last time—and I qualify I'm her mother." She laughed.

At the mention of Betty he became quiet, and his grandmother touched his hand. Betty, for him, was off-limits.

"What can I do for you?" he asked.

"Don't get formal on me. I came to get to know you. I had to. It's important to me."

He smiled again, not knowing what to say. He decided to go with the flow. "Do you want to go out to eat?"

"Oh, yes," she said, clapping her hands together.

They decided on a diner on Queens Boulevard and headed out shortly after she got there. As they were being seated, he realized that this is what Betty would look like when she got older, only she'd be taller. Bobbi was short, with dark skin like well-worn leather. Her eyes, brown and faded, betrayed her age, and they were filled with wisdom. There were wrinkles about her eyes and mouth, and when she smiled, he felt approval. She wore a green polyester pantsuit with a little white church hat pinned to her wig. After they were served, the conversation began to flow.

She told him about her parents and her childhood in Mississippi. They talked about how she met his grandfather, who was older than her, and how much she loved him. He found out that his grandfather had been in the service and had worked for mass transit for thirty years. She also told him about the births of her children, on down to his mother, and what being a grandmother meant to her.

He told her about living in Corona, and while he left out many of the gory details, he described how he had fought a lot as a kid. His grandmother asked him what he did for a living, and he told her about some of his business deals. They talked about his college life, the friends he had met there, and what they were doing now. Bobbi finally asked the question that she wanted the answer to the most.

"Are you planning to get married?" she asked.

He smiled. "Yeah, I am someday."

"Do you have a young lady that you're serious with?"

Here was his test. Could he say it? "Yes, as a matter of fact, I do."

"Why don't the two of you come for dinner? Your grandfather and I would love to have you both."

Betty's mother was quick on the draw, he thought. She laughed out loud, sensing the thought. They talked some more about him and his young lady friend, and Bobbi discovered that he was serious about her—from what he didn't say. She was proud of him: he was handsome, kind, and successful. He was a good man, but with sadness ever present in his eyes. She would start by just being his friend.

"Come by and bring the young lady. Meet your family; this is important. I want to be friends, and make no mistake—I'm putting in the effort because you are my grandson and I'm trying to catch up on time. With me, young man, what you see is what you get. Your mother will be there too—I won't lie. I'm honest, but I'm also too old to waste time lying."

"I'll think about it," he said.

It was a start. "Dinner will be on Sunday at 5:30 P.M. You'll see where I live when you take me home."

It was 8:00 P.M. when they left the restaurant and headed to his grandparents' house. During the ride, they didn't talk much, and Seven played some light jazz. In fact, the only time Bobbi spoke was when she would direct him to turn or go straight. She enjoyed the ride as far as he could tell, and he felt good to be in her company and to know that she felt good in his. They pulled in front of a little brick house with a well-cut lawn. When she opened her door to get out, he opened his and raced around to her side to help her. He helped her up the driveway to the side door. Inwardly, she was happy. She opened the door and he stepped into the kitchen behind her.

His aunt was standing at the sink, running water and talking over her shoulder to an elderly man seated at the table. When Bobbi stepped into the kitchen, the man's face lit up.

"I'm home, love, and I brought company."

Brenda was staring at him and smiling, "Seven, good to see you again."

He extended his hand by way of greeting. "It's nice to see you again, too."

The elderly gentleman stood, straightening his curved back as much as he could and staring Seven in the eye. "Damn, it's nice to meet you, son," he said.

Seven shook his hand and was surprised by the strength in his grip. "The pleasure is mine," Seven said, and it really was.

His grandfather went right into a topic that men were often comfortable with. "You like sports? Maybe you can come by and watch a few games with me?"

Bobbi, acting as an onlooker, was happy to see her husband excited about life. He was out of his seat and on his feet to meet his grandson. After all these years, she still loved him as much as she did when she first married him. When she saw him about to lead Seven off to the den, she put a stop to it, saying for everyone to hear, "Let's not overwhelm the man all in one day. He'll be back on Sunday with his lady friend for us to meet."

He liked his grandmother—there was no sense trying to convince himself that he didn't. She was funny, open, and very warm, and it appeared that she always got what she wanted. His grandfather was standing there awaiting his answer, and he couldn't disappoint him.

"We'll be here," he confirmed.

The older man smiled, and Seven decided that he was going to like him too. "Glad you'll be back," his grandfather said. "I'm very old. Don't miss any time with me."

Seven shook his hand and hugged his grandmother, because she would accept nothing less. Then he decided, *What the hell?* and hugged Brenda too.

Feeling a little lighter, he drove away. What could his mother have been thinking to subject them to the life they had lived when these people clearly cared for her? They embraced him because of their feelings for her—no questions asked.

He made some decisions about Lisa and himself, and before he knew it he was parked in front of her house.

*So much for not seeing her today.*

She came to the door looking a mess, but he found her to be as attractive as ever.

"Seven," she said breathlessly.

He smiled. Damn, he felt the same way. "I didn't come to stay. I just wanted to tell you that I'll pick you up for lunch tomorrow."

"Okay."

"Sorry I didn't get to see you earlier. My grandmother showed up unannounced, and I'm just coming from taking her home. We have been invited to dinner next Sunday. Is that okay?"

"Of course it is."

He kissed and hugged her. "I might not return you to work after I pick you up at lunch. Is that all right?"

"I'll use half a vacation day."

"All right, baby. I'm on my way. Tomorrow at 1:00."

"Okay," she answered, watching him head back to his truck and pull away. She worried about him when she didn't hear from him, and she was glad he came by. Their interaction this evening was so short that she didn't have time to be shy with him.

She went back into the house and up the stairs to get ready for bed. When she took off her clothes, she stared at herself naked in the full-length mirror. She was beginning to understand the passion that a woman could hold, and yet she looked no different. Lisa, however, knew that she was not the same person she was yesterday.

# CHAPTER 11

At work, she raced to get as much done as possible, since she was leaving early. Elise gave her half the day off with no questions asked. She also told her that she would be in charge of another major conference coming to the hotel, and that they would discuss it the next day. As the morning whittled away, she wondered where they were going. Wherever it was, she didn't mind if it meant spending time with him.

It was 12:45 in the afternoon when she noticed him in the lobby. He was dressed causally in jeans and a nice shirt. He stood staring at her and smiling. He was so handsome that he took her breath away, and after what they had shared, he seemed different too.

Walking to the front desk, he said, "Are you ready, Lisa?"

When he spoke her name, her heart leaped a little. He was killing her without knowing it. "Give me a few minutes and I'll meet you out front."

"Okay then, I'll go get the truck and be out front when you come."

After tying up a few loose ends, Lisa walked out of the hotel at 1:00 in the afternoon, as scheduled. He reached over from the driver's side and opened her door for her.

"Where are we going?" she asked.

Seven turned and looked at her with an odd expression on his face, and for a minute, she thought he wouldn't say anything.

"I made appointments for us to see the doctor."

His response produced butterflies in her stomach, but she said nothing. She was thinking about his answer to her question and how it made her feel. He knew what she was thinking, and he gave her a moment to come to grips with what he was saying. He wasn't pushing for sex—that wasn't what this was about. He was opening another door for them, changing the avenue along which they were traveling.

"Oh." There was nothing else to say.

"Do you not want to do this?"

She exhaled loudly and her facial expression showed that she was in deep thought. They had to move on to another stage. He was handling the situation correctly, yet she felt nervous, not about the test—she was a virgin, after all—but about what it represented. They were not children, but two responsible adults that understood where the relationship was heading.

Seven interrupted her thoughts. "Listen this is not about just sex. We still don't have to rush into anything. I just want this issue resolved between us because I want you to be sure about me and have no reservations."

"I know, and I want this too. I'm just shocked."

What he left out was that although he had never had sex without a condom before, he wanted that intimacy with her. There could be nothing between them—he was clear about what he wanted. This was the best time to clear up this issue, in a setting where sex was not clouding his judgment. Most important was that she felt safe. To him, that was a major component of their happiness together.

They didn't talk for the rest of the ride, both in their own thoughts. When he pulled into the parking garage, she knew she was taking the next step in the rest of her life. She asked herself if she was truly ready, and the answer was yes. There could be no one else; he would have to be her first. As that revelation came to her, she opened her door and stepped out. Seven walked around to the passenger side and took her hand. He leaned down and kissed her lips—with tenderness, not urgency.

They walked from the parking garage to the office building just up the street. In the lobby, he pushed the button for the elevator, and when it came, he waited for her to enter first. He pushed the button for the fifth floor, and when the door closed, he reached out and hugged her. Getting off the elevator, he led her to the left and down a long carpeted hall. He opened the door to the doctor's suite, and inside the setting was tranquil. There was a large fish tank in the waiting room, with many different-colored fish. Seven continued on to the desk and signed their names on the patient roster.

They weren't there very long when a thin white lady opened the door at the back of the waiting room and said, "Dr. Beniot will see you both now." She led them down a long hall and into an office.

"Please be seated. The doctor will be in to speak with you both first before he examines you." She shut the door, and it was just the two of them again.

Seven reached over and squeezed her hand to reassure her that he was there. After about three minutes, Dr. Benoit came in. He was an older African-American gentleman with silver and black hair and a genuine smile.

"Well, young people, how can I help you?" he said.

Seven spoke for both of them. "We want to be intimate, but we want full physicals before we take the relationship another step further."

The doctor shook his head in approval, wishing that more people, young and old, were this responsible. "All right," he said slowly. Dr. Beniot focused on Lisa, since he already knew Seven. Seven had just been tested about seven months ago, and he was healthy. The young lady looked a little pale. He would get this over with quickly for her sake because she appeared to be on the verge of passing out. He asked her, "Your name is?"

"Lisa Harris," she answered.

"All right then, Seven. I'll examine Lisa first."

"Okay."

Seven stood, gently squeezing her hand, and left.

"Step this way, Ms. Harris."

Lisa stood and followed the doctor into an exam room, where there was a nurse waiting. She was instructed to undress and cover up with a paper sheet. They stepped out long enough for her to change. When he returned, he asked her questions about her family history and she answered truthfully.

"How many sex partners have you had?"

There was a pause, and she exhaled, and the doctor looked up at her. "None," she answered.

The doctor stopped and stared at her with no expression at all. Years doing this work had helped him develop his poker face. Closing the folder, he asked, "Have you had a blood transfusion in the last few years?"

"No, sir."

"Why are you here?" Then he answered his own question: "The young man in there doesn't know that you are a virgin, does he?"

"No, sir."

"Why have you not told him?"

"I want him to want me for me and not to feel that dealing with me will complicate things because he is my first."

*I must be getting old*, Dr. Benoit thought to himself. That was one of the silliest answers he had ever heard. In his day, it was not a bad thing to be a virgin. "You want me to run the tests anyway?"

"Yes, sir."

He ran the required tests but did not offer a pap smear, since she was a virgin. He then did the same for Seven. It was about an hour and a half before they left the office, after making an appointment to come back Thursday at 1:00. The doctor thought that they were a nice couple and knew that Seven had taken this step because he was serious about the young lady.

Back in the truck, they rode in silence until she broke it.

"Thank you."

Humbled, he responded in kind. "No baby, thank you." He was about to tell her that everything would be all right, that they would make this work, but he said nothing, electing to let his actions speak for him. They stayed in a safe arena for the rest of the day, going to the movies and then to dinner. He dropped her off, kissing her at the door, and went home.

The next two days were pretty much the same. They went to see another movie, avoiding places where they would be alone together. This would make it easier for him to keep control of the situation. He was horny, but he was no child and he wouldn't behave like one. Lisa said nothing about the way he was handling things, but she was clear that he loved her, even though he hadn't said it. Everything he had done made her feel even safer in his presence. Wasn't that the meaning of a man-woman relationship, that a woman felt safe and protected in the presence of her man?

On Thursday at 1:00, they were back in the doctor's office. The nurse led them back to the inner office and Dr. Beniot appeared smiling. He sat with the two folders in his hand staring at them. "Shall I speak freely on both accounts?" he asked.

Staring at Lisa, Seven shook his head to give her the choice and she gave him the go ahead to answer for her. "Yes, please be straight with us."

"All right, then. Lisa, your tests were negative, which means that you are healthy." Then, switching folders, he said, "Seven, your tests are negative as well. Do either of you have any questions?" Both of them shook their heads no. The doctor normally recommended regular testing before the condom came off, but Seven had been tested twice every year for the past five years, and she was a virgin. They would be fine, as long as they understood the treasure they held in their hands.

# CHAPTER 12

Leaving the office they were both overwhelmed, not about the test but about what it represented. Their future was stretched out before them, and with it, endless possibilities.

They played it safe and had dinner with Gary, Valerie, and their girls at their home. Seven adored the girls, and they adored him. Gary took Seven down to the den and Lisa didn't see them again until dinner. Lisa helped Valerie with dinner and found her wonderful to spend time with. The meal was ziti with garlic bread and salad. They were all eating and enjoying their food when Michelle their older daughter said, "Are you going to marry Uncle Seven?"

Lisa looked at the beautiful child, with her long pigtail hanging on each side of her head. She was dark skinned, like Gary, whereas Kenya was light, like Valerie. She thought about what to say but could come up with nothing. It was Valerie who tried to save the day. "Michelle, don't be rude and nosey."

"But, Mama, I just wanted to know if she would be my auntie, since he's my uncle."

Seven, seizing the moment and wanting to keep her in the hot seat, said, "Are you planning to marry me?"

"See, Mama, even Uncle Seven wants to know. He's been wondering, like me."

"Child, would you be quiet?" Valerie said, staring at Lisa.

Looking out at the table at large, Lisa saw that all eyes were on her. "Yes, I suppose I am." She said.

Valerie's eyes watered up and Gary reached over the table to pat her hand. "Calm down," he said. Then he turned to Seven. "Now you see what you did? She's going to make me keep tabs on both of you until this comes to pass."

Seven laughed. He was enjoying himself and Lisa's discomfort. Gary's eyes narrowed as he watched his friend. *Shit*, he thought, *we never joke about marriage in front of women unless we're serious about it.*

On the ride home, they talked and laughed about the girls and Valerie. Lisa asked him if he would like to play cards at her cousin's house the next night, and he said yes.

"Good," she said. Then she cast a look of dread his way. "Can you play? Cause my Aunt Ruth will tear you a new ass."

"You just have to see."

"Oh, Lord."

He laughed. "Everything will be all right."

"My aunt Ruth is my grandmother's younger sister, and she is funny, but if you can't play, she will talk about you and me."

"You sound like you're trying to determine if I'm good enough to be your partner."

"No, no, I'm not. It's just that I want to beat her. When she's on the other side of the table, she's not my aunt."

He looked at her and couldn't believe what he was hearing. She wanted to win so bad that she was willing to dump his ass, if that's what it took. Seven leaned over on the steering wheel and laughed as hard as he could. "How could you have it in for a little old lady like that?"

"Little old lady, my ass. She's going to get it—if I can just get the right partner. Hattie, her church friend, ain't nothing but a card-counting heifer. Can you play or not, man?"

"I played once or twice in college, but I understand the concept of the game."

Lisa groaned, and Seven laughed his ass off some more.

When they arrived at Kim's house at 7:30 P.M., there were already several people there and a card game was in session. Aunt Ruth and her hangout partner, Hattie, were squatting. They had already won three games. *Shit*, Lisa thought, *I'm in for it. I'm going to have to be his partner since I brought him.* She smiled at how much she wanted to win and thought about him laughing at her.

She introduced him to her family, mostly her cousins who had come to play cards. Lisa explained that all her mothers' sisters and bothers had about three children, and once a month on Friday they got together to see who the boss was. Aunt Ruth seemed not to want to give anyone else a chance. Seven met Kim's husband and they hit it off. He saw Alex and his newest girlfriend, and he met several other cousins. Marie, Will Jr., and Theodore were her Aunt Hazel's children. Hazel was her mother's oldest sister. A.J., Steven, and Marc were cousins from several of her mother's siblings.

Seven met so many people that he couldn't keep up with the names, but they were a friendly bunch, and he immediately felt like family with them. They ate, talked shit, and played cards. When it was their turn to sit down, Seven studied Lisa's aunt and he could see why Lisa was stressed. She was very witty, and Seven figured she was about seventy years old. He learned from Lisa that her aunt had taught them all how to play cards, against her grandmother's wishes. Ruth was her grandmother's favorite sister, and although she had been married, her husband had died young and she never had children. It was decided that she would share her sister's children and grandchildren, and for them it was as if they had had two grandmothers growing up. Seven could see how Lisa ended up being the person that she was in spite of her beginnings.

"Lisa, it's nice to see you and your beau," Aunt Ruth said.

Lisa bent down and kissed her aunt's cheek. "It's good to see you too, Auntie."

Aunt Ruth turned to Seven and started right in with the mind games. She intended to win. "Young man, don't think 'cause you're good-looking you're going to distract me and Hattie. We've had our share of good-looking men, right, Hattie?"

"You better know it," Hattie cackled. Seven just smiled.

Lisa just looked at Seven, and the look in her eye told him he was on his own. Aunt Ruth started the deal, making it understood that she didn't play with a bunch of wild cards—that was for chumps. After the deal, and books were being counted, Seven looked at Lisa.

"How many do you have?" he asked her.

"Just two books," she answered.

"Sounds like board to me," Aunt Ruth said, starting with the old divide and conquer routine.

"We'll go seven," he said.

"I know your name. How many books you want?"

Lisa was looking pale. *I know he didn't just say seven books.* "Are you sure, honey?"

"Yes, sweetie. We'll take seven, Aunt Ruth."

"What you got, Hattie?" Aunt Ruth said, directing her words to Hattie now.

"I got three books."

Aunt Ruth turned back to Seven and said, "I got four, and three and four makes seven. One of us is lying."

"Are you going to bid your hand?" Seven asked.

"Oh hell, no. Is that a challenge?" Aunt Ruth inquired. At that, everyone in the room stopped what they were doing and began watching the game.

Aunt Ruth liked him, and she thought that if she were younger, she would give Lisa a run for her money. Chuckling, she said, "We'll go seven; there's only thirteen books, and that ain't no way for you to start the game, set."

Since Aunt Ruth dealt, Lisa threw out a low club and Hattie threw the ace. Seven cut it, winning the book for them. Lisa stared at him with renewed interest. He led with the ace of hearts, and Aunt Ruth started cursing. As the hand progressed, and Aunt Ruth threw the ace of diamond, Seven cut again, saying, "Diamonds aren't always a girl's best friend."

There were *oohs* and *ahs* coming from the spectators—it was on. The game ended with a score of 510 to 465 in favor of Seven and Lisa. It was a beautiful thing.

They ate some more and played some more and just had a great time. Aunt Ruth let everyone know, "Just because the rookie's won, don't get delusions of grandeur. I got something for your ass if you do." Everyone laughed, and Seven enjoyed himself thoroughly.

On the way home that night, Lisa couldn't help but stare at him. "Okay," she said, "why didn't you tell me you could play? Next time we'll be the champs, and they will want to take us down. You got to share any techniques that will help our game."

"Lisa, I don't know how to tell you this, but I've decided that in order to keep winning against Aunt Ruth, I'll need a savvier partner. I think I'm going to have to go with Alex."

She just stared at him. He had decided to go with another partner. Well, it served her right—she had planned on dumping him before she knew he could play. While she thought this over, they stopped at a light. When she turned to look at him, he was smiling, and then he started laughing in earnest. He was making fun of her, the bum, but she couldn't help it, and she laughed too.

* * *

Seven picked her up at 4:00 P.M. on the Sunday of the dinner with his family. He had gotten there early, as he needed time to decide if he should tell her about the situation with his family. His grandmother had told him that Betty would be there, and he had concerns about seeing her as well. Seven even contemplated not taking Lisa—he'd make the excuse that something came up—but that seemed underhanded to him, so he decided to let the chips fall where they may.

They arrived at 5:30 on the nose, and Lisa noticed that he had difficulty locating the house. She wondered about that, but said nothing. Seven's grandmother opened the door for them. When they stepped into the house, she hugged him. Seven introduced Lisa to his grandmother, and when Lisa went to extend her hand, Bobbi hugged her, as she did Seven.

"I'm glad you're both here," his grandmother said with tears in her eyes.

"Me too," he responded.

As they stepped farther into the house, she become aware that all eyes were on them. There was a crowd gathered in the living room, where his grandmother had ushered them. Everyone was smiling, but something seemed odd.

"Everyone, this is Seven and his lady, Lisa."

Collectively, everyone said, "Hello."

Seven and Lisa replied in kind.

"Seven, these are your uncles Michael and Calvin." Both men stepped forward and shook his hand.

"Good to see you again," they both said.

"Those three over there are your aunts Evelyn, Pat, and Brenda." They stepped forward, following their brothers' example. Brenda, however, was the brave one, and she hugged him.

"Good to see you again," she whispered.

Betty just stepped forward, but she didn't hug him. "I missed you. Did you get my message?"

Betty had lost weight, Seven noticed, but her hair was cut and curled very nicely, and her clothes were a little more stylish than usual. They were rolling into June, and she dressed for the season: a khaki skirt with a brown shirt that flowed as she moved and a nice pair of brown clogs. She looked younger and more carefree, and he felt a pang at the thought that maybe she looked better because he was no longer around.

"You're looking well, Betty," he said. He missed his mother, and seeing her made him realize it, but he wasn't willing to bend. Gesturing toward Lisa, he said, "You remember Lisa, don't you. She's the little girl that lived down the hall from us in Corona. You remember her Aunt Jenny."

"Ms. Thomas, is that you?" Lisa asked.

Betty stared at the young woman standing at her son's side. The little girl came into focus, and after a few moments she was able to connect the little girl to the woman standing before her. Betty was shocked. "Is that you, Lisa? I often wondered about you. I worried over whether I did the right thing. How are you?"

"I'm fine. You did the right thing. My mother's family is good to me. What you did was the best thing that ever happened to me."

Seven watched the exchange, and he was about to say something when he spied his grandfather gesturing toward him from the couch. "Excuse me, ladies."

Betty and Lisa were so deep in conversation that they didn't respond. Seven approached his grandfather, "Hello, sir," he said.

"Sir? I know you're a man and we're just meeting, but call me Pop. Everyone else does."

"Okay, that works for me."

"Your lady is pretty."

"Yes, she is," he said, smiling.

While he was talking to his grandfather, three young men and three young women came forward to introduce themselves. A young woman introduced everyone with her. "I'm Ebony, and this is my sister Nicole. Evelyn is our mother. This is Rae. Her mother is Aunt Pat. This is Kevin and David. Their father is Uncle Michael. And last but not least, this is Patrick, Aunt Brenda's son."

The men stepped forward and shook his hand. "Grandma said you were coming. We just figured that she bossed you, like she does us," Kevin said, smiling.

"Glad that you could make it to dinner," David said.

"Good to meet you, man," Patrick said.

"Nice to meet you too, and you're right—she did boss me around. I think it's hard to tell her no," he said admitting that he had been beaten.

Turning to the women, he said. "The pleasure is all mine." They smiled. The evening was off to a good start.

Seven sat and talked with his grandfather about a little of everything. "What do you do to support yourself?" his grandfather asked.

Seven explained some of his business deals, including the issues with the developer in Georgia. He told him about how he just had a knack for recognizing a good deal. His grandfather was impressed, and Seven felt good. Seven told Pop that most of his ventures were in real estate in different states, but he would try anything legal that turned a penny.

His grandfather told him about his life in Mississippi with his parents and siblings. He told Seven about meeting his grandmother. She was younger than him, he told Seven, and he didn't think it would work, but he was wrong. "Your mother," he said in a whisper, "is my favorite child, not because I love her more—I love all my children. She's my favorite because your grandmother and I decided that we wouldn't have any more after Brenda. When your mother came, she looked so much like my mother I couldn't believe it. It was love at first sight."

Seven stared at Betty. She was still talking to Lisa, and they were laughing. Lisa was enjoying herself, and he knew when they were alone she would have questions. He saw the way she stared at him when everyone started introducing themselves. She went with the flow. She understood that now was not the time. Lisa was genuine and his family seemed to pick up on it.

Seven's cousins walked up to Lisa and started talking to her. Ebony was telling Lisa something in an animated way when he saw Betty excuse herself and start toward him. Well, how long did he think it would last before his mother wanted a word with him? Walking over to them, she said to her father, "Daddy, can I borrow Seven for a moment?"

His grandfather hated to relinquish his grandson—their conversation had been so interesting—but he said, "Of course you can."

She led him into the den, and his grandmother watched them go. He saw her looking into the den when his mother closed the door. "You never answered my question."

"Yes, I got your message."

"Oh, I see."

They stared at each other—mother and son—but said nothing for some time. Betty broke the silence. "I was worried about you. I got used to you coming by in the middle of the month to check on me. You think that you might come by next week to check on me and Butch?"

What could he say? She was offering a truce. To continue holding a grudge put too much out in the atmosphere. Still, there were a lot of questions in his life that had gone unanswered for far too long. What would they do about those issues? According to Betty, nothing. She just wasn't willing to tell him anything. If Seven had to be honest with himself, his interest in his father really stemmed from feeling that he didn't know his mother. Many children grew up without a mother or father, but they were sure about the one parent they did have. Because of Betty's indifference, he needed to identify with something. There was also the big mystery that seemed to surround his father, but he was the only one who would be enlightened if the truth was revealed. If Betty had had a baby as a young girl with a man who walked away, what would be the secret in that? Things like that happened every day.

"Betty, let's not beat around the bush. What do you want from me? I feel like an intruder in your life, not your son. What you want is to pick up where we left off, when you had no respect for truth in our relationship. I love you, Betty—you're my mother—but a relationship where I'm in the dark and everyone else knows more than me about me just won't suffice."

"I know," she whispered. "Can't we get to know each other before we let *his* shadow in?"

"What are you saying to me, that you want to open up and be my mother? It's a little late for that, don't you think?"

He was antagonizing her again, and he knew it. Why, he didn't know. He didn't have a history of being a bastard to any woman, let alone his mother. Why was he so angry?

She looked at him and broke down and started crying, turning away to shield herself from his ugliness. Her hands were over her face and her shoulders shook, and he was ashamed. He wanted to hurt her, and now that he had, there was no satisfaction in it, only emptiness. Seven felt desperate to stop the hurt he had caused her. Stepping forward, he placed his hand on her shoulder.

"I'm sorry. I didn't mean it," he said.

"Yes, you did, and you're right."

"No, Ma, I missed you too. I want to try and be friends."

Betty turned and looked at him, and she saw his concern over hurting her written on his face. "I'd like that too," she said. "I don't want to share you with him. You're mine, not his."

It was the most feeling he had ever seen his mother display, and Seven didn't know what to say, so he just hugged her. Betty cried some more and hugged him back. Whoever his father was, Betty didn't like him. The thought gave him pause. He wouldn't push her—she would talk to him in time, and he would wait. Now, he had a life that he just wanted to get on with living.

There was a light tap at the door, and his grandmother's head popped in. He was facing the door while he hugged his mother and smiled at his grandmother. Seeing them hugging made Bobbi's heart sing, and she got in on the action and hugged them both. "This is a good day," his grandmother said.

From the living room, Lisa could see what was happening, and it was clear that she was witnessing a private moment. Seven looked over the two women's heads and locked eyes with Lisa. She didn't look away. It was then that he knew he would marry her. Finally, he was able to touch the past while still looking to the future. He felt good, and it showed on his face.

They stood around the table holding hands while his grandfather said the grace. When the prayer was finished, the family sat down to a wonderful meal of fried whiting, porgy, and steamed red snapper. The side dishes were coleslaw, rice pilaf, and a colorful salad. Dessert was red velvet cake.

Lisa uncovered, through talking to Kevin, the oldest of the cousins, that Seven was actually the seventh grandchild. She found that interesting, but Seven just smiled. She noted that none of his cousins were married, even though all of them were older than him. There was talk, though, about Kevin marrying his longtime sweetheart. She also learned that his three aunts were married to three best friends, all of whom worked for Mass Transit and were at work today. His uncle Michael's wife had passed away the previous year, so it was just him and his boys. Calvin wasn't married and didn't have any children, although he has been seeing the same woman for ten years, and she was older than him. She didn't want to marry him because of the age difference, so he just decided not to marry. Nicole told her that bit of information, and Lisa thought it was romantic.

When it was time to go, Seven offered to take his mother home. Lisa offered his mother the front seat, but Betty refused, opening the back door and climbing in. They rode and talked about the weather and other superficial things. Lisa asked Betty if she worked far from her house, and to Seven's chagrin, his mother responded that she worked rather close. She volunteered at a women's crisis center in Queens, three times a week in the evenings, and during the day, she worked at a PS 32 in the cafeteria.

Although he had been angry with his mother during their estrangement, he continued to put money into her account. If she worked, it was because that's what she wanted to do. Listening to the conversation between his mother and Lisa, he realized that his mother never spoke about herself at all, but then he never asked her anything. Betty gave off a certain vibe that said, "Don't ask me about me and I won't ask you about you." Going over the discussion he had with his mother earlier, it was clear that he didn't know much about her. His mind focused in on her reaction over the mention of his father—she obviously didn't like him. He wondered if her pushing him away had to do with her intimidating him into not asking about his father.

Zoning back in on the present conversation, he heard Lisa saying, "Can you take me home first, honey? I have to get ready for work."

Looking at her over the glow of the dashboard and the stereo, the only lighting in the truck, his eyes locked with hers. He smiled at her and Lisa smiled back to hide her disappointment with him. She leaned over to the driver's side and patted his leg, to comfort herself more than him. He took his hand from the steering wheel and placed it on top of hers. He wanted to be with her and she wanted to be with him—*but not tonight*, she thought.

Betty, seated in the back, noticed the whole exchange and smiled. She liked Lisa and thought that she would be good for her son. They were in love, Betty could see, and the sexual tension fairly cracked like thunder about them. She had never had that with anyone, but she was glad he did. The two seemed to have forgotten that she was back there. The always-serious Seven had never smiled or laughed so much. His happiness made him look younger, and Betty could see the burden of the life they had led being lifted from his shoulders.

They parked in front of Lisa's house, and they both turned to the back. "It was so good to see you again, Mrs. Thomas," Lisa said.

"Oh, sweetheart, the pleasure was all mine," Betty said.

"Get in the front and I'll be right back. I'm going to walk her inside," Seven said to his mother.

Seven walked Lisa to her front door and kissed her, just placing his lips on hers. "Back to work tomorrow," he said, pulling away and touching her lips with his thumb. "Shall I pick you up tomorrow after work?"

Lisa stood there staring at him in silence. She was a little hurt that he would take her to his family's house, where he was clearly meeting many of them for the first time, and say nothing about it. It was why she had requested to go home first. She knew he wasn't going to say anything unless pushed, and she wanted him to feel as though he could talk to her. Maybe she was expecting too much; maybe it was none of her business. The way he was treating her certainly made her feel that way.

"Yeah, tomorrow will be fine. I need to pick up some things from the grocery store on the way home."

"I thought we could go out to eat and you could tell me why you're so pissed off with me. Although I'm sure I can guess," he said, sensing her anger and deciding that meeting the issue head on was the best way to deal with it. Her head popped up and she looked him in the eye. He saw hurt there, which he knew came from the feeling of being shut out.

She wasn't biting. He was going to have do more than be witty—he was going to have to trust her. "Eating out tomorrow will be fine," she said as she put the key in the door and went inside. He stood there for a moment to get himself together before going back to the vehicle where his mother waited. Good thing he had parked up the street a little, where the exchange he had with Lisa couldn't be seen. What did she want from him? He really wasn't much on talking about himself. He was like Betty in that regard. Although he loved it when Lisa told him things about herself, he felt as if she was being intimate with him on a whole other level. Maybe that was what she wanted, to know the man that she was going to sleep with.

Back in the truck, Betty was sitting in the front seat with her eyes closed. When his door opened, she looked over at him and said, "She is a very nice young lady. How did you two find each other again?"

Seven told his mother about the meeting at the Plaza, how Lisa was the coordinator. "We literally bumped into each other, and the rest is history."

They talked about the house, Butch, and how everything was coming along okay. Then Seven asked, "What made you start working?

"I'm not rich," she said, and when she thought he would protest, she hurried to continue. "Yes, I know that you will take care of me, but your job is to take care of yourself and the family that you make. I know that you don't mind, but I have nothing to do during the day and I'm not old enough to retire. Volunteering gives my life meaning; helping women get on their feet after abuse is rewarding. I do like it when you help me, though. I don't have the same worries, because I know that you will help me, but I must try to stand on my own two feet. Do you understand? Please say that you do."

Seven laughed. He had never heard Betty string together more than two sentences, and if she did, it was usually because she had no other choice. He wasn't going to give her a hard time; ultimately, he wanted a truce with his mother.

"Yeah, I understand."

He came in with her instead of merely dropping her off in front of the house. Butch was excited to see them. Betty let him out in the yard to do his business, and Seven went into the living room to wait. Betty had hung up some pictures in the living room, and he noticed that they were of him at various ages. He didn't even remember them being taken. Several, he noticed, were of him asleep.

When she came into the living room with Butch at her heels, Seven turned and looked at her. "You are full of surprises. How much do you want? And before a deal can be struck, I want the negatives."

Betty laughed, and before he left she told him again how much she missed him. They stood talking at the door for a few moments. Seven invited his mother out to dinner with him and Lisa one evening soon. Betty accepted, and Seven told her that he planned on taking her mother out soon as well and that she was welcome to come. He told her that he was fond of Bobbi, and Betty admitted that just like him, she was glad to have her mother back in her life. After hugging they parted for the evening, both feeling *his* shadow in the background. Seven was still determined to bring him to the light, while Betty was determined to keep him in the shadows and away from her newfound happiness.

# CHAPTER 13

Mondays at the hotel were always hectic, and now there was the added pressure of her personal life. They had taken a responsible step toward intimacy, yet he still wasn't talking to her. Who was he? Lisa's old fears began rising. She understood that there were no guarantees in life and love, but the images of the abuse that she and her mother suffered still came to the forefront of her mind. One day, while her father was at work (or wherever it was that he went during the day) she asked her mother, "Why do we stay with him when he doesn't like us?" She could still hear her mother's reply.

"Your dad wasn't always like this. He just changed one day out of the blue. I know through love he'll change back to who he was."

The thought had made her leery of men, and she steered clear of male/female interactions because of it. She fought it every day, the fear that every man was like her father. She trusted Seven and feared that since he showed no signs of trusting her, she must be missing something.

Seven had gotten very little business done today, preoccupied as he was with the fact that Lisa was mad at him. She had left him standing on her doorstep. If Betty hadn't been with him, he would have pursued the issue last night. Normally she would have called him by now, and when he tried her on her cell phone, it rolled straight to voicemail.

*Talk about your cold shoulder.*

He would pick her up later, he thought, and they would talk until the inevitable came up. Seven turned his mind back to the work at hand, mostly to pass time until they were together.

Mary came in at eight, as she did every Monday, and started in the kitchen. Seven hadn't seen much of her, since he had been spending most of his time at Lisa's house. Lately he had been handling business at his lawyer's office, so he was usually leaving as Mary was coming in. Being tired of his own company, he figured that he would bug Mary.

"What's up, beautiful?" he said.

Turning to look at him, she said, "Nothing much. Just trying to get some things done that were on my list from last week."

He sighed and she turned to look at him over her shoulder. Seven was so deep in thought that it was clear he hadn't heard her response. Mary went back to what she was doing, taking inventory of the cabinets so she would know what to buy when she went shopping. He really didn't eat at home much, so the items she would need to replace were minimal.

"The young lady you're seeing has got that head of yours in a fog, I see."

Laughing, he said, "I don't know that you can blame that on her—my head was in a fog before I met her."

"True."

He told her a little about Lisa and mentioned that they had a date tonight. She smiled, feeling a little less worried about him. Seven seemed to be a loner. She hadn't met any of his friends or family, and that seemed intentional. He looked younger somehow and more carefree. The young man standing before her was not the same young man who worked all the time. They talked about a variety of things, and Mary gained a little insight. He appeared to be more than interested in this young lady. It was as if he was practicing the art of conversation with her, learning to communicate about himself.

He was out front to meet Lisa just as she was stepping out of the building at 5:30 P.M. Seven was happy about his timing, because he didn't feel like driving around until she came out, which he would have had to do in Manhattan at this time of the day. Watching her approach, he saw that she had not changed out of her uniform.

Yeah, she was pissed.

When she opened the door and climbed in, she smiled and said, “Hey, honey.”

He leaned over and kissed her. “Hey, baby,” he said against her mouth.

“Where are we going? I’m starving.”

“I thought we would go back to the Japanese joint. Is that okay?”

“That’s fine with me.”

Neither said anything else for the rest of the ride, and the only sound they heard was the jazz playing in the background. They were in their own worlds. Seven had doubts about her feelings for him. Lisa had insecurities about his lack of trust in her. He wanted to hear her say that she loved him. She wanted him to confide in her so that she could better understand the man that she loved. They sat in silence fighting their worry and concern, never realizing it was unnecessary—each had the answer the other was looking for.

Seven let Lisa out in front of the restaurant doors and went to park. She waited for him and they entered together. They were seated in a secluded corner, and they waited until after their food was cooked and they were alone before they talked. Lisa decided that she would not push him to talk about his family—it was his right to talk about it or not. In the end, he wasn’t being dishonest; he simply didn’t want to talk about himself, which was consistent with who he was from the beginning.

She wondered if she was creating this wedge between them because of other fears as well. They had spent a lot of time in the company of other people over the last few days and weeks, and Lisa suspected it was to help her understand that he wasn’t pushing for sex. The fact was that she wanted sex and intimacy with him, but doubt was starting to play a part of her thought process which was uncommon to her—doubts about whether he trusted her, who he was, and whether she was being realistic in her expectations of their relationship. Her grandmother once told her that broken hearts come from hearing our own wants rather than hearing and seeing realistically, what the other person is saying and doing.

Lisa was subdued tonight, Seven noticed. Gone was the animated person that could pique his interest for hours. She held up her end of the conversation as politely as ever, but she made no effort to elaborate on anything said between them. In other words, the ball was in his court. As he sat there talking about things that went nowhere, he realized that he wanted to remove the wedge that was growing between them. He knew that he was in love with her, but he was afraid of what would happen if she saw the real him. The real him had been hurt as a child and did not wish to be rejected again. Lisa had not rejected him, though; she had accepted him. She had not questioned him or been demanding. She had risked herself by baring the truth of her feelings to him, and she had not required that he do the same. He realized that he would have to open up in order for her to understand that it was not her.

Breathing in deeply, he watched her with her head down concentrating on her food. Now was as good a time as any. "Betty and I are not very close, not because we fight a lot—we just don't talk to each other."

Lisa's head popped up, and she looked at him. He continued before she said anything and he lost his nerve. "I suppose the very thing that puts distance between me and my mother is happening to us, and I don't want to lose you. When you lived down the hall from my mother and me, you may have been too young to know it, but my mother paid the bills by selling herself. I'm not judging her, but for years, it was just me and her. She won't tell me who my father is, and often I wonder if the reason she doesn't tell me is because she doesn't know. Maybe he was one of her customers—hell, I don't know. Betty and me—I hate to admit—are a lot alike. She didn't talk about herself, so when I showed up to her house, imagine my shock to see all her siblings standing in her living room and learning that she was the youngest of seven children. I guess that's where I get my name. We became estranged after that, and what you saw was us burying the hatchet, although I know it's just a matter of time before we dig it up again."

"You two seem to love each other. Have you thought of just telling her how it makes you feel."

"I have, but Betty can be very evasive when she wants to be, which is most of the time."

"Isn't it funny how ironic life can be. Take me, for instance. I'm sorry that I ever knew who my father is. Has it ever occurred to you that when you find out, you might wish you hadn't?"

"Yes, it has but the thing that bothers me is that my mother's family seems to know who he is. It pisses me off that people who this doesn't involve know more about me than I do."

Lisa knew that a man like Seven would never tolerate vulnerability in his life.

"I suppose I see your point. What do you think of me not wanting to see my mother or father ever again? Even as an adult I couldn't deal with seeing them."

"In your case, you understand what it is you're rejecting. I see nothing wrong with self-preservation, although I have a question about your mother. If she didn't abuse you, why do you dislike her?"

"As silly as it sounds, I guess I feel like she chose him over me even though he was the one doing us both harm. Can you understand that?"

"Unfortunately, yes I do."

They talked on about their feelings regarding their parents, and Seven had to admit that he felt better. Hearing her take on it and listening to the issues that still troubled her regarding her parents pushed them closer together instead of tearing them apart. "Did you ever think that leaving you behind was your mother's way of protecting you?" he asked.

"Yes, I thought about that as I got older, but to keep it real, I asked myself a few choice questions. First, if she left me behind to save me, why leave me in the schoolyard, where I couldn't even find my way home? Second, if she had so much family, why would she not leave me with them? Third, and most important, you saw that apartment. They took their belongings and left my things and me behind. If you hadn't come along or your mother hadn't searched that apartment, there is no telling what could have happened to me. I didn't know her family either, because my father didn't like visitors or to go visiting. I didn't even know that I was with the right family after her sister came to get me; it wasn't until I saw pictures of her in their homes that I knew for sure. Tell me, what do you think?"

He didn't have an argument for that. She was right. "I agree. I hadn't thought about it like that."

"As for my father's family, I wouldn't judge them by his actions. Maybe his mother is nice, too—who knows?—but no one in my mother's family knew anything about him. My aunt told me she just showed up with him, and the next thing you know, they were married."

"I can identify, but I think it's even worse when you feel betrayed by both parents. Even then I see how your grandmother and your aunt Ruth made the difference between your life becoming a nightmare and you persevering in spite of everything. My mother showed a lot of indifference, and she continues to sidestep the issue of my father. I have this feeling that when it comes to the light, it won't be pretty."

They talked on, not even noticing that the hour had grown late. Seven didn't want to take her home. He was tired of being without her in the evenings and he didn't know how to approach the matter. "Come home with me," he whispered. "Please."

Lisa sat there looking into the eyes of the man she loved. What could she say? This was where they were heading. They took the long route, but the destination was the same. She thought to make an excuse about work, or a change of clothing, but Lisa wanted to be with him this evening too. She really wanted to be with him forever, and honesty with herself wouldn't allow her to hear what she wanted to. He had asked her to come home with him *tonight*, not forever. She answered accordingly: "Yes."

They both knew that she had agreed to more than just coming home with him; it was unspoken but communicated nonetheless. Her answer made Seven euphoric, and he had to control himself. He would go slow and savor this feeling of oneness with her. He paid the check and they made their way out to the parking lot. Again, there was no talking between them as they rode to his home.

Lisa, to her surprise, felt at peace with her decision to be with him tonight. The pressure was gone and in its place was the anticipation of the pleasure they would share. It occurred to her to tell him that she had never been with a man before, but she decided against it. She wouldn't add tension to the moment or expectations that couldn't be satisfied. She would just be the woman and let him be the man, and the rest would work itself out.

As he sat behind the wheel, he could think of nothing to say. Then he thought it might be for the better that he couldn't, since it ensured he wouldn't say the wrong thing. He couldn't understand the pressure he was feeling—he was no adolescent with his first woman. There were many encounters for him to draw from. What made this so different? His thoughts crashed into each other until he found what he was looking for. What was different about this encounter was the intent. She wasn't holding the pussy hostage in an effort to control him, and he wasn't trying to manipulate her into feeling that she was more special than she really was.

They walked from the parking deck to his building, holding hands. Seven couldn't take the silence any longer. "Are you all right?"

She smiled and contentment showed in her eyes. "Yes, I'm fine."

The absence of manipulation and control caused him to have to deal with the real issue at hand, his feelings for her. He had never engaged in sex with a woman that he was in love with, and he was unsure about himself; in that respect, he was a virgin too. He wanted to please her, and while they were walking to the elevator, he tried to calm himself so that it would be an experience they would both enjoy.

Lisa, deep in her own world, thought about her dreams of what her first time would be like. She would meet a strong man and he would right the wrongs of her life. He would be sure of himself, and the world would bow down to him—and also her, because she was with him. He would be sensitive and understand that she had never been naked in the company of a man, and he would treasure her even more because of it. The setting would be romantic—like in a waterfall—and when they came together the world would stop, not to start again until they climaxed. A beautiful child would be the product of that union, and he would be elated that she carried his seed. Seven had not fallen short of her dreams; he had in fact enhanced them with reality. He had taken her mundane reality and turned it to fantasy. Yet their setting was anything but romantic.

When the elevator door opened, he stepped aside and waited for her to enter first. After pushing the twelfth-floor button, they stood apart like strangers waiting for the elevator to bring them to his apartment. The door opened and they walked to his door, still in the heavy silence that had surrounded them during the ride to his house. He opened the door and they stepped in, but he did not turn on the lights. Reaching up over her head, he shut the door, placing his palm flat against it. He was agitated at the thought that this moment could incite insecurity in him. He became aggressive, not toward her but the circumstances, and in an effort to control his feelings, he whispered, "Are you sure, because now is the time to say?"

When she didn't respond verbally, he felt a rhythmic jerking of her body and realized that she was nodding her head yes.

"Say it," he said. "Say you want it."

"Yes, I want it," she whispered.

Pressing her firmly against the door with his body, she felt the rigidness of his sex against her pelvis. He leaned down and grabbed her bottom lip between his teeth and suckled it. It was mind blowing. They had danced this suggestive dance before and she had tasted a slice of satisfaction, and so had he, but now he was looking for the kind of satisfaction that comes with having deprived yourself for a cause. He wanted to fuck, and the thought was crude and unromantic, but it was a moment of clarity that could not be denied.

He unbuttoned the blazer of her uniform and pushed it back off her shoulders, removing it. He fumbled with the buttons of her shirt until, like her blazer, it was on the floor at their feet. He cupped her breasts through her bra, and he could feel the soft protrusion of her nipples, but it was not enough, so he groped at her clasp to remove the offending garment. When the bra loosened, he heard her gasp and he kissed her, pushing his tongue into her mouth to keep her focused on what was important, fulfillment.

Lisa was panting, and the more she tried to control her breathing, the more harsh it sounded. The door was cool on her back, and he was hot against her front. He teased her nipples with the rough pads of his thumb while kissing her. She could still taste the wine on his tongue from dinner and, the combination of taste and feeling caused a deep sensation to pool between her legs. Lisa began to whimper, and her own sounds were turning her on.

He popped the buttons on his shirt too, impatient to feel her skin against his. It was like an electric current running through his body at the slightest contact of her breast against his chest. "Baby, you feel so good," he groaned.

His words further inflamed her, and in her desperation she reached out, mimicking him, and touched his nipples. His chest and nipples were hairy, and the contrast made her feel even more feminine. She heard his sharp intake of air and deepened her kiss, afraid that he would pull away. Lisa felt his hands at the zipper of her skirt, and then she felt it sliding from her body. Finally she stood there in the dark, still at the front door of his apartment, naked with the exception of her panties and a pair of sandals.

Seven touched her everywhere, fingering her breasts, and then palming her ass. Her skin felt incomparable to softest of silks. Pushing her moist panties aside, he stroked her love button, and his name rolled off her tongue. "Seven…Seven…"

Hearing his name on her lips was his undoing, and he stepped back, removing the rest of his own clothing. Their attire forgotten at their feet, he placed both hands on either side of her head and kissed her, not touching her anywhere else. "Please," she whispered, and he leaned in, giving her, her first male/female contact. His skin felt like fire, so intense was his heat.

Reaching around her waist, he palmed her ass cheeks, separating them, and she shivered at the erotic sensation. He pulled her forward against his rigid member, and as he pushed himself between her thighs, he could feel the heat of her core. The softness of her panties brushed his member, and he groaned. The perfume she wore was like a melody that danced around his head, making him want to take her where they stood. He readjusted her panties from behind and they rode up between her lips, and the connection was intense as his sensitive head brushed her clit.

She hugged him around his neck to steady herself, but he took advantage of her position and lifted her, forcing her to wrap her legs around his back. She could feel his rigid member push up between her buttock, and she felt exposed, but not at all vulnerable. They continued to kiss as he turned and walked them deeper into the apartment. The darkness that surrounded them was profound; neither had ever been so aware of another's presence, and it was sexual in the extreme.

As he passed his office and the other bedrooms, making his way to the master suite, streams of light danced off their skin through the Venetian blinds. She could feel the rippling of muscle in his powerful body as he walked toward his bedroom. When he got to the doors, he kicked them open and stepped in. Then, she broke the kiss to take in her surroundings. There was a large window to the right of the room reaching from the floor to the ceiling with the curtains drawn back to let in the moonlight. Outside, one could see the river and the buildings behind it all lit up, indicating life outside their world. Although she had been to his home many times, she had never been in his bedroom, and the view took her breath away. Lisa turned to look at him and something caught her eye, causing her to look in the opposite direction. They stood in front of a full-length mirror, and the image she saw was beautiful. He stood potent and very male, wrapped in obscurity, and all that she could make out was their silhouettes, her arms wrapped around his neck, her feet locked behind his back, and his strong hands cupping her bottom.

"We're beautiful," she said with no shyness.

He stepped toward the bed and then, as if changing his mind, he made his way to the window, her sandals dropping to the floor along the way. Releasing his hold on her, he let her slide down his body to her feet; then, threading his fingers into the string of her panties, he pushed them down over her hips and she stepped free of them. Her body was washed with moonlight, and it was a remarkable sight. Reaching out, he caressed her breasts, and they fit in his big hands perfectly. Leaning down, he kissed her again, not urgently but appreciatively, showing that he understood the honor that she had bestowed upon him by sharing herself with him. He wanted the exchange to be mutual, so he stepped back and watched her eyes grow wide with curiosity.

The moonlight splashed over him, making his skin darker and his physique more imposing. It was her first time seeing a man naked, and she could not control her inquisitiveness. She wanted to explore him with her eyes, her hands, and her mouth, if he would let her. Seven was a tall man with very broad shoulders; his arms bulged with muscle and in the moonlight, his outline was art. His chest was sculpted, leaving his stomach muscles in the shadows, further illustrating his strength. Looking down, she could see the very essence of his masculinity jutting forward at the juncture of his lean thighs, and her lips parted involuntarily. If she had any inhibitions left, they fled at the sight of him. Stepping forward, she could feel his manhood pressing against her stomach, and she leaned in and kissed his chest, and his head fell back at her touch. Placing her hand around his waist, she grabbed his ass, and it was like marble. She was starting to feel frantic in her quest for pleasure and asked, "What do I do now?"

Seven was burning inside and tried to hold still for her to explore him, but her question was the invitation he was looking for. He carried her to the bed, pushing away the pillows and comforter and laying her across the middle. He kneeled down between her parted legs and placed his hands on either side of her head, kissing her forehead. In the same fashion he kissed her eyes, nose, mouth…

To Lisa's surprise, he didn't stop at her mouth; instead, he kissed her throat and neck and then moved down to her nipples, and she discovered that it was not a fluke as sensation pooled between her legs, just as it had done before. Her nipples, still wet from his kisses, hardened as the cool air touched them. He kissed her belly, causing her stomach muscles to contract. Pushing her legs further apart, he leaned down, placed his lips to those between her legs, and simply kissed her there. She tried to close her legs, but he would not let her, and she surrendered—to him and the bliss that enveloped her. His tongue was rough against her sensitive flesh and the first stroke of it was almost traumatic, causing her to die a little in order to experience life. It was only the beginning, she learned, as she felt his tongue on her again and again, bringing her to an awareness of her body and her man. The build up was so great that she cried out, and the sound of her ecstasy alleviated some of the tension, but not all of it.

He kissed her neck, and moving down to her nipples he licked one and then the other, feeling them harden in his mouth. As he moved down to her belly, he could see them glistening in the moonlight, and his dick started pulsing. He had never known that foreplay could be this intense. He inched farther down between her legs and instinctively she tried close them, but he grabbed her by her thighs, stopping her. She understood what he was trying to convey, and although she was tense, she gave in. Inhaling her sweetness, his body clinched with anticipation, and then, without warning, he licked her clit. She stiffened beneath his touch, and he became frenzied as he stroked her flesh with his tongue over and over in the same spot. When he thought that she would break apart into tiny shards of ecstasy, he would suckle her to calm her then restart the process over, driving them both insane until finally she cried out, releasing some of her tension and making his mount. He stayed in direct contact with her, riding the wave until she could take no more, and then, in one motion, he was over her, holding himself up on his hands and pushing her legs apart with his knees to give himself better access. Leaning down, he kissed her with the dew of her body still clinging to his mouth and beard. This was rapture, he thought.

The taste of herself on his lips intensified the exchange for her. She hadn't known that intimacies like this existed. How had she lived without him and his touch? She returned his kiss with the same urgency that he was giving her, and when she felt her legs being nudged apart by his knees, she knew that they would be one. She needed him, and the realization scared her.

His breathing was harsh in her ears, and she was unsure of what to expect, but she wanted him. Opening her legs wider for him, she felt his manhood bouncing as it jutted forward in its quest for fulfillment. At the mouth of her womanhood, he pressed his sensitive head into her, encountering her moisture. She felt herself stretching and wiggled to accommodate him, and he stopped, closing his eyes before he moved again. She felt him withdraw a little and was about to protest when she felt him plunge forward, burying himself within her to the hilt. Involuntarily, she pushed at his chest and attempted to close her legs, but he began kissing her face and whispering words that made no sense. She was hurting, and she wanted it stop. Tears began to roll backward from her eyes, and she held herself still beneath him, wanting to fade away. She didn't understand; she wanted him and she was aroused, but now she felt like cold water had been thrown over them both. Unable to help herself, she cried, but instead of turning from him, she turned her face up to his, accepting his kisses and the comfort he offered, even though the hurt came from him. She cried softly and he spoke softly, and yet each understood the other because they spoke the language of love.

Seven was so frenzied after loving her with his mouth that he could not wait another moment. He wanted to be surrounded by her scent, her heat, and her moisture. He wanted to be joined to her, as he had no other human being. Pushing himself against her wet opening, his tip sank into her, causing oblivion for him. She was dewy, hot, and so taut. He withdrew and plunged forward, burying himself within her tightness, unable to restrain any longer from her sweetness. In his mindless state, it took a moment for him to understand that he had breached her. Struggling to bring his urges under control, he began kissing her and speaking words of love to stop her fight to dislodge him. He felt his chest constrict at the pain that he caused her, but his male instinct would not allow him to stop; he would not lose her to pain when pleasure awaited them.

He was unsure of how true it was, but he whispered it anyway, for himself as much as for her: "It will stop. The pain will stop. Stay with me."

She shook her head yes, unable to trust her voice for a moment. "I love you. I trust you," she said, tears still in her voice.

Hunger pushed him, and he could stay still no longer while her muscles tightened and loosened around him. He withdrew from her again and felt her squeezing him as he reentered. He was dying. A deep moan escaped her, and he knew they were on the same page. She opened her legs wider, and a rhythm overtook them as she began meeting him thrust for thrust. He wanted to be gentle, but he began pounding himself into her, unable to stop. Instead of pulling away, she wrapped her legs around his, giving him control over how wide she opened to him. His body started tingling, and her body began to stiffen—both signs of their approach to a beautiful destination. They were speeding toward satisfaction and it had a color—it was orange—and when they touched it, a red hue engulfed them, making them cry out in unison, changing the darkness under which they started their lives into a brilliant light that held them both. When they fell back against the bed, panting and breathing hard, it was not a tangible thought but somehow this experience showed them that where they started in life was not as important as where they would end up. Like their lovemaking, it started out rough, but it would end up beautiful.

As their breathing calmed, he moved to get up, but she squeezed his hand. "Don't leave me yet."

Seven wanted to get a warm cloth to clean her, but instead he moved to the head of the bed, reaching over the side for a pillow and a sheet to cover them. She lay with her head on his chest and both legs wrapped around one of his, and he held her. He did not verbally respond to her request—he just leaned down and kissed her forehead. Seven was unsure of what to say; he was saturated in emotions that he could not name and was already hard again. He knew she would be sore, and he didn't want to appear the brute, so he held her, waiting for her to fall to sleep. He needed to think.

"Is it always like that?" she said into the darkness.

"No." He didn't mean to sound so abrupt, but he had been with many women, and it was never like that.

"Are we all right?" she asked with insecurity in her voice.

They were more than all right; he just didn't know how to convey all that he was thinking and feeling. "You should have told me."

She didn't pretend ignorance. "I didn't want to change the course of our relationship, and you can't take responsibility for a decision I made for me. It was the way I wanted it. More importantly, it was the man I wanted."

He lay there thinking of her innocence and how much he loved her, and it occurred to him that although he had tried to bind her to him, the opposite had happened. Smiling into the darkness, he thought he loved being her first, but he knew it would hurt him more if he were not her last. It was important to him that she understood that she was his now, and the past was the past. *Mine,* he thought.

His silence spoke volumes, and she said, "The same things that are important to you are important to me." Leaning up on her elbow, she kissed him.

He growled, and she was on her back with her legs straddling his hips. They made love again, and their lovemaking was so intense that when he came, she felt his juices splash her soul. They slept in a tangle of limbs until the sun shone through the window, waking them.

# CHAPTER 14

Seven woke first. He was a little disoriented, until he felt the warmth of her body next to his. He turned to look at her in the sunlight and smiled thinking about how honest even her beauty was. The light of day held the same beauty that he witnessed in the shadows, and it was refreshing. She had beautiful skin and large round breasts with deep brown nipples. She slept wild, with the sheet tangled about her, and he could see that the hair at the juncture of her thighs was soft. Remembering the feeling of it, he tried to control himself. Gazing at her, he noticed the stain of blood on her thighs, and his arousal decreased. He would give her some time to heal. He was worried that she might be sore. It struck him that it was Tuesday and she had to go to work. Staring up at the ceiling, he sighed.

Lisa began stretching as she awoke, and she could feel him next to her. She felt shy this morning, realizing that she had kicked the sheet off them in her sleep. She felt like a cake on display in a bakery store window. The thought made her want to laugh, but she decided to pretend to be asleep instead. The bright red behind her eyelids let her know that the sun was shining brightly.

"How long are you going to pretend to be asleep?" he said.

"I'll pretend until I get up the nerve to look at you."

He laughed at her, a deep laugh that rumbled from his chest, and she could feel the vibration because he was so close. She opened one eye to look at him and gauge her shyness and her heart squeezed at his male magnetism. Sometimes, she thought love can be scary, but she didn't want to be anywhere else. That's when she remembered that she needed to make her way in to work.

"What time is it?" she asked.

"Eight forty-five. You're not going to make it even if I drive you, so you might as well call in."

"I can't," she said, thinking about the fact that she had no clean underclothes and her uniform was still catching dust on the floor wherever she had left it. This was bad.

"Call in," he said again, handing her the phone.

Lisa called and spoke to Elise, who sounded annoyed about her calling in but told her that she would see her tomorrow. She needed her job, and this was just plain irresponsible. Thinking about her grandmother and all that went into caring for her, she realized that this was her first bit of living. She would be back to work tomorrow and things would get back to normal. Hanging up, she turned and looked at him. He had propped himself up and had the sheet covering him at the waist, his strong chest exposed, and she admitted to herself that things would never be normal again. She even prayed that they wouldn't be.

Picking up the phone behind her, he called the senior manager at the hotel and let him know that he needed to plan another conference, this time three months ahead instead of six. He inquired about the nice young woman who had handled things the last time he was there. "Lisa, I think her name was. Can you see to it that I get the same person for this conference?" he asked, waiting for the response that he knew he would get, and when he hung up, she laughed.

Swinging his legs over the side of the bed, he stood, heedless of his nudity. "Come, let's bathe."

He was asking a lot, she thought, as she tried to do her best not to look down, staring only at his face. He was enjoying her discomfort. In an effort not to appear the coward, she cast the sheet aside and stood. Looking back at the bed, she saw the blood stain, and for the first time she was embarrassed. There was a lot to intimacy, and she was learning that it wasn't all perfect.

Seeing her eyes bounce over the stain, he knew what she was thinking. Taking her hand, he led her into the bathroom. He ran water for them and she stood still as a statue, waiting for him to tell her what to do next. Trying to act nonchalant was hard for him—she was perfection in her nakedness, and it was driving him mad. Focusing on the temperature, he turned to her and asked, "Is this too hot?"

Leaning over the tub, she let the water run in between her fingers and then replied, "That's fine."

"Hold on a moment," he said as he left the bathroom.

Alone, she looked around at the bathroom—it was very nice, and she now noticed that the tub was round. She breathed in to get herself together. She would be all right, she could do this, bathe with him. He appeared in the doorway with towels and directed her to get in. The tub was big, as if made for a man of his size. He stepped forward, squeezing bubble bath into the water, and she watched as the bubbles appeared as if by magic.

He knew she was nervous, and it took effort for him to keep his need from her. He stepped into the tub behind her, and when he seated himself, she was between his legs, with bubbles concealing her nudity. They sat in silence for a time, taking in the quiet—no TV, radio, or anything, just the sound of the water and their breathing. He knew when she gave in and relaxed, because she let her back press against his chest and he held her. It was strange, this connection that he felt with her, it seemed to grow stronger in the light of day. He felt more protective of her and in love with her, and again he experienced the inability to convey his feelings. Leaning his head back against the wall, he closed his eyes, and he was elevated to an emotional plane that he had never visited.

"I love being here like this with you," she offered.

Lisa's honesty was contagious. When she spoke, you didn't have to decipher her; she was such an open book. He knew that to continue experiencing honesty with her, he would have to be honest too. "I love you, and I love being here with you too." It was the first time he had said the words, and they sounded strange to his ears. He felt his chest constrict as if the words were being ripped from his heart, but somehow he felt lighter for having shared the piece of himself that he kept closed to others.

She turned, her shyness forgotten, and kneeled between his legs, placing her arms around his neck. Lisa looked him in the eye and then kissed him, "I love you too," she whispered. "Can we make love again?"

His arms closed around her waist and he could feel himself growing in the water, but he responded, "No, baby, you're not going to be able to walk if we keep on like this." It cost him, but he would give now to get later.

She laughed and kissed him, and they talked for a time while soaking. They held each other, splashing the water and just having fun. Seven told her that he was hungry, and she had to admit that she was hungry too. Rinsing off, they stepped from the tub to dry themselves. He gave her a shirt, which fit her like a dress, coming to mid-thigh. He put on a pair of shorts and they headed for the kitchen with food in mind. Lisa was a little off kilter, both because he had not put on a shirt yet and because she had no clean underwear. He left the bedroom first, and she doubled back into the bathroom after finding her panties. She washed them and then headed for the kitchen. She didn't want this feeling, to end. When he took her home tonight, she would dream of the hours she had spent in his arms.

He turned on some music and as it filled the air, so did the smell of breakfast. She made scrambled eggs and toast with turkey bacon. He ate about five eggs and ten pieces of bacon, as well as a pile of toast, and she couldn't understand where he put it, since he didn't appear to have an ounce of fat on him. They danced around in the living room for a while, she trying to control how far her shirt rose up, since her underwear were in the bathroom. When they finished dancing and were feeling sleepy again, they went back to bed and held each other, watching TV until she fell asleep.

When she had fallen asleep, he made his way to his office for the first time all day. His work had been his constant companion, keeping him too busy to face his life. While she slept in the next room, it felt more than right. He could barely concentrate on business, as his mind kept drifting to her, but he needed to get some work done, so he buckled down to take care of his affairs. Checking his messages, he saw that Betty had called, as had his grandmother. He would get back to them later.

About two hours passed when he looked up in the doorway to find her standing there staring at him.

"You left me," she said, poking her lip out.

"Never," he responded, and they both knew he meant it in every way.

At about 3:30, she knew it was time for her to get dressed and go home. "I need to get dressed and get ready to go."

He stood behind the desk, and she wondered how often he did business dressed like that. "I'll take you home," he offered.

Her heart sank a little, but she smile and answered, "Okay."

"You need to pick up some clothes and uniforms so that you can go to work from here."

It was a statement, but she could hear the command in his voice, and she responded, "I can't stay here every night with you. What will my family think?"

His nostrils flared, and he replied (a little more forcefully than he would have liked), "I don't give a damn what your family thinks. I can't sleep without you now."

She wanted to argue, but she wanted to be with him too. She was sure there were rules about this shit, but she decided to follow her heart.

"I'll stay, but I have to go to work. I have bills to pay. I also need to be independent. I can get to work on my own. You have business to tend to, and I don't want to get in the way."

"Fair enough, but if I have to go into the city, I will take you to work. I'm going that way anyway."

"Okay."

"By the way, I have to go into the city tomorrow, so it looks like you will have a ride." He wanted to take care of her, and he knew that he had to go slow, wanting her to feel cherished, not owned. They both laughed, and they knew that life was good.

They dressed and headed over to her house to get a few things. When they arrived at her home, it felt like they hadn't been there in ages, even though it had been only about a day and a half. She went directly to her room to get some clothing. Since the weather was mild these days, she chose her clothes accordingly and then packed a few uniforms. When she turned in the doorway, he was standing there. He had been upstairs in her house only once, and he looked strange but not out of place. As a couple, they had come a long way since then. There was no turning back now.

"You mind if I walk around?" he asked.

"No, not at all."

Next to her bedroom door was the bathroom, with an antique tub. Down the hall there was what looked like a guest bedroom, and to the right of it was a sizable master bedroom. Turning on the light, he stepped into the room and noticed that everything was laid out as if her grandmother still lived there. There was a large bed with a dresser at its foot. The mirror was square with many old pictures stuck in its edges—of children, grandchildren, and other family members. It was as if time stood still in this room, and in other parts of the house as well. When he turned to make his way back to her room, he found that she was standing behind him.

"I haven't felt ready to clean out her things yet."

He understood, even though he had never experienced the death of a loved one. "There is no rush."

It felt good to say she wasn't ready and have him understand. Her grandmother had been her best friend. She needed time.

❧ ❧ ❧

They fell into a routine in the weeks that followed. Lisa went to work every day, and when she returned home, he was there waiting for her. Seven conducted business from his office and wrapped up each day just before she got home. They would go out to eat twice a week, and other days Lisa would cook something nice and they would watch TV. They talked about whatever came to mind, and debated which shows they would watch. He was learning her likes and dislikes, and she was learning his.

She found that he really didn't like cheese, except on pizza. He found that she hated walking around barefoot, as it made her feet feel creepy. She found that he shaved every morning and by evening his face was darkening with five o'clock shadow. He found that she hot curled her hair some mornings and was very concerned about it getting wet when they showered together. She found that she was very rarely in the bathroom alone, because as soon as he heard the shower running he would come and get in with her.

Kim called her on her cell phone, wanting to know when she would be home, and Lisa felt shy when she said, "I'm not sure. I've been staying with Seven. It's just easier to get to work from here."

"Easier to get to work, my ass," she said.

They laughed, and Lisa told her how much she loved him and how good it was to be there with him. Kim told her that she had better come by and see her or she would bring Aunt Ruth and Hattie over there. Lisa laughed, knowing the heifer would do it. Kim was happy that her cousin was doing well and that love was working out. They made plans to see each other soon.

Mary, Seven's housekeeper, was another issue. The day after they made love for the first time, Lisa had gotten up a little late that morning. She was supposed to ride in to work with Seven but had decided against it. He left her a set of keys and grudgingly went on to handle his day. While she was dressing and combing her hair, an older woman appeared in the bedroom. She started for the bed when she noticed Lisa standing in the bathroom.

"Oh, I'm sorry. I didn't know anyone was in here."

Lisa, not used to this type of situation, felt hot with embarrassment. She could have killed Seven—he had forgotten to tell her that his housekeeper was coming today, and, knowing him, he wouldn't care if he did remember. "That's all right. I was just leaving."

Mary smiled, backing out of the room to give her a few more moments to collect herself. Staring at the bed, she was glad that she had talked him into taking that sheet off the bed and throwing it away. She didn't want his housekeeper seeing the bloodstained sheets. The thought made her want to sink into the floor.

Gathering her purse and keys, she headed to the front door. Mary stood in the kitchen drinking coffee and smiling.

"Nice to meet you. I'm Lisa."

"I know who you are. He speaks highly of you. I'm happy to finally meet you," she said. "Do you have any errands that you want me to handle for you today?"

Lisa smiled. "No, thank you."

"Well, you have a wonderful day, and if you change your mind, call and let me know."

"I will, and thank you," Lisa said, opening the door to make her escape.

That evening, when Seven got home, he laughed at her reenactment of the scene that morning, and he reassured her that he was his own man. No one would dare tell him how to live in his own house. He knew Mary, though. She would have been interested in the young woman who had spent the night, since she had never met any of the women he dated. Seven was sure that Mary understood that this woman was special to him.

After the incident with Mary, everything went well. Lisa became comfortable and both his family and hers realized that she was never really at her own house anymore. When she would run out of things to wear, he would order her more clothes and shoes from Spiegel's and other women's catalogues. He was spoiling her, and she knew it, and to be truthful she loved it. Every day, her feelings for him deepened.

They took his grandmother and grandfather out to dinner, and all had a great time. Gary came by with his family for dinner one Saturday, and Lisa was glad to have them. Rhonda and Sean couldn't make it, and Lisa was sorry, as she wanted Rhonda to see that cousin Sherri was out.

Seven went by to check on his mother at the middle of the month, like he always did, and Betty came by one evening and had dinner with them. She was happy to see her son so happy.

Seven and Lisa entertained regularly at what was becoming *their* home rather than just his. They went out often, even going over to his grandmother's house again for Sunday dinner. He hung out with the men, watching sports on the tube, and she hung out with the women, talking and laughing. When it was time to go, his grandmother immediately told him to make certain that they came by again soon. His grandfather, she told him, missed his company. Seven kissed her and promised that he would.

They rode home in a comforting silence that Lisa was coming to recognize as sexual tension. Seven, she realized, wanted to make love all the time and was trying to curb his appetite to be considerate toward her. He had a way of making her feel sexy and wanted. Their sex life was wonderful. He was a patient and caring lover, helping her explore her body and his. Nothing she did was wrong, he was open to answer any questions that she might have, and he was always willing to demonstrate whenever necessary.

When they arrived home that evening, she walked toward the bedroom to change her clothes. Seven began taking his clothes off in the hall, and he was sporting a full erection.

"Come," he said. "Take your clothes off."

She was still a little shy, and she felt like she was being stalked as he walked toward her naked. She began removing her clothing, and when they both stood naked, she realized that she was just as aroused as he was. When he neared, she reached out her hand for his, walking him into the bedroom. Placing her hands on his chest, she pushed him to sit on the side of the bed and, stepping between his open legs, leaned down and kissed him deeply.

Caressing his face while she kissed him, she began suckling his tongue. She realized that she wanted to taste him as he had done to her so many times before. Breaking free of their kiss, she got up her nerve and kissed his throat and then his chest, until she was on her knees in front of him. His manhood strained forward at her, and without preamble she leaned in and licked his tip. She heard him hiss at the contact and she looked up at him. His head was back, and in the moonlight she could see his Adam's apple bob up and down. He was clutching the sheet on either side of his legs, and she became bold in her stroke as she sucked him again and again. The taste was so arousing and masculine that she tried to fit as much of him in her mouth as she could, and for all her efforts, it was just the tip of the iceberg. Taking her mouth away, she kissed his sac, and he groaned, turning them both on. She trailed her tongue along his shaft, and when she came to his tip again, she suckled and felt him pulse in her mouth. She pulled on it one more time before taking her mouth away. His body tightened, and she felt a spurt of warmth touch her lips. With her tongue, she tasted the essence of him, and when she would have licked him again, he stopped her. Sliding off the bed, he turned her, pushing down on her hands and knees. Placing himself, at her opening, he pressed forward, stretching and bearing down on her until he was buried to the hilt. When he started pumping into her, he realized that she could not hold herself up—his thrusts were too powerful—so he maneuvered them to the opening of the bathroom door, where she clutched the door frame. At this angle, he was able to touch her very soul, and the current that flowed only intensified with each stroke. He hammered himself into her until she was mindlessly calling his name. The sounds that she made inflamed him so much that he stiffened, grinding himself into her so that she would catch every drop of him. They collapsed, gasping and panting into each other's arms.

Later, as they soaked in the tub and she sat between his legs with her knees up, he noticed that she winced when the water touched her skin.

"Are you hurt?" he asked with concern.

"I think I have carpet burn." She laughed, showing him her elbows too. "It just felt so good."

He smirked before saying, "You are crazy."

She stood in the tub and turned, showing him her skinned knees close up, and he kissed them both. *This*, he thought, *is living.*

# CHAPTER 15

It was the middle of June when Lisa agreed to stay with him for a week. It was now the first week in September, and they had been together nonstop. She went to work, and he conducted business in the office down the hall from where they shared their bed. All was going well until she started feeling sick. It was like she had the flu and couldn't get rid of it. She felt so bad in the morning that she had called into work twice the previous week, but as the day progressed, she would start feeling better, and she began to think it was all in her mind. Then, the next day, it would start again. Eating was out of the question, since she couldn't hold anything down. When Seven wanted to go out to eat she would decline, telling him that if he wanted to go out he could; she just wanted to sleep.

Seven noticed that she hadn't been feeling good, and he was worried about her. When he asked her what was wrong, she didn't want to worry him, so she would respond, "I think something's going around."

A week and a half later, she didn't seem any better, and he made an appointment for her to see Dr. Beniot. She protested, until she started throwing up. He had a business meeting that day, but he said that he would cancel it so he could go with her to the doctor. Lisa refused, saying that she would come straight home after she saw the doctor and tell him what was wrong. Seven went to his meeting, and Lisa went to the doctor.

In his office, the doctor listened to all her complaints and asked a few questions of his own. "When is the last time you had a period?"

Lisa was about to answer, but she slowed down as she realized that she didn't remember. She counted backward, and the further she counted, the further back she had to go. Worried now, she tried and tried, and June popped into her head. *Oh*, she thought, *this isn't good*.

"I believe it was June."

"Are you using any birth control?"

It just hadn't crossed her mind. What could she have been thinking? She hadn't been sexually active before him, but she understood preventing pregnancy. He would be angry with her, and things had been going so well. She started to feel like she couldn't breathe, and the doctors voice sounded far away. She felt like she was going to faint—how could she have been so stupid? He might not want her now that she was pregnant. He might even think that she was trying to trap him.

"I'm not using any."

The doctor did a urine test, and it was positive. She was pregnant. He prescribed prenatal pills to help her get her strength up. "Make an appointment with the nurse," he instructed her, "and I will see you the same time next month."

After leaving his office, she decided to go back home instead of to work. She needed to think and rest, but mostly rest, since her only option was to tell him and she would need strength to do that. There was love in her heart for this child already, because it was his. She could not get rid of his child—she loved them both too much for that. All she could think about on the ride home was resting, and she hoped it would help make her thoughts clearer.

When she arrived home, he was in the living room talking on the phone. He hung up when heard the key in the door. He was pulling at the knob as she was pushing. "What did the doctor say?"

The concern in his eyes made her feel bad. She wouldn't lie; she just wouldn't tell him today to give herself time to get it together. "I'm not dying; I told you something was going around."

It was the first time that she had ever told an untruth to him, and he could feel it. She never looked at the ground when she talked to him. He was hurt and he didn't know what to make of this. What was it she was keeping from him? He decided not to push the issue.

She walked in past him and headed straight for the bedroom. After pacing the living room for a half-hour, he head back to the bedroom, and as he entered he heard the shower turn off. Her hair was pulled back in a ponytail and he noticed, of all things, that it had grown. She was drying off, and when he stepped into the bathroom, she covered herself from him. It was like a blow to the chest. He pretended not to notice the change in her and asked if she needed anything.

"I'm all right. I'm just going to lie down for a while."

He watched her closely. Maybe she hadn't noticed, but she was clutching the towel to her and standing as still as a statue. She wanted him out. "All right," he said, and he turned and left the bathroom.

Evening was approaching when she climbed into the bed, and although she was tired, sleep would not come. How could she have let this happen? The only explanation could be that she wanted his child. If he rejected her, she wouldn't be able to take it. This was her last thought before falling into a deep sleep.

Seven had gone out for a ride in an attempt to control his rage. He stopped at a bar and began drinking shots of tequila. He felt like fighting, and it scared him that she could drive him to such a point so easily. Shit, he hadn't felt this way since he was a kid. He stopped at some bar on Queens Boulevard, and he must have looked like he was spoiling for a fight, because no one spoke to him at all. When he was tired of his own company, he headed back home.

After he walked in the door, he realized that he should have stayed away longer. Entering the bedroom, he found her still asleep, so he sat in a chair in the corner brooding in the dark. She was his one true love, but there had been a breakdown in communication, and he wanted to know why she would lie to him. She tossed and turned after he entered the room, feeling his anger, he thought. When she sat up in the bed, he could see that she was disoriented, and like a predator, he waited until the moment was right to ask.

"Why would you lie to me?"

She sat up, trying to focus her eyes. There was nothing to say—she had lied, and he was angry. The silence stretched out between them for long minutes as she fumbled with her thoughts. Focusing her eyes on the chair where he sat, she could just make out his outline, tall and erect. He was pissed, and it seemed she had made a bad situation worse.

"You're taking too long to fucking answer me," he said, his voice low and menacing.

Lisa had never seen this side of him. He was like a different person, and she was just a little afraid. She didn't want to move for fear that he would pounce on her. She knew he had a temper, didn't she? Yes, she did, and she was cowering.

"I just didn't feel like talking about anything."

"Why didn't you feel like telling me the truth? Why didn't you just say you would talk to me later?"

He had a good point, and although he made perfect sense, she could tell that he had been drinking. Seven was definitely on point, but the drinking seemed to heighten his anger instead of calming it. "I didn't know what to say."

"Did you even go to the doctor?"

She deserved that, she supposed, but still it hurt. "Of course I did."

He was tired of this dance. He wanted answers. He stood, flicking on the lamp next to the chair. She made not a sound—at least she hoped she didn't. Seven stood blocking the doorway; he wore a t-shirt and some black jeans, and his eyes were red with anger. His five-o'clock shadow made him intimidating as he stood there glaring at her waiting, his patience running thin.

This confrontation would not end with him in the dark; he had enough of that with his mother. She knew that he wouldn't accept secrecy with her. If she told him the truth and lost him, at least she would still have their baby. Staring at her hands, she heard rather then saw him approaching the bed. He grabbed her chin and made her look at him. "You're hurting me. Please don't," she whispered.

He saw the fear and tried to control himself. He needed her honesty like he needed air. Lisa's eyes were the window to her soul, and when she looked at him, it was as if she were welcoming him. She had embraced him with her love and honesty, and it was all or nothing for him. He did not want her fear.

"You hurt me. That's how we got here." Releasing her, he turned and headed for the door.

It was true, and there was no way around it—her untruth had brought them here. When he reached the door, she said, "I'm pregnant." Her voice shook with the emotion she felt saying that, as well as the fear. The words just hung there in the air, and in the silence she could hear them echoing through her head. She didn't move or breathe, waiting to hear his rejection.

He stood still in the doorway to their bedroom, looking down the long hall in the darkness. The light on behind him seemed to make the outside of the room even darker. He had heard what she said but he did not respond right away; he didn't trust himself to speak. Relief was his first feeling; he wasn't losing her to something he didn't understand. He was in fact gaining, not losing. Carefully he said, "You decided not tell me because you don't want the baby. Is that it?"

"I didn't tell you right away because I was trying to get up the nerve."

"Get up the nerve about what?" he asked, angry.

"We had not discussed having children, and I was afraid that you wouldn't want it. I have to keep this child. The only thing that I can do now is be truthful. I made a mistake not telling you right away, but I don't want to choose between the man I love and child I made with the man I love."

As she said this, the burden lifted from his shoulders. The crazy woman thought that he wouldn't want the child. "I thought that we weren't using birth control to get pregnant. You see this as a mistake? I have never been with a woman without a condom before you. I thought we didn't care about being pregnant; in fact, I thought you wanted to have my child."

He said all of this with his back to her. He then turned to see her, really look at her, and in her eyes he saw the fear of rejection, and he understood it. Fear of rejection had influenced him a lot in the way he had lived his life before her. Still he was hurt that she didn't understand the depth of his love for her. "Lisa, how could you doubt me, a man who is still hurting from not knowing his own father?"

She could hear the pain in his voice and wanted him to know that if she had hurt him, it was due to her own inadequacies, not his. "I wasn't thinking…I was just afraid. I didn't want you to send me away."

"Oh, baby." He opened his arms and she was up off the bed running to him. She wrapped her legs and arms around him and he held her. Lisa felt so safe with him, and both of them felt as if their lives were back on track.

They made love that night, and another layer of intimacy unfolded for them. He was gentle and loving, while she was receptive and willing, and the world for both of them seemed to come off its tilt. They lay facing the window, basking in each other's love, Lisa feeling safe and Seven feeling the need to protect her. They slept that way all through the night, feeling reassured by the other's presence.

# CHAPTER 16

They decided to tell his mother and her Aunt Ruth at the same time. The couple decided to have a dinner party to announce the birth of their child. They had to plan it quickly considering that she was pregnant, but with Mary's help they pulled it off. Seven had been doing a little planning of his own, ordering Lisa a beautiful engagement ring. He planned to ask her to marry him in front of their friends and family. Lisa, being old fashioned, wasn't thrilled about telling her family that she was having a baby with no commitment from the father, and he didn't want to be viewed as nonchalant either where she and his child were concerned.

Mary worked late that evening answering the door and taking coats. His mother and grandmother were there for him and for Lisa, her aunt Ruth, cousin Kim, and Wayne, Kim's husband. Seven's grandfather couldn't make it because he was feeling under the weather. The guest list also included Gary and Valerie, along with Sean. Rhonda couldn't make it.

Mary served appetizers and then started mingling. She was pleased to meet his mother and grandmother, and both were very sweet to her. The meal consisted of broiled salmon with a steamed vegetable medley and baby potatoes cooked to perfection. A colorful salad was added to the menu to finish the meal. They ate and talked, and it was clear that Valerie and Betty were too excited to enjoy their food—something was up, and they could smell it.

When dinner was finished, they retired to the living room for drinks and conversation, and Lisa decided that she would announce her pregnancy after everyone was seated in the living room. Pulling Seven aside in the kitchen, she told him that she was ready, and he smiled saying that he would back her. Back in the living room, Lisa raised her hand to get everyone's attention, but before she could start speaking, Seven cut her off.

"I'd like to thank everyone for coming out tonight to be with us. I'm not one for long speeches, so I'll just cut to the chase. Some of you may not be aware of this, but Lisa and I have known each other since I was ten and she was eight. She was my friend then, and now she is my friend, lover, and soon to be the mother of my child. It is with honor and respect that I ask her to be my wife."

Kim, Valerie, Betty, and his grandmother started crying, but Aunt Ruth said, "It's about time, you scalawag. I thought I was going to have to give my niece lessons on cows and the buying and selling of milk."

Seven started laughing, and then he focused in on Lisa. "Baby?" he said.

She stood there frozen for a moment, and then she started to cry. "Yes," she said, over and over again. He placed a rather large diamond on her finger and kissed her thoroughly. Everyone clapped, and Lisa's aunt capped off the evening by telling him that if she were younger, he wouldn't even remember Lisa's name. Kim wanted to die; Aunt Ruth was too damn frisky by far.

The evening ended for the young couple with Lisa modeling the ring for him wearing nothing but her birthday suit. She learned how to ride him, and she found that the ring was even more breathtaking when she splayed her fingers out over his chest. In the glow of candlelight she found that his dark skin made it twinkle all the more. Their intimacy level had risen to another plane—the man that she loved showed her the ultimate respect by giving his name to her and his unborn child. They would now be one in the eyes of God.

Lisa's belly was not big, but it was definitely rounding, and Seven found her more beautiful than ever. When she bathed and he himself wasn't in the tub, he sat and watched her. If she combed her hair, he sat and watched. When she ate, he took pictures and she complained. He was moved by her condition, and so was his mother. Betty came by more than ever, making excuses about her house, her dog, or her bank account. He found it funny, but what bothered him was that she felt she needed to make excuses. His mother wasn't intrusive—she never overstayed her welcome, and Lisa enjoyed having her around.

When Lisa had her next doctor's appointment, his mother came along to support her, and he appreciated it. Dr. Benoit examined her and told her that she was about twelve weeks in. He also referred her to Dr. Kembro, a very good obstetrician. All went well on the visit, and seeing the new doctor wouldn't be a problem since she was in the same building on the second floor. Before leaving, they made an appointment with the new doctor.

The three went out to eat at a Jamaican restaurant, and the food was great. Seven had steamed red snapper, Lisa had goat roti, and Betty had ox tails with rice and peas. After lunch, Seven went to a meeting. Lisa and Betty spent the rest of the afternoon window-shopping. When they got tired, they stopped for tea at Starbucks. Betty seemed to be deep in thought and bothered about something, and out of concern, Lisa reached over the table, touching her hand. "What's wrong? Is there something I could help you with?"

Betty smiled, squeezing Lisa's hand lightly in response. "No, baby, there's nothing that you can do. It's my father. I don't think that he will make it to see the baby. Things were going so well for you and Seven that I didn't want to tell you."

Lisa knew Seven was very fond of his grandfather. This would be hard on him. "What's the matter with him?" She asked afraid to know the answer.

"He's old. This is no tragedy in the scheme of things—he's old and has lived a good life, and he can say that he was good to his wife, children, and even his grandchildren. How many can say that?"

The death of her grandmother gave her insight into Betty's situation. She knew that when a loved one dies, the living can only accept it—because choosing not to accept death would leave a person in a continual loop of despair, unable to move forward—and see all the good that life still had to offer.

"I understand. I still feel that way about the death of my grandmother. You need to tell him so he can make time for his grandfather, and it needs to come from you."

They stared at each other, thinking about life on 104[th] Street in Corona. They had come a long way—all three of them.

Betty broke the silence. "I'll talk to him when I see you home."

Lisa was pleased and let Betty know how she felt. "We're family now; we'll be there every step of the way with you."

Seven took the news about his grandfather as well as could be expected. Pop was old, and the writing was on the wall. Outwardly he appeared untouched, but both Lisa and Betty knew better. As it turned out, he would have some free time in the afternoons for next few weeks, and he decided that he would go by and hang out with his grandfather.

The routine for Seven and Lisa changed—Lisa still worked, and although Seven wanted her to quit, he wouldn't try to bend her to his will. He handled business in the mornings, wrapping up at about one. Three days a week, he hung out with his grandfather until 5:30 and then met Lisa at home. He felt as if he was grasping what was important in life. The time spent with his grandfather was invaluable.

They talked about everything—sports, politics, women, and life. His grandfather was happy about the baby and the upcoming wedding. He seemed weaker to Seven, and it bothered him. Seeing the worry in his eyes, his grandfather decided it was time they talked. "It would seem that we can't beat around the bush any longer."

Seven didn't think he was ready for this conversation, yet it would be a sin to not hear his last thoughts and ideas about life and death. "I don't suppose we can. It would seem time is of the essence."

His grandfather laughed—his grandson was refreshing and had a good head on his shoulders. "You know, it is said that if you have children, you never die."

Seven said nothing, just listened to the jewels being dropped. "You can't stop what's coming—none of us can—but in some ways, by coming and facing death with me, you make the road for yourself less rocky. Understand that when I go I will be happy, because I enjoyed life. I got the woman I wanted and had wonderful children, and if life is good to you, you will die with a younger version of yourself at your side. I'm seeing my bloodline carry on, now even with the knowledge of a great grandchild. Life has been good. I don't want to go, mind you, but I find it better to focus on life in the face of death."

They had these types of discussions whenever he came, and he found that he learned without even trying.

His grandmother doted on him even more, and even though he was a grown man, he loved it, and them. She fixed plates for him to take home to Lisa and spoiled them both. It got to a point where if he came home without a plate, Lisa accused him of eating it. Even in the face of the inevitable, life was good.

❦ ❦ ❦

Dr. Kembro turned out to be a very nice woman. She answered all of Lisa's questions and made certain that she was taking her vitamins. They checked for protein in her urine and did a sonogram to determine the date of the birth (although they didn't ask about the baby's sex). The baby, she told Lisa, was due March 20. Seven and Lisa were both excited. When Seven went down to get the truck, she turned to the doctor and asked shyly, "Is it all right if we…"

"Yes, you can continue a healthy sex life. If there are any problems, I will let you know. If you feel different, or if you have any pain, you let me know; otherwise, you should be fine."

Lisa's morning sickness was becoming an issue of the past, and all appeared to be going well. Seven started picking her up from work, and though she didn't say anything to him, she was thankful.

❦ ❦ ❦

In the early part of November, Seven arrived at his grandparents' house to find an ambulance outside. He felt disloyal, because he had promised that he would be strong. Now, confronted with the possibility of good-bye, he felt burdened by that pledge. Unable to change what awaited him, he entered the house. He could hear the commotion coming from the back near the den. Stepping with purpose, he headed in that direction, searching for his grandmother.

As he approached the den, an officer stepped into his line of vision. "Are you family?" he asked.

"Yes," Seven responded. "I'm their grandson."

The officer looked at him and nodded to the paramedic as if to say, "It's okay." Seven broke the silence with a question. "Where are they?"

The paramedic was a tall guy, the officer a little shorter and fat. He knew he was being impatient, but Laurel and Hardy weren't answering fast enough. Pushing past the two, he stepped into the den. On the couch in front of him sat his grandfather. He was crying while the other paramedic was checking his blood pressure and trying to get him to calm down. In front of the TV on the floor was a sheet, and it took a moment before the scene made sense, but once it became clear, he still asked, "Where's my grandmother?"

The paramedic taking care of his grandfather looked up and then stood. "Sorry for your loss," he said. "Her husband said that she laid down for a nap and never woke up. We won't know the cause for sure until an autopsy is done." The paramedic could see that Seven was stunned and tried to get him focused on what he could do to help the old guy. "Your grandfather is a little disoriented and very upset. His vital signs are elevated, and at his age we don't want to take the risk. We want to take him in to be checked out, but he's refusing to leave. There's nothing he can do for her now."

Seven felt like he was standing in a vacuum. The man's mouth was moving, but he couldn't hear a word being said. He felt like a prizefighter, out cold on his feet, with the possibility of having to say good-bye now a reality. He searched the room for her again before realizing she was lying on the floor in front of the TV, covered by a sheet. He moved toward her, kneeling at her side. The paramedic looked as though he would protest, but seeing the look on Seven's face, he changed his mind.

Removing the sheet from her face, he studied her, detached from the reality before him. His sweet grandmother lay there with a smile. Reaching out, he caressed her face, and her skin was cool. He thought about her showing up to his house uninvited. She told him that he was worth the effort—he was her grandson. Holding his feelings in check, he realized that she was his first family, even before Betty. She showed him unconditional love and friendship in the few months they had known each other. Now it seemed that those few months would have to last him a lifetime. She was gone.

Behind him, he became aware of the presence of his grandfather, who was crying softly. He was so immersed in his own grief that he had forgotten him. He stood and walked over to him and placed his hand on his shoulder. At his touch, his grandfather came out of his stupor. "She left me," he said.

What could he say to that? His grandfather's eyes glowed with pain, and his frail body shook with sorrow as he reached up to touch Seven's hand. At the touch of his grandfather's hand, he felt comforted. It was a small consolation against the unpredictability of life. They had no choice but to move on, and they would have to start now. Turning to the paramedic, he said, "When will she be taken away?"

"When the coroner gets here. Sometimes they can be awhile," he responded.

Nodding his head, he turned to his grandfather. "Pop, they want to take you to the hospital. I'll stay here and handle things while you go and get checked out."

"I'm staying with my wife until they come for her," his grandfather said with conviction. He was a man in Seven's eyes, and he would treat him as one.

"My grandfather and I will stay until my grandmother is removed. I will bring him to the hospital later. Thank you for your time."

The men began packing up, since there was nothing else to be done. The police stayed. Seven sat on the couch to wait with his grandfather. They sat that way for a time, until he heard a familiar voice coming from the next room. Patting his grandfather's leg, he said, "I'll be right back."

The police were blocking his aunt Brenda off in the kitchen, and when she saw him, she broke down.

"Daddy?"

Seven grabbed her first and held her. "No…Grandma."

He could see the moment when his words finally touched her. She wailed, "Noooooooooooo."

He asked himself if he would be able to stand replaying this scene over and over again, as it surely would for the rest of the day and into the evening. He would endure, but each time the realization set in to another pair of eyes, he would relive his own reaction, and the unpredictability of life would be laced with the unavoidable weight of sorrow.

Seven was afraid to face Betty, to see her pain, but when she came through the door, she came straight to him instead of her father. He held his mother and she cried softly, and when she got herself together, she went to her father. Lisa crossed his mind as he watched his mother walk away. She would be waiting for him. The house was full with his aunts, uncles, and cousins, so he felt all right leaving his grandfather to get her.

Heading toward the door, he found his Aunt Brenda standing near the kitchen sink. He told her where he was going, and she told him she would let his mother know. They would come straight back, he reassured her. His cell phone was ringing as he stepped out of the door. It was Lisa, and he told her he was on his way and that when he got close he would call her back. The mere fact that he was late was cause enough for concern, but when she heard the tone of his voice she was certain something was wrong. Lisa pushed redial with the intention to call him back, but she changed her mind, knowing if he was going to tell her over the phone, he would have done so already. Her cell phone started ringing, and she knew that it was him and that he was waiting outside for her, so she headed for the door. It took him some time to get there, but he made it.

When she stepped out of the door and headed for the truck, the sight of her restored him. The weather was cool now, and she wore a beautiful charcoal-gray cape that wrapped around her. Even though the cape concealed her, her stomach was becoming noticeable. Her hair was curled in a style that caressed her face, and her skinned glowed with life and health. He realized that he missed her today, and the thought made him smile. She looked concerned, and he knew that she was in tune with his feelings. Even though he hated to tell her and make her worry for him, he decided to tell her the truth.

"Is everything all right?" she asked.

It was a rare moment of weakness for Seven, as he sat there facing his own limitations. He wanted to protect her from hurt in whatever form it took, but the lesson to be learned today was control. He suspected that power in life came from understanding what one could not control. By understanding what was not in our power one could become proficient in matters that are.

Pulling away from the curb, he kept his eyes on the road. As they came to the first traffic light, he said, "We have to go to my grandparents' house tonight. Are you feeling up to it?" He was merely filling up space until he got up the nerve to say what had happened.

"Yes, I'm fine, but are you all right? Did something happen?"

"My grandmother died today."

Lisa cried, because she understood his plight in all this. Bobbi had made the effort to get to know her grandson. He was important to her, and she didn't try to hide her feelings. She was an open book where Seven was concerned, and now she was gone. The presence of his grandmother in his life encouraged him to build his own family. Family for Seven meant understanding who he was by understanding from whom he came, which has its place, ultimately though family is the collection of people with a common denominator. Understanding that heredity is not always the tie that binds is key—love, friendship, and respect can turn a stranger into a family member.

Everyone had been worried about his grandfather and had been blindsided by the unforeseen. She even felt sorrow for herself and her unborn child, who would never know the great grandmother that loved unconditionally.

"What happened?" she asked, unsure of how to approach the topic.

"I wish I could tell you. I got there around 2:00, and when I pulled up, I saw the ambulance outside and feared the worst, but not for my grandmother. I got myself together and went in, and he was sitting on the couch crying. My grandmother was nowhere in sight. The paramedics had her lying on the floor, probably to work on her."

"I'm sorry, honey. I love you, and I'm here for you."

Just hearing those words made him feel supported. He discovered something unpleasant about loving another—the risk of loss triples in the face of love. "I'm all right. I have you in my corner."

She stared out the window and concentrated on the ride until the house came into view. There were more cars out front than when he had left, and although he didn't understand why, he wanted them to go. After parking and helping Lisa from the truck, he headed with her into the house. When the door opened, it was his uncle Michael's face that he saw, and his pain was tangible.

"My man, they told me you were coming back. Granddad is looking for you. You made the right choice not letting the ambulance take him."

Seven nodded and shook his hand, but his uncle pulled him in close, hugging him and patting him on the back. When he noticed Lisa, he turned and hugged her too, and feeling her belly against him, he said to Seven. "The next generation is at hand—there is still something to celebrate."

Seven smiled, placing his hand on her belly, and she could feel a current of intensity flowing from him. His mother, aunts, and cousins came into the kitchen at just that moment to witness the exchange, and though there was sorrow, there was optimism about the future. Needing to see his grandfather, he whispered that he would be back, leaving her with the women. Betty glowed with pride as she put her arm around Lisa.

In his grandfather's room, he found him sitting up in the bed with some pillows behind him to prop him up. At his entry, he turned and looked at Seven. He said with a smile, "We had a hell of a day, didn't we? We lost our girl." His voice cracked at that statement.

Seven's heart squeezed at his grandfather's acknowledgement that she was his girl too.

"Yeah, we did."

"She loved you, you know. I love you too. I'm proud to be your grandfather." Seven made not a sound, yet he wiped his eyes. His grandfather continued, "I was sitting watching television. She came in the den to sit with me. She always does that. She said that she was tired. I felt her grab hold of my hand, and then she fell asleep. After about thirty minutes, she started leaning very heavily on me, and I nudged her to tell her that she should rest, that I could take of myself. She slumped over the other way, and when I called her, she didn't respond. I called 911, and they laid her on the floor to work on her. I knew she was gone when one of the paramedics said to the other, "No need to move her. Call it. Call it, he said. The other one tried, though I think it was for my sake."

Seven stood helpless, unsure what to say. "I love you, Pop."

"I know you do. Could you do me a favor? Help me get your grandmother put away properly. And marry that girl so that I can be there. I have decided to stay until the baby is here. Can you do that?'

"I can do that."

"I figure that the wedding and the birth of the baby will help all of us."

"Yes, sir. I can do that. Do you want to come home with me and Lisa?

"No, I want to rest and think. I will see you tomorrow bright and early."

"Yes, sir. I'll be here."

When he shut the door, he could hear him weeping, and Seven was shaken. He found Lisa, and after a lengthy goodnight, they left heading home. He told her that he had to help his grandfather with arrangements in the morning. Now, he just wanted to go home and get himself together so that he would be some help to his grandfather.

He attempted to change the subject to something more mundane. "Are you hungry?"

"Yes, starving. Can you go for pizza?"

"Pizza it is."

They stopped at a pizza shop on Sutphin Boulevard and then jumped on Hillside, taking it to Queens Boulevard. From there, it was almost a straight shot home. They ate in the truck and talked very little. On the elevator, he took the box from her. When they got to the door, he opened it and stepped aside, letting her in first. He headed straight for the kitchen, while Lisa kicked her shoes off and headed straight for the bathroom.

After undressing, she ran a tub of water to bathe in. It was clear that he would need time to himself; taking a bath would allow him to do just that. The water felt good, and she soaked for a time, thinking about Bobbi and reliving the death of her own grandmother. Even before his grandmother had died, she was somewhat depressed that her grandmother, dead a year, would never see her child. So much had happened in such a short time—she was already five months pregnant, and yet it seemed as if she had been with him forever.

When she stood to get out of the tub, he was there holding the towel open to her. She stepped into his embrace. Seating himself on the edge of the tub, he gently toweled her dry. Taking the towel from him, she closed it around her and headed into the bedroom. Seven noticed that she was a little self-conscious about her appearance now that her stomach was rounding. Following her into the bedroom, he undressed. When she asked him to turn the light off, he only dimmed it and started for the bed.

"Don't hide from me, please. I think you are beautiful. I've never been around a pregnant woman—this is all new for me, too. Living with you and seeing the transformation is fascinating. Please share."

She reached out her hand to him and he climbed in next to her, the dim light forgotten. He pulled back the cover and touched her. When she relaxed, he leaned down and kissed her. It was a long, lingering kiss to her belly. As he sat back in the bed, he palmed her, and looking down at her rounded stomach, he found her beautiful. As he ran his dark hands across her honey-brown skin, she felt cherished. She knew they would make love—not to fulfill a sexual need but to feel a connection to life. He was testing his vitality, and she welcomed him. Turning on her side, he spooned her entering, her from behind. They faced the window, and when he was deep within her, lightning lit up the sky.

Grabbing her by her hips for leverage, he pushed himself deep within her and withdrew. Placing his lips to her ear, he whispered, "I love you."

She whimpered, and he had to prevent himself from slamming into her. He didn't want to hurt her or the baby; he just wanted to be apart of them and feel life surround him. Reaching around her, he placed his finger on her clit and rubbed it in the same rhythm of their lovemaking it until she came, letting go once he felt her pleasure. He scalded her womb with his heat and juices, and it was at that moment that he heard it thunder outside.

He turned off the lamp, spooning her again, as they watched the rainfall. Neither spoke, but she could feel him crying inside. God knew of his hurt and the world cried because he could not, and when they felt the baby move within her, they continued in that same silence, both thinking deeply about the miracle of life and the mystery of death.

# CHAPTER 17

They arrived at his grandparents' house at nine in the morning and found most of the family still there from the day before. Obviously, they hadn't wanted to leave his grandfather alone. Everyone, it seemed, had a job: His mother and her sisters had to get an outfit for their mother. Ebony, Nicole, Rae, and Lisa were to plan a menu for the gathering afterwards. They were warned not to make too much food, because the church they were attending would provide a lot of it. Seven, his grandfather, and his uncles Calvin and Michael were going to the funeral home to get everything in order. All would meet back at the house at 4:00. Everyone wanted Pop to rest, and Seven intervened on his behalf, telling them this was his wife and that he was capable of making decisions regarding her burial. Betty smiled at her son and watched her father walk from the house with dignity as he went to handle her mother's final business.

The men got back at 5:00 from handling their tasks. There was tension in the air when they came through the door, and Seven noticed it. In the living room sat Kevin and David, Michael's two sons and the oldest of the grandchildren. All eyes were on Seven as he entered the room. Michael and Calvin had gone into the bedroom to help their father.

Looking from his mother to Lisa, he knew what the issue was, and both women looked nervous. "Good evening, everyone," he said.

The woman spoke with their heads down; only Lisa and his mother looked at him. Kevin broke the silence. "You're trying to take over. You probably think you're going to get some money. We don't owe you shit—you or your mother."

Lisa paled, and Seven forced himself to calm down, trying to show consideration for the women. "Behave, Kevin, before I make you."

"Behave," he said indignantly. "Who the fuck do you think you're talking to? I'm the oldest grandson in this family."

His aunt Brenda got up from the couch and stood behind Seven, taking hold of his hand. He smiled inwardly at her. She was sweet to show him that she stood with him, but it didn't stop him from checking Kevin. "I don't give a fuck whose grandson you are. I will bust your ass. Think long before heading my way, son. I will spank both you and your brother."

David had the sense to say nothing. Michael, their father, stepped into the living room at that moment. "Kevin, can I see you outside for a moment?"

Kevin looked at his father, a little relieved that he was being asked outside. He couldn't beat Seven, and he knew it. Seven was younger and in better condition. As Kevin walked past Brenda, she said, "Your father just saved you from getting your ass beat."

Kevin, not wanting to be outdone, said, "Maybe I should call Seven's father to see if he would be interested in him. But that's still a big secret, isn't it?"

"Kevin," Michael said harshly, and all were silent as they exited the house.

Then, to everyone's amazement, Brenda said, "I can't stand when men act like bitches."

Seven coughed at his aunt's words and smiled, but inwardly he died a little. Clearly, everyone but him knew who his father was. Staring at his mother, he smiled, trying to release her. She had just lost her mother and he didn't want to see her hurt. Betty was pale, and Lisa started talking to her, telling her she was feeling a little nauseous. Before Seven could say anything, Calvin came in and told him that his grandfather wanted to speak with him.

He entered his grandfather's room and saw the old man in bed, looking very tired. Seven was concerned, but what could he say? He was certain that if he was in his shoes, he would be worn out too.

"Is everything okay?" his grandfather asked.

"Yeah, everything is all right."

"Calvin came in and told me that Kevin was causing problems. He's my first grandchild, but he disappoints me sometimes."

"Everything is all right."

Seeing that Seven wasn't going to tell him anything to upset him, he said, "It's been a long day. Take your woman home so that she can rest."

Seven agreed, knowing that his grandfather was trying to defuse the situation.

"What time will you be here tomorrow?"

"What time do you want me here?"

"When Lisa gets up and feels up to it."

"You got it. I'll be here as soon as she's ready."

He left, needing to get out of the house. Lisa was in the kitchen looking tired. He motioned for them to leave; she stood and he put her wrap around her. Betty walked them to the door and he hugged his mother. They stepped outside just in time to see Kevin pull away from the house. His tires were singing, and from the look on his face, Seven could tell he was pissed.

Michael stepped up to shake his hand and hug Lisa. It was understood: "No harm, no foul."

They pulled away and Lisa burst out laughing as soon as they were out of sight. She was wheezing with laughter, and he couldn't help from laughing along with her. "What the hell is so funny?"

Getting herself together, she said, "I was glad when you came in. He was yelling at me and your mother, about how you were trying to take over. When you came in the room, he changed his tune."

Seven was boiling now—this shit wasn't funny anymore. "What do you mean he was yelling at you?" He said it softly, and she was afraid.

"It wasn't a big deal, baby. Emotions were high today."

He started to yell at her for not telling him when they were at the house, but looking at her, he saw that she looked tired and there were circles forming under her eyes. Lisa was going straight to bed when they got home, and he would hold her tonight—nothing more.

At ten in the evening, they were lying in bed holding each other while he watched TV. She was sleeping soundly, pressed warmly against him. Involuntarily thoughts of what his cousin said came to mind.

*Maybe I should call Seven's father to see if he would be interested in him. But that's still a big secret, isn't it?*

It played over and over again, and he was unable to stop it. The other shoe was about to drop, and he could feel it.

The viewing was on Monday and Tuesday evening, and the funeral would be on Wednesday at 11:00 A.M. It was nice turnout, with family and friends coming to pay their last respects to Barbara Thomas at Collins and Sons Mortuary. She wore a pretty white dress and white gloves with a purple flower in her hand. Her face was serene; she was peaceful.

His grandfather sat in the first row with his head held high, his children and grandchildren sitting around him. Lisa was included in the group, as she carried his first great grandchild. Seven and Kevin kept their distance, and David, his brother, stayed away from both of them. Betty went in early to greet people as they came and went, signing the book. Lisa was happy to see her family show up in support of them.

The first two days went by uneventfully, but on the morning of the funeral, Lisa took ill and couldn't get out of bed. When Seven saw her face, pale and drawn, he asked whether she was in pain. She told him that she wasn't—she just felt queasy—but when she tried to get out of the bed, he ordered her back in.

"I want to be with you today."

"Baby, please. I can't have you getting sick. I'll go for us both. You stay and rest. Try to eat something. I'll be home as soon as I can. Call Kim and have her come and stay with you."

Feeling tired, she gave in, getting up only to help him get dressed. He called Kim and asked her to stay with Lisa while he was gone. Kim was happy to do it, understanding that he needed to be there to see his grandmother on and to support his mother. Seven left happy that she was getting rest. He would hurry home as soon as he could.

The funeral was in progress when the doors to the parlor opened, admitting two people that he was sure he had never met before. Beside him, his mother stiffened, making him take notice of the couple as they made their way down the aisle to a seat on the side where friends were sitting. The woman was small and appeared to be in her late sixties, or maybe early seventies. She wore a black hat that was stylish for a woman her age and a black dress. She held a cane in one hand and in the other, the arm of a younger man, in his late fifties or early sixties. The man was tall and in very good physical shape despite his years. He was dressed elegantly, making the woman beside him look even older. His hair was gray at the temples, and his beard was trimmed neatly. He stood tall and erect, as if the world owed him.

When Seven looked into his face, he knew that he was staring into the face of his father. Locking eyes with him for a moment, Seven saw smug pride on his face. Turning back to his mother, Seven saw that she appeared to be faint. That was all he needed to confirm his suspicions, but the self-satisfied look on Kevin's face gave it away. He was the author of this bullshit.

He betrayed no curiosity; he kept his eyes straight ahead and behaved as if he was clear about what had just happened. Seven resented the stares and whispers and the fact that this would happened to him here, at his grandmother's funeral. He would endure because he would not be broken down or show weakness.

Seven was a pallbearer, and once his grandmother was in the hearse and everyone headed to the cemetery, he and Betty got into the truck alone. They didn't ride in the limo, as they both wanted privacy.

"Looks like the other shoe has dropped, wouldn't you say, Ma?" he asked, addressing her that way to take the edge off the tension.

Betty looked straight ahead, and for a moment he thought she would say nothing. "I guess it did."

"Do you really want me to hear this from someone else, or do you want to tell me?"

Taking a deep breath, she said, "What do you want to know?"

"Old habits die hard, I see. Since I am unclear about what I should be asking, why not just tell everything, from the beginning, as it pertains to me. That was my father, right?"

He knew it was. When he had left the church, the older man had stared at him, but judging by his reaction, or lack thereof, it was clear that there would be no love lost between them. Betty was having a hard enough time, so he focused on the road to give the illusion that he was only half-heartedly listening. He hated to corner her at a time like this, but he could not let another person get the upper hand over him.

Betty had tried to avoid this conversation, and now there was no way to get around it. She realized now she should have gotten up the nerve sooner to tackle this ugly business. Maybe if she had, she wouldn't be on the way to cemetery to bury her mother and still dealing with this issue. There was no more stalling—it was time to face her son and hurt him herself so that no one else could. She needed her mother, she thought. No, she could do this; she had been working at the battered woman's shelter now for months, and she had learned some things.

"Yes, he is your father." Before he could respond, she held her hand up. "I need to get this out before I lose my nerve."

He nodded, and she continued, "When I was twenty-two, I found a job down on Jamaica Avenue at a clothing store. My mother and father wanted me to go to school, and I promised that I would. I was making my own money, and like most kids, all I wanted to do was work and buy new clothes. The job was going well, but traveling there was becoming a problem. When I look back, my aunt's house was really no closer to where I worked. I just wanted to be away from my parents, because they were still treating me like a baby. I moved in with my aunt Bea and her husband, Clarence. My aunt was older than her husband by ten years, and it showed. When I moved in, she was happy to have me there, because she had never had children of her own and she always loved us children. When we were children, she would bring dolls for us girls and basketballs for the boys. She was my mother's younger sister, and my mother adored her. It was no leap for me or any one of us to stay with her—all we had to do was ask." Seven just listened, and when she stopped to collect herself, he didn't press her; he just waited.

"After the first week there, I noticed that her husband treated her like shit. He stayed out late, and when he was home, he was always watching me. I wasn't afraid of him, because I thought he was harmless. I thought his malice was only for my aunt Bea. One day, while I was home alone, I decided to take a shower. When I stepped from the shower, he was in the bathroom waiting. We had words, and when I tried to step past him, he threw me down and took me on the floor in the bathroom." As she relived her nightmare in front of her son, she realized that she had gained power by speaking out loud about what he had done. What they said at the shelter was true: silence gives the abuser power. She didn't understand why the burden of secrecy lies with the victim and why the victim has to be concerned with who will be hurt by the truth. In most cases, the victim is hurt and no one cares.

"It was my first time with a man. I left the house and the family and never looked back. I thought they blamed me. My aunt did, but my mother, father, and siblings never did. My mother told me that he was sick; she said that he had a stroke. I see now that she lied to get me to come home."

After finishing her story, she asked him to pull over. She was feeling sick. She went to the back of the truck and threw up.

When she climbed back in, she didn't look well. It was plain that this ordeal—the death of her mother and the appearance of her aunt and Clarence—had taken a toll on her. As he listened to his mother, he felt something pop loose in his head and start dripping. Betty had just told him that he was the product of a violent union. The puzzle pieces of his life had been small and unidentifiable, making it hard to put together, but as his mother spoke, they became larger and more defined. The only problem with that was as the puzzle came slowly together in his mind, the more he realized that he already knew what the picture would look like.

He thought about Lisa, the first time they made love and how sweet it had been. The idea that his mother's right to choose her own mate had been taken from her was appalling. Yet, what Betty had to endure was worsened by his presence, as it reminded her of the worst time of her life. He could say nothing; to verbalize what he was thinking would be to trivialize her ordeal. Seven knew that to offer an apology would degrade them both, so he said nothing. Yet the silence that blanketed them spoke volumes.

He pulled into the cemetery and parked with the other vehicles, and then he and his mother made their way to the grave site. He stood behind his grandfather, as did the rest of the grandchildren. Words were spoken and tears shed. But for Seven, a numbness had set into his being, leaving him feeling hollow. His detachment continued as the coffin was lowered into the ground. As he looked on, he felt as if he were witnessing the lives of people who had no association to him. As he started back to his truck, he realized that he had changed; he would never be who he was again. There was a moment of insecurity when he feared an introduction to his new self.

Betty wanted to hide and take a ride from someone else, but she loved him, and somehow she knew that he would need her. He never commented, and that worried her, but what was there to say? She climbed into his truck, and though she was tempted to stare straight ahead and ignore him, she could not. He had been part of her peripheral vision for far too long; it was time for him to be her main focus. There was her grandchild to think about, and Lisa. She could not leave things as they were.

"I love you," she said to her son.

He remained silent, feeling disgusted with himself—she was still trying to care for him despite all that had happened. He loved her too—he had always loved her. Shame was waiting for him, but for now, the numbness was keeping it at bay.

"I want you to know that I never blamed you. I was a bad mother because of me, not because of you. I should have sought help for both of us. I knew this day was coming even when you were a baby. There were times when I felt selfish for not putting you up for adoption, but I wanted you—you were my baby, not his. I knew nothing about caring for a child, and I had no real means to support us, but you were mine, not his." Her voice shook.

He saw his mother different, and not selfish as he once did. She wanted reassurance, and he supposed he owed her that much.

"Everything will be all right…I'll be all right." It was a lie, but necessary.

At the house, he could see there was a gathering from the number of cars out front. When he and Betty entered the house, they both noticed the pinched look on Brenda's face. Betty knew without stepping farther into the house that her aunt and her husband were there. Bea was her mother's sister—she would have come regardless—but he was there as well. Betty decided that she would not be a coward today; she had just as much right to be there as anyone. With her head held high, she moved into the crowd and mingled, thanking people for their support in her family's time of bereavement. When her aunt noticed her, she looked her up and down but said nothing, and Betty smiled at her nerve. Both Bea and her husband looked out of place, not really speaking to anyone, especially the family. Betty's brothers came over to her, and she could see that they were angry.

"We wanted to put them out, but daddy didn't want a scene."

"Daddy's right. How would it look to put Mom's sister out at a time like this?"

"I'm not interested in appearances. You have the right to grieve in peace," Michael said. "I'm sorry about Kevin. He can be an ass sometimes."

"I love you, Michael. You have always been a good brother," Betty said.

Looking around the room for Seven she instead saw Clarence, her aunt's husband, and she felt tension in her shoulders as her eyes locked with his. He had a drink in his hand, and he raised it as if to salute her. She turned her head, pretending not to see him. Calvin was saying something to her, but she excused herself, making a dash for the bathroom. She rinsed her face, and when she looked in the mirror, she felt humiliated that she still felt fear in his presence. She had thought that was behind her.

After a few minutes, she decided she had been in the bathroom long enough. The house had only one bathroom, and they had guests. She couldn't hide there forever.

After checking her appearance once more in the mirror, she opened the door and came face to face with Clarence. He stood there smiling as if they were old friends who would be happy to see each other after so many years. The bathroom wasn't in a high-traffic area, so they were alone. Life had come full circle for her—she was standing in the doorway of a bathroom facing him. She saw this as a tasteless trick that life was playing on her—or was this as an opportunity to do something different?

She spoke first. "What do you want?"

"I was just waiting for the bathroom. It is good to see you. though. I think of it as a bonus to be in your company today."

He was goading her, and what was worse, it was working. Losing control now would give him power. She didn't acknowledge his comments but pushed past him and headed back out to the living room. He grabbed her arm, and her skin crawled at his touch. She wanted to jerk away out of fear, but instead she stood there looking down at his hand in disgust. It was another violation against her at his hand, and the dam broke from the pressure.

"After all that I have lost and endured because of you, you would come here the day my mother was buried and corner me. Take your damn hand off me, and don't you ever touch me again."

Betty had always been plain, but he always saw the beauty that she tried to hide. Clarence had prided himself on his understanding of women, their wants and their needs. He wanted her now, but he didn't want to cause a scene. He was her first, and he had been more than disappointed when she left him. He had thought that she would come around and want to be with the man who had taken her virginity. He had plenty to teach and she had plenty to learn. The combination would have been heaven for them both.

Months later, he learned that she was pregnant—his old-ass wife had come bitching to him about it. Bea had been hurt because she was never able to conceive. She said that Betty called her for help, but Bea was jealous and wouldn't have dreamed of helping her. She never called back. The young man with her looked just like him. It had to be his son.

He released her and stepped in front of her to stay her. "I was happy when I heard that you were pregnant. I would have left Bea for you and the boy, but you never came back."

She stared at him as if he had two heads. How could he speak to her as if they had had a relationship. He was her uncle by marriage, and he had raped her, taking her innocence. Her blood boiled at his mention of Seven. He was her son, not his. She thought about her grandchild and the boil began to roll out of control, and before she could contain herself, she slapped him as hard as she could, feeling her shoulder pop with the force of the blow.

His head jerked from the blow, and when he turned to look at her, his eyes told of his intention, but when he would have reared back to slap her, he looked over her head to see the younger image of himself standing behind her.

Seven had seen the exchange from the living room, and he had seen his mother leave the room abruptly, looking ill. Locating his father again in the crowd, he saw him follow her from the room. Seven followed them both, standing just beyond sight, listening to the exchange. Betty was not the kind of person to get riled up, and when she slapped him, Seven almost laughed. He stepped into view and saw his father's intent, he prayed that his father would see his and understand the danger he was in by contemplating hitting his mother. In an effort to get him to understand where he was at he spoke.

"I pray God smiles upon me and gives you the courage to strike my only parent."

Clarence opened his mouth to speak but thought better of it. Stepping around Betty and his son, he left. Betty turned to look at her son, and what she saw frightened her. As he stood there staring at her, she saw a pain in his eyes that he did not yet fully understand, and it worried her that she could not recognize him.

Seven and Betty didn't talk, but they understood that they stood on the same side in a fight. His mother didn't try to hug him; it was better that way. When they reentered the living room, they saw his father and his wife leaving.

Seven walked over to his grandfather and paid his respects, letting him know that he would see him in few days. Looking down, Seven could see concern in his eyes, and he tried to reassure him, squeezing his shoulder.

"I understand, but don't stay away too long. Son, I want to let you know that when you judge yourself because of the actions of another, you'll never get a fair trial."

Seven smiled and said, "I'll see you, Pop."

Heading for the door, he had one more obstacle—his mother.

"Are you leaving?" she asked.

"Yeah, I've got to get going. I'll see you in a couple of days."

"I'll come by your house to check on Lisa as soon as we get Dad situated."

He nodded, opening the door. "I'll call you."

They both knew that he wouldn't.

# CHAPTER 18

Once on the road, he didn't know where to go, and he felt alone again. It was late afternoon, almost evening. He decided on a sports bar in Jackson Heights. He entered the place and took a seat at the table in the back. A very friendly waitress came over to take his order.

"What can I do for you?" she asked suggestively.

"What's on the menu?" he offered, and both knew that he wasn't talking about the menu.

She gave a throaty laugh that was practiced and promising. He felt like taking her to the nearest motel and working off some of his frustrations, but he didn't think she would be able to handle him in the state that he was in. She wouldn't get good company from him.

"Whatever you want," she replied.

As if throwing cold water on her, he said, "I'll have a burger, well done, and a Heineken—nothing more."

It was her turn to smile. She didn't give up easy. "Are you sure?"

She was a beautiful woman with skin of deep chocolate; her hair was braided, giving her the look of a Nubian queen. She wasn't slim but she wasn't fat either, and she had nice-sized breasts. The woman was a find, but he had nothing to offer. Fucking her wasn't going to change the problem at hand. He stood firm.

"No, sweetheart. Not today."

She was an optimist. "Another day then? I'll get your order in. Should you change your mind, let me know."

He nodded and gave no verbal response, the signal that he was ready to enjoy his own company again. When she was gone and there were no other distractions, he was faced with the events of the day—his grandmother's death, his mother, and his confrontation with his father. It was all too much, and he felt over stimulated. He was glad to be alone; he had felt stifled in the company of so many who knew the secret.

When the waitress came with his order, he told her to keep the beers coming. He never touched his food, but it seemed that the more he drank, the more sober he got. Betty was on his mind. He could see her as a young woman again, handling her customers. Now he saw things that he had never noticed before, like the times when he was hungry and wanted seconds, how she would let him eat off her plate, casually saying that she was full, even if she couldn't have been. Then there were the arguments that ensued when a customer didn't want to pay for services rendered. Their lights had never been turned off for non-payment, and although people had been evicted, they had never even received a notice.

Betty was a warrior who gave everything, including her body, for them to survive. Even now, she was taking this awful experience and making something good out of it by volunteering at the battered women's shelter. Images of things that made no sense when he was a kid were now filling his head. The images were clear now, and he wanted to hide from them. He loved his mother, but deep inside he knew he had judged her, and he wondered why his mother was "Betty the Ho."

Clarence was another issue. It was disturbing to think of him as an actual person. The worst part was that he could no longer delude himself into thinking that his father was some type of fallen hero. Clarence was a rapist and a thief of innocence, and Seven, who had never lifted a hand to harm a woman, was the product of such a man. The more he thought about his father, the harder it was to look his mother in the face.

He felt guilty that he had given his absent parent the benefit of the doubt while giving Betty, who was there trying, nothing but his judgment. He loved her, and wanted a relationship with his mother, but he wanted her to be truthful with him, and he blamed her for that as well. His arrogance had allowed him to believe that their lack of a mother-son relationship stemmed from Betty's detachment. All these years later, it was clear now that she had been trying to protect him. Even as a grown man, she continued trying to protect him. Remembering the exchange between his mother and his father, he knew that she had become unglued and struck his father when he spoke about him. The thought made his guilt even more severe.

He had spent enough time drinking, but it was not doing the job that he needed it to do. After his third beer, his thought process was still too lucid, so he called it quits, paying his tab and heading for his truck. Once on the road he played no music, letting his thoughts haunt him. Some thoughts repeated in his head, but these were just self-recriminations. Each time a recollection grabbed him, he was faced with the realization that reality as he knew it was skewed. It was no easy conquest to admit that what he thought was reality was in fact a picture drawn by his mother and colored by him in order to function. Seven discovered that weakness plagued him in ways that were not visible, and it appeared that his strength lay only in his ability to fool himself. There was an understanding that filled him with dread—he was not who he believed he was and, more importantly, he was not who he wanted to be.

It was a little after midnight when he stuck his key in the door, and when he stepped in, he saw her making her way from the living room to the hallway. At the mouth of the hall, she stopped and he saw that she was dressed in a sheer nightgown that emphasized the roundness of her belly. He stared at her, taking a minute to understand how she had come to be there. Apparently the drinking had had some effect. Her hair was around her shoulders, not combed but curly, and she was beautiful. While looking at her, a new reality set in—the innocence that she shared with him had not changed him, and he was in fact still jaded, tainted, and unworthy. The truth was that the roundness of her belly only confirmed that the opposite had happened.

He appeared not to recognize her for a moment, and she became concerned. Burying his grandmother must have been hard on him, she thought. "Are you all right, baby?" she asked.

Seven continued to stare at her for a moment before he spoke. "What are you doing still up? I thought you would be resting." That was a lie; he had forgotten she was even there.

"I was worried about you. Your mother called looking for you and she sounded worried. Are you all right?" she asked again.

"I'm fine. Why don't you just go to bed?"

She got the message: *Leave me alone*. She wasn't angry; she had felt no differently when her grandmother died. "Are you coming to bed?" she asked in a last-ditch attempt at closeness.

"Go to bed, Lisa, please."

His words hit their mark, and he saw the hurt in her eyes, but she said nothing more. She turned and walked away, heading for the bedroom. There was no desire within him to go after her. He didn't want to remember that she carried his child and that he had ruined her life too. They had played at normal, and now it was time to face the fact that he had not a clue what normal was or how to simulate it.

After she went to bed, he stayed up pacing the house, wondering how he was going to deal with her and a baby. The thought of her being tainted by him was too much to bear. What could he offer them other than financial stability? They deserved better than him, but, like Betty, he was selfish and he would not let them go. It was his last coherent thought before he fell asleep at his desk.

❧ ❧ ❧

Morning was rolling through the window, and when Lisa turned to look at him, she realized that she had slept alone. She thought about the previous day and the pain she had seen on his face. But today was a different day, and she would show him love and patience in his time of sorrow. As she swung her legs over the side of the bed, she felt the baby move, and she was excited to share it with him. She walked to his office. The door was cracked, and because she heard nothing, she peeked in, thinking that he must have gone out.

He was there with his head on the desk, sleeping. From the office door, she called his name softly. He stirred, lifting his head at the sound of her voice, and she saw that he didn't look well. It was as if he didn't look like himself; he seemed like a stranger, and she was concerned that his grief was severe.

Seven sat up and looked at her in the light of day, and it was clear to him that she had made the wrong choice in a mate. He shook his head to clear out the thought, but the web of sleep still held him. He stood and walked to the door, and the insecurity he felt didn't show as he approached her. He didn't touch her; he just stood there staring at her.

No longer being able to stand the silence, she reached out and touched his unshaven face. "Are you all right? I'm worried about you."

He felt so unworthy of her touch that his skin began to crawl. He stepped back a bit out of her reach. "I'm fine. Don't you have to go to work?"

Dismissed again, she let her hand fall to her side and looked at him. He wasn't himself. Whatever it was, it was more than just his grandmother's funeral. Being pregnant was taking a toll on her, and she wanted to cry at his treatment of her. She was being shut out—that was clear—and it was a hard pill to swallow when they had such a good relationship. When she could trust herself to speak, she said, "I took the rest of the week off when Bobbi died…to be with you."

"Oh, well, I have some business to handle, so I hope that you can find something to entertain yourself."

Anger welled up inside of her, but she said, "Don't worry. I can keep myself busy. I have a doctor's appointment today. I thought you would like to come."

"No, I'm sure that you can handle it."

"Yes, I can. I'll stop by my cousin Kim's house afterward to see how she is doing. I'll be in late." She then turned and walked away, heading for the bathroom.

He didn't want her to go to her cousin's house. He wanted her to be with him. As for the doctor's appointment, he wanted to go with her, but he said nothing. It was better that way. He took a shower in the smaller bathroom and dressed in his office, giving her privacy and himself a chance to hide. Dressed, he seated himself behind his desk, leaving the door open so he could watch her leave. It wasn't long before she came to the door to tell him she was leaving.

"I'll be back later," she said, but he just looked at her and didn't respond, so she left.

He sat there for a moment thinking, about her and about their life together, before he poured himself into his work for the day. It seemed the more he kept his mind occupied, the less time he had for the demons that plagued him. Betty called a few times, but he didn't answer. *Not today*, he thought. He just couldn't take hearing her concern for him. Uncle Michael called too, but he didn't answer his call either. He stayed on task all day and got a lot of work done.

He owned some land in North Carolina, and he decided that rather than sell it he would build a 102-unit complex on the site. After going back and forth with the developer in Georgia, they worked out a deal in which he would receive a discount on the building of the complex in exchange for a better price on the land in Dallas, Georgia. The builder was desperate now and was willing to see reason. Seven ended up killing two birds with one stone.

As for his storage space, he sold his 1969 Corvette, making a pretty penny, and was set to buy a 1970 Mustang. The Mustang was beautiful, but what he really wanted was the dealer's orange Barracuda. He was told, however, that it wasn't for sale. He would wait and bide his time until the right moment came.

Gary had let him know that some developers were building in upstate New York and told him to check out the property. He spent some time researching it on the Net to see what he could find out. The information that he stumbled upon was enough to get him thinking about going up and having a look around. He started a checklist and made this number one on the list.

He paid some bills and balanced his personal checkbook. He transferred money into his mother's account and then spoke with a bank representative to have it done automatically so he would have one less thing to do next month. He gave a call to his accountant to have his statements delivered so that he could track his money and see just what it was doing. Finally, he had made some purchases for Lisa and the baby. He bought clothes for them both and some furniture for the nursery. He paid those bills as well, thinking that in the future he would give her an account so that she could buy what she wanted for the baby without having to ask him.

She never asked him for anything, really. Any purchases she made came from her own money. Since she wasn't the type to ask for much, he bought her whatever moved him, and he enjoyed doing it. Lisa was always happy with whatever he gave, and her excitement made him feel content. As for the baby, he had just started purchasing things for his child, and he loved it. Now he just wanted to give her the money and let her make those decisions. His reason for doing this, if he was being honest with himself, was to maintain a cool distance from his life and the people in it.

It was late when she came home, and he was asleep on the couch. She had spent the day with her cousin and seen the doctor. Kim asked if everything was all right, and Lisa assured her that it was. The appointment had gone well—the baby's heart rate was fine, and she was feeling great. Dr. Kembro's nurse did her regular tests of urine, iron, and weight, and she got good news on all counts. The doctor refilled her vitamins and then she was on her way, after making a new appointment for December. Despite all the good news, it wasn't the same without Seven.

Walking into the living room, she grabbed the remote, turned off the TV, and shook him. "Honey, wake up, and come to bed."

He was awake, but he kept his eyes closed long enough to feign sleep. When he opened his eyes, she stood over him, still in her wool wrap.

*Where the fuck had she been, and how did she get home?*

He didn't ask those questions; in fact, he didn't ask her anything other than "What time is it?" It was his way of telling her that she shouldn't be out so late while pregnant. She needed to be home, where it was safe.

She didn't bite. It looked as if they were about to travel down the same avenue they had been traveling for the last day, and she was having no part of that. He looked angry, but she wasn't going to participate in a discussion in which she was the child. Instead, she said again, "Come on to bed." She was taking off her coat as she spoke to him.

The next question came out of nowhere. "Do you drive?"

She gave it some thought, and when she decided it wasn't a trap, she answered, "Yes, I can drive."

"Good, because I'm buying you a car so you can get around easier when the baby comes. Plus, this way, when you go out, you can get your ass home faster. Oh, and I had better get you a watch, too, so that you don't lose track of time."

She just stared at him, and she could think of nothing to say at first. Stepping back a little, she gathered her belongings and said, "I'm tired. I'm going to bed."

Whatever she expected him to say, it wasn't what he said. "Maybe you wouldn't be tired if you stayed home and rested."

She left him shadowboxing himself and slammed the bedroom door. It was the only outward indication that she was mad. Pacing the room, she thought about him sneering at her about her lateness. It was just ten o'clock, and she had let him know before she left that she was going to be late. If he was upset, why didn't he talk with her, why be accusing? She missed the man that she moved in with, and she wanted things back the way they were before his grandmother died, or before whatever happened to upset him.

He opened the terrace door and stood outside for a moment to clear his head. It was the middle of November and freezing, but the cold seemed to match his mood perfectly. She had been gone all day and he missed her, yet when he saw her, he wanted to fight. He wanted to know how the doctors' appointment had gone, but he wouldn't ask. It seemed that his demons were active tonight, and where he could have cuddled with her, they were now strangers who lived in the same space, avoiding each other.

His mind grabbed on to the thought of Betty vomiting after merely telling her story, and he was lost again in thoughts of unworthiness. As for Lisa, when these thoughts struck him, he was unfit to be in her company. The thought of telling her what had happened at the funeral was out of the question—he just couldn't share this. He was out of control, and he didn't like the feeling—it was yet another sign of weakness.

He decided after closing the terrace door that he would not sleep without her tonight. They would not have sex; he would just be in her company tonight, and maybe her presence would push away his doubts. He waited until he thought she was asleep and then he headed down the hall. Undressing in the dark, he climbed in next to her on the side facing the window. But sleep would not come, and he just stared out the window thinking and measuring himself up against his father, not liking the results. Listening to her even breathing became hypnotic for him, and he finally abandoned his thoughts and began dozing off. At some point during the night she turned, spooning him in her sleep. He could feel her belly on his back, and it was good, but just as he was about to fall back to sleep he felt it, the baby moving. Seven lay there well into the night feeling his child move against his back, and he knew he would not sleep in here with her again. It was an intimacy that he didn't wish to experience. Still, he was fascinated at how active his child was and how she was able to sleep through it all.

❧ ❧ ❧

Thanksgiving was just about a week and half away, and Lisa had decided that she would not cook. After all that had happened in the last few weeks, she thought it would be better if they spent the holidays with family and friends. Seven was depressed and not really himself, and had not been since his grandmother's funeral. She thought that if he was around friends and family, they would get back to where they were. In all honesty, she was desperate to regain what they appeared to have lost. They had previously had familiarity, trust, and love—or so she had thought—and of course they had their baby. Now it seemed that he avoided her and any conversations about the baby. She didn't know where to turn to, so she kept the hurt that she was feeling to herself.

Their routine had changed tremendously: he did most of his work at night and she could no longer deny that it was to avoid seeing and talking to her. During the day, when she worked, he didn't call her to just talk. He never inquired about her health or the baby's, and that made her heart squeeze. When she got home most evenings, he wasn't there, and when he came in he had nothing to say other than, "Why aren't you resting?" She understood that he said it so she would go back to their bedroom and leave him alone. Lately, she had started going to bed before he came home so that he wouldn't have to dismiss her. As for sleeping together and making love, they were doing neither, and they hadn't been since his grandmother's funeral. To put it bluntly, she was lonely.

There was an unkindness about him that almost frightened her when she was in his company, and it stood out in situations when they were thrown together and had to speak. The night before, when she had gotten home from work tired, her back and feet aching from standing all day, she headed for the bedroom to fall into bed. But when she entered the room, he was coming from the bathroom still dripping with water from a shower. When he realized she was there, he stopped and looked at her, saying nothing. The silence for her was too heavy, so she said, "Oh, excuse me."

This was the worst blow of all. They had shared so much, and now she was reduced to feeling as if she had just walked in on a roommate. She felt her face heat up with embarrassment, and she turned to leave to give him a moment to get dressed, but when she would have left, he stopped her and said, "This is your room. I'll go."

She turned back to look at him, and her awkwardness deepened because he was at a full erection, and when she looked him in the eye, he was smirking, rubbing her face in the humiliation she felt. She was still in the doorway, looking at the floor, when he approached, still naked. At the door, he slid past her making certain that his tip brushed her as he did. Closing the door behind him, she placed her back to the door and cried. It was at that moment that she realized that she didn't have to live with him; she could go to her own house, where she would no longer have to be a guest.

The thought of leaving and not seeing him every day was too much for her heart to take, but she had known it might come to this one day. She was just thankful for their child, because no matter what, she loved him and wanted their baby. It hurt to think about it, but if things didn't turn around soon, she would leave. She couldn't be her mother; she had to be stronger, if not for her sake, then for her child.

# CHAPTER 19

Betty had called a few times, but he was never at home. She was concerned, but when Lisa asked if something had happened that she was not aware of, she was evasive. Betty would change the subject asking after her health and the baby. Lisa told Betty that she was worried about Seven—he just wasn't himself—but all Betty would say is "Just tell him I called." Lisa understood that she would get no help from his mother, probably out of loyalty. She felt weary and didn't know what to do. She waited for him in the living room that evening and it paid off. She had worried that she would fall asleep before he came, but when he stepped into the hall, she greeted him with her "I'm happy to see you" look.

"Seven, I'm glad you're home. I need to talk to you," she said cheerfully.

The look he gave her said, *Not now, not you. I don't need this bullshit.* This wasn't starting out the way that she wanted, but she pushed forward, needing to try. She loved him, and she was trying to reach him. Naively, she thought that if she could just get him to talk about whatever troubled him, he would see that it wasn't so bad, because her love was steadfast and constant. But then she would see his disinterested look and the tension that he obviously felt in her company.

She began by saying, "I miss you and I would like to spend some time with you." When he didn't respond, she continued in a hurry to get it all out. "My cousin invited us over to her house for Thanksgiving, your mother too. I thought we could go and have a good time, and if you want we could swing by to your grandfather's house or whoever is doing the cooking in your family and eat there too. I basically just want to bum food off people." She thought that he would laugh, but he didn't.

"I have plans for Thanksgiving, but you're welcome to go anywhere you want," he said with the intent of dismissing her. He was done with her.

"Can I come with you then?" she then asked, and she hated herself for asking it.

He stared at her for a moment, his heart constricting with love. She was filling out, and he could see that she was heavy with his seed. Her skin glowed with health, and her hair was pulled back from her face in a large barrette that sat lopsided on top of her head. She wore one of his shirts, and on her feet she wore socks that looked like gloves. Just looking at her, he felt like snuggling and watching TV. He could see that her eyes were glassy with unshed tears, and he wanted to stop the hurt for both of them, but he didn't know how. He could see his life running out of control, but he couldn't stop it. The silence stretched out between them, and he knew that she had just opened herself to be hurt by him.

"No, you can't." It was all he could say, anything more would let her know that he was hurting too, and he just didn't want her to know that.

She swallowed, letting the rejection set into her being so that she could embrace it and move on. Why were they living like this? He didn't want her there, and in this last failed attempt to bridge the gap, she no longer wanted to be there either. His answer cut, leaving a wound that would never heal. She suspected this might be melodramatic, but she thought that this rejection, while she carried his child, would shape her future relationships with men. You could only be new at something once, she thought, and however that experience played out would teach a person how to handle it the next time.

She had seen young women pregnant with no men in their lives carrying the brunt of the failed relationship for their friends and family to see. This was the twenty-first century, and having a child out of wedlock was a common occurrence, but there was still shame attached to it—the shame of a young girl or woman bearing the rejection of the child's father. To be rejected by the very person that your child ties you to for eternity makes it difficult for a woman to trust her own judgment from then on.

She was a grown woman who worked, and she could take care of them both. Her family would help her, but she would still have to face her family's reaction, the look in their eyes if not the words from their mouths. *How could you let this happen? How could you be so stupid? Girl, you know he don't love you. He ain't gonna do nothing for you or that baby.* The stares she knew she would get would hurt all the more, because they would make her ask herself why she hadn't asked those questions sooner.

Ultimately, that rejection is sometimes so great that women continue to make the same mistake in order to heal the first rejection, having child after child with men who don't care. But it is insanity to continue doing the same thing while expecting a different outcome. She would leave him, and she would not announce it to him, because she was not trying to wring a reaction out of him. They could not continue on this path; it was unhealthy for both of them, and more importantly she wanted to understand her mistakes so that she would not repeat them. She did not want to be her mother, allowing an unhappy situation to fester until the child paid because she was too weak to make a decision. Turning to him, she said simply, "I understand."

She headed to the bedroom and shut the door—there was really no more to say on any level. He had clearly made some decisions that she wasn't aware of, in regards to their relationship, or lack thereof. She thought about his comment, "This is your room"; she remembered feeling slapped. He had obviously felt that since she was a virgin, he couldn't say that the child wasn't his, so he had let her stay. Maybe he felt stuck with her, but he didn't need to worry about that; she was going to *unstick* them. Looking around the room, she took inventory to see what she would take, and she quickly decided that she would leave with what she had brought here. The things that he gave would stay, as would the ring. Although she hated facing her family, she would need their help to move a few of her things. She would make a new start, even switching doctors. As she made plans, she decided that she would wait until he wasn't home to leave. Leaving while he was away would be less awkward for them both.

His soul bled from every blow that he had dealt her. He wanted to keep her at a distance, yet he did not want her out of his sight. When he glimpsed her coming home from work on the street or when he came into the room to watch her while she slept, he realized that there was some perversion to the pain he caused himself. Why keep her at arm's length when he could have her closeness, her warmth, and her love. The answer was simple: his association with her had not changed the stain on his existence. In fact, their association had changed her life forever; she was now bound to him, and though he pushed her away, he would not let her go.

At night, he felt tormented by the thoughts in his mind, playing Betty's words over and over in his head. Lately he'd been giving his mother and his life as a child a lot of thought, and he realized there were realities he had never contemplated. His mother had taken many men to her bed, yet he had never seen Betty in the company of the opposite sex unless she was conducting business or they were family. Never had he witnessed his mother enjoying life the way a woman of her age should have. He could not remember her ever having a male companion who adored her, or vice versa.

As he examined these facts now, he understood that Betty was still seriously affected by yesterday. This truth made his facing Betty even harder.

When he looked at his mother, he could still see the man standing behind her when he rushed out to save her. It seemed a million years ago and, at the same time, yesterday—the memories were still so fresh. Even though time had passed, his memory continued to play the scenes, and he would have to blink to stop the visual. With the truth out in the open, he couldn't control when the flashbacks came, and often he wanted to vomit from the memory of his mother making a living on her back. He had acted like a coward around his mother because he knew too much about her, things that a son shouldn't know.

As for his father, he had had no other contact with him other than the exchange in his grandfather's house. Clarence had made no attempt to see him, and it was better that way, but what concerned him was his father's obliviousness to the hurt he caused. He spoke to Betty as if it was her fault that they weren't a family. There was also the fact that his mother had conceived him through rape. He would hold his head high, but the pain and embarrassment were so great at times that he felt dirty. Although no one would say, he could hear their thoughts: *Poor Betty, having to bear a child from a man that she hated. How could she love him? It's human nature to rile against the cause of hurt, isn't it?* Seven knew that although others might be thinking such things, so was he, and that hurt even more. He saw them as reasonable thoughts. He tried to move beyond the pain, but the inevitability of his own child made him afraid.

Betty had had enough of waiting for her son to come to her. She tried to respect that he lived with Lisa and that he was making a family of his own, and she didn't want to intrude. But he was leaving her no choice: she was worried about all three of them, and like her mother, she was a grandmother now, and she couldn't let Clarence ruin her family. It was what her mother would expect.

It was what she had done for Seven, and she could do no less. She loved her son, and she didn't want to lose him.

It was a few days before Thanksgiving when she went over to see them. Seven wasn't home. When Lisa opened the door, Betty hugged her for a moment before speaking. She looked tired and had lost weight.

"He's not home," she said, turning and heading for the kitchen. Lisa realized that she was angry with Betty and Seven because of something that had happened that she didn't know about. Then, as fast as she got angry, she calmed herself, remembering all that Betty had been through.

"Maybe it's good that he's not. I need to speak to you."

She evaded Betty's statement because she knew she was about to hear something unpleasant. Instead, she said, "How is Grandpa, and how are you? I know that the last few weeks have been hard on everyone. I wanted her to be here when the baby came. Your mother was a treasure."

Betty smiled at Lisa's concern for her. She loved the girl and wanted Lisa and her son together. "My father is coming along. He's worried about you two. His favorite grandson hasn't been by to see him since my mother died. He's hurt; he misses Seven. Where is he? Did he have a meeting? I thought at this time a day you would be at work and he would be here working on whatever he does in that office of his."

"I took a few days off because I haven't been feeling well." Lisa wondered, did broken hearts count?

"Oh, what did the doctor say?"

"She doesn't seem too concerned, just told me to rest."

"How many months are you? Do you feel the baby moving a lot?" Betty asked.

Lisa found that she wanted to talk with someone that was interested in her well-being. She wanted to talk to someone that cared about the baby too. Seven just didn't give a shit. "In December, I'll be six months and, yes, the baby moves a lot."

Lisa made them some herbal tea and the two women, having gotten past an awkward moment, went to living room and sat down to talk. It was there that Betty broached the subject of how things were going between her and Seven.

"Is everything all right? I haven't heard from him since my mother passed either."

Lisa smiled and was about to lie, but unable to hold in her hurt any longer, she started crying, and Betty was at her side immediately. "No, don't cry. Everything will be all right."

When she could finally talk, she told Betty about how he'd been treating her lately. She told her about how he was never home, how didn't sleep in the same room, how he refused to talk about the baby or go to any doctor appointments. Lisa cried when she told Betty that she didn't think that he loved her and that she thought it would be best if she moved back home. She talked about the way he spoke to her without respect, and how he avoided her at all costs.

It was then that Betty realized that Lisa wasn't wearing her ring, and she became worried. Seven wasn't telling her anything, and the poor girl thought that he didn't love her. For the child's sake, Betty would tell her. Seven was making the same mistake that she had made with him and the rest of her family. She had to help him break the cycle.

"Look at me," Betty said, and when she was sure that she had Lisa's undivided attention, she continued. "Seven's father showed up at my mother's funeral."

Betty described everything that had happened at the funeral, and then she told Lisa about the past. She told her about being raped and about the man who had committed such a crime against her. Betty opened up about the fear that she felt in the beginning of her pregnancy. She told Lisa that one day, after contemplating adoption, she felt the baby move and she knew that she loved the child no matter what. Betty told the whole truth about her life on 104$^{th}$ Street in Corona, and she was shocked to see no judgment in Lisa's eyes.

As Lisa listened, her heart went out to him. She knew that he was facing his demons alone. The story that Betty told reminded her of the time that they had gone to the Japanese restaurant and talked openly about their childhoods. She remembered him predicting that when the truth came out, it would be nothing pretty. The day he came home from the funeral, he seemed different, and she could only imagine the humiliation that he experienced at the sight of his aunt on the arm of his father. Worst of all, the whole family knew of this atrocity, and there was no room for him to deal with the unexpected encounter without an audience.

They talked awhile longer, and Lisa felt better—now she would be able to help him. It was like the sun had started shining again. She would be patient and show him love. If she could just get him to open up, everything would be all right, and they would go back to the way they were. She would get him excited about the baby, and he would see that he was worthy of her love and their child's love.

While they spoke, Seven stepped off the elevator, and his mood was foul from a combination of things. He had had a meeting today with his lawyer. His wife had given birth a week ago, and Larry could hardly focus. All he could talk about was the baby. Seven was jealous and he hated the feeling. It took up a lot of energy, and it made him pissed off with himself and the other person, who had tapped into emotions that he didn't want to acknowledge. He'd also gotten stuck in traffic, and he was tired, because he wasn't sleeping at all due to all the bullshit that danced in his head in the wee hours of the night.

The other issue was Lisa. He had to face her every evening, and things only seemed to get worse for them with every encounter. He stood in front of the door for a moment before finding the strength to put his key in the lock.

Dropping his briefcase, he headed for the bedroom to find her, since she had not met him at the door. Funny that he would expect her to greet him when he came in, only to be shunned by the ice he was shooting. He heard them at the end of the hall, heard his mother's voice, and he wanted to turn and leave, but this was his house; he wouldn't run. Walking into the living room, he said, "Hello, ladies."

The two words were laced with suspicion, and he intended to make Betty and Lisa cringe under his stare. Betty held eye contact with him, refusing to be goaded. She noticed that he looked angry and unsure of himself. He reminded her of when he was a little boy, fighting all the time and getting into trouble. He might not like hearing it, but he was her baby and always would be.

"I called, but you didn't call me back. I had no choice but to come see about you."

"I see you can't take a hint," he said with bite, but Betty didn't flinch.

"Seven," Lisa said, apparently shocked at the way he was talking to his mother, but he had something for her ass, too.

"Did you call my mother over to question her? If you wanted to know something, you should have just fucking asked me."

Lisa was so hot with anger that she couldn't think for a moment. It was one thing for him to be shitty when they were alone, but he wasn't going to be talking upside her head crazy in front of other people. "I'm sorry. Who are you talking to?" It was her attempt at giving him another avenue to travel.

"I already spoke to Betty. I'm talking to you now."

She struggled to her feet and faced him. "I think I have had enough of your shit. You're worried about being like your father, but you're really like mine, a damn bully. I'm leaving. I can't take it anymore." She stomped off, heading for the bedroom to dress.

He didn't respond. He couldn't. His anger was so great that he shook from the intensity of it. They were finally having the fight that he was pushing for, and she had decided that she wouldn't even stay to witness his rage.

When she was out of earshot, Betty looked at him and shook her head, but before she could say anything, he said, "You had no right to tell her anything I didn't want to tell her myself."

"I was trying to help you. You're losing your family. Open your eyes. Can't you see it?"

"Do you even know anything about a relationship that doesn't require the exchange of cash? Don't tell me how to run my life." He was sorry as soon as the words were out, but she had pushed him by butting in where she didn't belong.

Betty was jaded too, and he wasn't ready for her response. "I have been disrespected my whole life to take care of us both. I will not take disrespect from you, but you're correct—I haven't had a relationship with a man where money didn't change hands. I will offer a word of advice to you: if you don't stop traveling down this road of destruction you're on, you're going to end up paying. You're my son, so even though you're acting like an ass, I'll be back in few days to see about you."

She stopped there and smiled at him, and he got the feeling that his mother had just called him a john. She picked up her coat and she left without a backward glance. As he watched her go, he heard some movement coming from the bedroom and he remembered Lisa. Heading back, he pushed open the doors to find her dressed, pacing the room as an overnight bag sat on the bed. Stepping into the room, he stared at her, and he could see that her chest heaving with anger. The look she gave him was one of pure contempt, and he experienced a moment of apprehension.

"Where do you think you're going?" he asked.

Stopping at the window, she responded, "Home."

"This is your home."

"This is not my home, and I'm leaving. I won't marry you. In fact, I never want to see you again. I wanted to try after your mother told me what happened, but then it occurred to me that *you* should have told me. You didn't trust my love, and you never have. This thing we're doing is done. I am no longer afraid to say it—it's over."

Standing in the doorway, he smiled to cover his pain, and when he spoke, he was calm. "The child is mine, too, so I don't have to make you understand that you will see me again."

"Don't threaten me—it won't work—and don't try to manipulate me either."

There was no love in her voice, and he felt it. This was what he was looking for—rejection. He had pushed her away so that when she left it would be under his terms, but now that the moment had come, he feared being alone. It was in him to tell her that she wasn't going anywhere, that it was his child that she carried, but he no longer wanted to push her. Faced with the idea of being without her, he wanted to stop the situation from getting out of control. "I think you should stay here. This is your home. This is my child's home."

"You don't even want this child, or me. Why the interest now? I told you—don't try to manipulate me and I won't try to control you. Actually, I don't care what you do anymore, as long as you're not doing it to me." At that point, she picked up her bag and started for the door, but he stood in her way.

He was about to tell her that she wasn't leaving when the doorbell rang. They stood facing each other, both knowing that the visitor had come to take her away.

"Who's at the door?" he asked.

She pushed past him and headed to the door, opening it to find her cousin Alex. Seven was hot on her trail and stood over her shoulder, mean-mugging him. Lisa took matters into her own hands. "You don't have to come in; just take my bag. I'm ready to go home."

Alex reached for the bag, and Seven shut the door in his face. "Don't do this. You won't like the outcome."

"What are you going to do, beat up my cousin because you don't know how to treat your family? You are such a fucking bully. Maybe you shouldn't beat him up. Just beat me, here and now, and get your anger out."

Seven was appalled at the idea of hitting her, but she was right. Giving Alex a good thrashing would make him feel better. It was petty, he knew, but young Alex needed a lesson in boundaries and not crossing him. Placing his palm flat to the door, he whispered for her ears only, "Send him away and we will talk."

"Seven," she said with a sigh, her eyes filling with tears, "it's too late. I don't want to talk to you. I can't stay with a man who takes it out on me because he can't deal with his life."

She was crying now, making her pain visible to him, and through her tears she said, "I want you to know I'm not leaving you because I'm ashamed of what Betty told me. The only person who should feel shame is your father. Your mother loves you no matter what your father did, and I understand, because I love our child no matter how you have treated me."

She spoke with the honesty that he was used to, staring him in the eye and leaving him no room to deal with what he was feeling uncensored.

"Don't go." It was all that he could manage.

As she stared at him, she could see the old him emerging and she hoped that he would find peace within his life, but it would not be with her. Seeing him change to what he had become resurrected demons for her too. Placing her hand on the hand that rested against the door, she said, "Please. Alex is waiting for me. Don't make me look any more the fool than I already do."

He had her pinned in the corner with his hands on the door and the wall when she placed her hand on his. The contact was excruciating, and he wanted to kiss her, but instead he removed his hand from the door and placed it on her stomach. He looked toward the floor, not in shame but to hide how overcome with emotion he was. Now that he had pushed, and gotten exactly what he *didn't* want, he realized that if he kept her there, he would be doing what his father had done to Betty, taking her right to choose.

He stepped from the door and she walked out without looking in his eyes again. Alex waited at the door, pale from the last exchange, and when she stepped out, he grabbed her bag and directed her to the elevator.

He didn't touch the door, and it slammed on its own. He stood there alone, hating his own company. He heard the elevator door open and close again, and he knew that he had just done what Betty had told him not to do twenty minutes earlier. He had ruined his life and, in the process, his family. Seven had existed alone for so long, but after living with Lisa, the solitary life he had led seemed a million years ago. What would he do now that the best part of him had walked out?

# CHAPTER 20

It was Thanksgiving, and Lisa had not left the bed. The phone rang several times, and she didn't answer. She had gone down to the kitchen, eaten some toast, and gotten right back in bed. At around 1:00, after falling into a deep sleep, she awoke when she heard someone on the stairs. Kim was here—she knew her footsteps anywhere. She didn't have to wait long before her cousin opened her bedroom door.

"Lisa, it's me, Kim. Are you awake?"

"Yeah, I'm awake. What are you doing here? I thought you were having guests."

"I am, but I slipped away to come and get you."

"Alex told you what happened?"

"No, he didn't tell me anything."

"Then how would you know that I was here?"

*Shit*, Kim thought. She had always been a bad liar. "All right, he told me, and I was worried, so I came over. Get dressed so I can get back to my guests."

"Kimmy, I don't feel like it. I just want to stay in bed."

Kim looked alarmed. "Are you sick?"

"Seven and I are not together anymore, and I just feel like dying."

She sat on the bed and hugged her. "Oh, sweetie, everything will be all right. All couples go through hard times."

The damned tears started again, so she shook her head before saying, "This is it. We won't be getting back together. He isn't who I thought he was."

Lisa told Kim everything that had been going on, and to her surprise she felt better. She didn't know what she would do without her cousin's support.

Kim insisted she get dressed and go with her to her house to enjoy Thanksgiving. When she got there, her family was playing cards. As usual, Aunt Ruth and Ms. Hattie were kicking ass and taking names. Alex met her at the door and explained that Kim had twisted his arm and that's why he had told her. He ended up being Lisa's partner and even though they lost, it was the best time that she had had in a long time.

Seven had been drunk since she left, and he hadn't gone near the master suite. She hadn't really taken anything, and her belongings were still where she had left them. He wandered into the bedroom closest to the room they shared, and he found that she had been planning to turn this room into a nursery. The weight of everything that he lost came crashing down on him, and he felt suffocated by his own hand. The phone rang, and several times he thought he heard the doorbell, but he didn't answer. He didn't want to speak to anyone.

He cried and was disgusted to find that it was hard to stop once he got started. Yet when he stopped, he felt better. Now, instead of the old demons, he was fighting new demons. He cringed when he thought about what he had said to his mother, but Betty had taken it in stride, warning him to get it together. He hadn't listened. Betty may not have known it, but she was his hero—she had been his father as well as his mother. Although he knew that his mother was just a call away, he couldn't bring himself to call on her.

On Thanksgiving, after days of not answering the phone and ignoring the doorbell, he heard the bell ring again. This time, the person was persistent. He had fallen asleep on the side of the bed, and it took a moment to get himself together. After staggering to the door, he opened it to find his mother and grandfather standing there.

"You stink," his mother said, and his grandfather laughed.

"What are you two doing here?" he said, annoyed.

"We came because we were worried about you. Where is Lisa?" Betty asked, putting him on the spot.

His grandfather hobbled into the living room and sat down. "She left you, didn't she? You don't have to say, because that's how I looked when your grandmother left me. I'll bet you were acting like an ass."

Betty laughed, and Seven wanted to throw them both out. "How you feeling, Pop?" he asked, changing the subject.

"If you cared about how I was doing, you would have come to see about me."

"We're going to your Aunt Brenda's house for dinner and we want you to come. I'm helping with the cooking," Betty said.

"Betty, you know that you can't cook," his grandfather, said and Seven had to laugh. Just when he was about to tell his mother that he didn't feel up to company, his grandfather said, "I don't want to go either. I'll stay here and take care of Seven. The man needs a bath and a shave."

Betty didn't even attempt to try to persuade them to come. "All right," she said. "Seven, will you bring him home when he's ready to go?"

"I'll look after him."

Betty kissed them both and left. Afterward, Seven felt awkward, because he didn't feel like talking. He exhaled loudly, thinking his mother was nosey and just wouldn't butt out. Turning to his grandfather, he said, "What do you want to do, watch a little TV?"

"First go take a shower and get refreshed so we can talk."

Giving his grandfather a curt nod, he headed for his bedroom to get himself together. It was his first time being in the room since Lisa had left him. Pushing his feelings down inside him, he showered, shaved, and changed clothes. When he returned to his grandfather, he found him with the terrace door open, standing there in his coat staring at the skyline.

"You did well for yourself in the finance department. What about your child and your woman?"

There was the million-dollar question. What was he going to do about Lisa and the baby? He decided that since Pop had come all this way, he would give him the truth. "I messed things up and I don't know what to do."

Walter stared at his grandson, and he was reminded of the time that Bobbi left him when she had caught him fooling around with a woman closer to his age. He thought the age difference was too great between them, and Bobbi had left him, having had enough of his nonsense. They were apart for about two months, and it had been the worst time of his life—until now.

"You have to let go of the hurt about your father and mother—that's the best place to start. You can't change the past, and it's not your past to change."

"You don't understand," Seven said walking to the terrace door, which was now closed, and looking out the glass.

"How could I not understand? Your mother is my daughter. You think that I didn't torment myself about taking better care of my children. I didn't even know that she was pregnant until your grandmother's sister called and complained about how your mother was trying to take her husband. I worried about your mother and you for years. I was thankful when she was found, and you too. Make no mistake, I was a younger man then. I kicked your father's ass, but it didn't stop the hurt I felt. As for you, you're my favorite grandchild, like your mother is my favorite child. I love you. Don't let this stop you from living your life or he wins all over again."

What could he say in the face of such wisdom? His pain was physical, and he never understood that emotional and mental pain could hurt so badly. What was he going to do about the baby and Lisa? He needed them. That became clear when she left. Was it too late? He wasn't sure, and he turned to his grandfather, but before he could get the words out, his grandfather said, "It's not too late."

Seven's knees almost buckled with relief as the answer to his question came from his grandfather's mouth.

"I'll go and talk to her," Seven said.

"She doesn't want to see you now."

Frustrated, Seven looked at his grandfather and said, "Are you confusing me on purpose?"

Walter smiled now that he knew his grandson was alive and still in the game. "I'm not trying to confuse you at all, but if you go rushing over there, you will only further alienate her. You are a brute. I used to be just like you."

Seven laughed, and it felt good; he hadn't done that in a while. His grandfather was his partner and he was sorry that they were at different stages in life; he wanted Pop around for as long as he could keep him. Friends like him came only once in a lifetime. "What do I do?"

Pop stood and began pacing. Seven noticed for the first time that his grandfather was in a neatly pressed shirt and black pants with his cane in hand. His pacing was slow going, but his thoughts were coming fast. "When is the baby due?" he asked.

"March 20 is the due date."

"It's almost December. You have time to see Lisa and make things right." He paused a moment, as if giving serious thought to what he was about to say. "You may feel a little better now, but you have to find yourself and face your fears. I know that you have had a lot happen to you over the last months—meeting your family, your grandmother dying, facing your father and hearing truths that could break a man down. Son, you have to start with you before you can navigate a family."

"I want her and the child home with me."

"Yeah, I know that you want them back, but you don't even want to be in your own company. Take a moment to get to know you, and you'll find that the basics of who you are won't change. Seven, you will find pieces of yourself that you haven't even tapped into yet. Life comes in stages, and when you get to the point that you no longer know yourself, then it's time to take a moment to reintroduce yourself to the one person that should care about knowing you, and that's you."

He wanted to say that he had no fears or weaknesses, but he decided not to lie. "For a long time, it was just me and Betty. As a kid, I worried that if something happened to her, I would have no one. I used to dream that my father would save us. Sometimes all you have is your dreams."

"I know," his grandfather said.

"We lived hard, often with no money. I used to think that when I grew up and made money, I would have no problems. As an adult, I see now how unrealistic that was. I blamed Betty for our living situation when *he* was the one who put us where we were. I feel like I fell into a deep hole and I can't climb out, but I can see people walking by looking down at me. It seems that no matter how much I try to climb out, I can't get a good foothold. The dirt just loosens every time I think I've found a secure spot."

"I've been there in my life—many times—but the truth is when you hit those patches in your life and you're serious about making a change, you grow strong from the experience."

"Guess you're right," Seven responded.

"When it's time to see Lisa, you need to show interest in your child so she can see that you're ready. She's going to be a good mother, and she's not interested in a half-assed father for her child. Your mother told me about what happened to Lisa when she was a child. You both had it hard, but it's time to break the cycle."

They talked for hours about the shit that men deal with, and Seven felt he was better for the experience. His grandfather told him about when his grandmother left him and all that he went through to get her back. He told him about the soul searching he did to deal with his own insecurities so that his family could be whole again. Walter told his grandson that all his insecurities hadn't just vanished because of some soul searching.

"You have to decide what reality is and what idealism is. The key to life is bringing reality and your perception of it into the same arena to compare. You will come up short, but you will be the better for it. To put it simply, the enlightenment of one's self can make for a better understanding of reality."

Seven and his grandfather shared a bottle of vodka while they bonded. Seven told him that he feared he would lose Lisa and the baby for good, and he didn't think that he could handle that. He admitted that he wanted to drag her home and tell her to stop it, that he couldn't take anymore. Pop laughed, saying that he remember feeling like that.

"I almost beat the shit out of her cousin just to relieve some stress," Seven confessed.

"I'm glad that you didn't do it. Women hold that kind of shit against you forever."

Seven smiled. "Who did you beat up?"

"Your grandmother's brother, for trying to tell her in front of me that she shouldn't marry me. I heard about that for twenty years."

Seven laughed his ass off, and it occurred to him that he was like his grandfather, and he felt proud of this.

Pop spent the night, and when Betty came in the morning, they were asleep in the living room, both smelling like liquor.

"Daddy, I brought you to straighten him out, and look at you." Turning to Seven, she said, "I thought you were bringing him home last night. Brenda called me to tell that Daddy was missing."

"I'm your father and I'm a grown man. I can stay the night with Seven if I want to."

Betty turned and looked at her father. She decided to shut him up. "I'm telling Brenda that you've been drinking."

His grandfather opened his mouth to say something, but his fear of Brenda stopped him, and Seven fell off the couch laughing. "You ain't nothing but a turncoat," his grandfather accused.

Betty made some coffee while the men got it together. When they sat at the table, they talked about his grandmother, and it felt good to be in the company of others who understood his loss. They told funny stories about her and how pushy she was. Seven talked about the day she showed up at his house. His mother and grandfather laughed. "That sounds like her," they said.

They left shortly after with Seven promising to start his routine of seeing his grandfather regularly again. At the door, just as Betty was leaving, she said, "I'll be stopping by to see Lisa. I know that you two are going through hard times, but she is carrying my grandchild. I have to remain neutral. I won't be deprived of my grandchild for anyone."

Seven nodded, saying nothing, and she hugged him. As he watched her walk away, he thought that his mother was a cut above most women.

# CHAPTER 21

As the days passed, Lisa was finding it harder and harder get to work. She was tired, plain and simple, and she couldn't understand how most women worked up until the day before delivery. The hotel was offering just six weeks of paid maternity, and she knew that she would have to dig into the money that her grandmother had left. She would wait until January to go on leave, but she would be fair and tell Elise now what her plans were.

When she tried to switch doctors, Dr. Kembro's nurse wanted to know why to determine if they had done anything wrong. She informed the nurse that it was a matter of convenience. The nurse told her that Dr. Kembro had an office in Queens, near Jamaica Hospital. Lisa then decided that she would keep the doctor and switch locations. She felt some relief sticking with the same doctor, and she made an appointment.

Betty had Lisa's cell phone number written in her book, and when she finally got up the nerve, she called. As always, Lisa was warm and receptive to her, and she was happy that she wouldn't be deprived of her grandchild. Betty asked after her health and the baby's. She also volunteered to go to her next appointment with her. Lisa thought that would be great, and Betty was elated to be included.

On the day of the appointment, Lisa took the day off work, and she and Kim waited for Betty. After Betty arrived in a cab, all three of them would then go to over to the doctor's office. When Betty pulled up, Lisa and Kim were just stepping outside. It was a cold and cloudy December day, the kind that makes you want to stay in the bed. Lisa had filled out a little more, and she was beautiful, her face and hair shining with health. Betty stepped out of the car and hugged her, and they both cried.

"I still love him," she said.

"I know you do, and believe it or not, he still loves you."

"I told her that," Kim said.

The doctor's appointment went well, and the doctor let Betty and Kim listen to the baby's heartbeat. Betty cried, and so did Kim, and Lisa realized that although she loved them, she wanted Seven. He was the baby's father, and should have been there. She had to admit that even in a crowded room she felt alone without him. She kept her feelings to herself, though, because whenever she thought that she would bend, she would remember her father and how Seven had changed. It was enough to deter her from pursuing him. She wanted her baby to be happy.

It was the second week of December, and he had thrown himself into his work. He made a trip to upstate New York to see some of the new homes that were being built. His interest was in rental properties that would generate a monthly cash flow and give him the flexibility to venture elsewhere. Nothing caught his eye, so he headed back home empty handed. It just wasn't what he was looking for.

Betty called while he was on his way back to tell him that she had heard the baby's heartbeat. She said that Lisa was doing fine. He was also informed that she had changed locations for her doctor's visits and was now seeing the doctor in Queens. Betty was excited about the baby and how well things were going, and it showed. She also told him that Lisa's next appointment was on the sixth of January. He listened but made no comments, thankful to hear something about them. Before she hung up, she let him know that his grandfather was doing well and that he wanted to see him.

It was twilight as he rode home. He was lonely, and it was by his own doing. He missed her and being part of her pregnancy. He could see that his grandfather was right—soul searching was no easy task. Taking a hard look at himself, he had to admit that work was all he had had before her. He had side-stepped serious relationships because he hadn't thought that he had anything to offer. The most disturbing revelation was that he got rid of any woman who treated him like a prize catch. *Her decision-making process must be off if she was choosing him*, he thought.

His parents were another issue, and in truth, he still hated that his mother had been a prostitute. However, he had learned that he didn't have to like it.

For both him and Betty it had been demeaning, but they had risen above it, only to find that it was still in the background. He wanted happiness for his mother, and he wanted her to understand that companionship could be good. The hardest part of the lesson was coming to terms with the fact that he couldn't live Betty's life for her. He wanted someone to love Betty; she deserved that. Until he had tasted love with Lisa, it never occurred to him that his mother was lonely.

As for his father there was no love lost. He had looked his father in the eyes and he had felt nothing, unlike when Betty looked at him. The realization hurt—he was nothing to the man who fathered him, and vise versa. It said a great deal about his father that he could stand in the same room with his son and not speak, but he could chase his mother to the back of the house for ass. The fact that his father's wife was his great aunt wasn't lost on him either. After all the pain that he had caused Betty, he spoke to her as if she had missed out on a great life with him. His reality was no longer skewed in that department—he wanted a father, and Clarence wasn't it.

Finally, he did a lot of thinking about his unborn child, and he realized that he couldn't wait to see his child. He wanted fatherhood, and he felt excitement when he thought about it. The decorator he commissioned had given him a good price, and he had ordered furniture for the nursery. He wanted Lisa to see it and be proud of him; he found that he wanted her approval when it came to the baby. He could see clearly now, and he knew that he would be there for the birth of his child. It was his place, and his right.

He wanted to marry her. He knew that he would have to work hard to regain her trust. She needed to see that he could control his temper. His mind thought back to the day when he was in the hall and heard her screaming from the beating her father was giving her. He remembered thinking that he must have killed her, and though he tried to stop it, the memory persisted, and he saw her with a sling on her arm and a black eye. She needed to feel safe with him and he needed her to feel safe with him—it was just a part of the male/female interaction.

As he rode home through the countryside of New York, the sun was dipping behind the hills. The setting was beautiful and relaxing, motivating him to think. There were fields as far as he could see, and they were dotted with livestock. He thought about the hustle and bustle of the city, and how different it was here.

And that's when he saw it—a small white church with a bell tower, nondescript by itself but with scenery that made it magical. He knew that he would marry her here. Turning his truck on the dirt road, he headed for the church.

His birthday was December 20, and he decided to go shopping for her and the baby. He also did some Christmas shopping for his mother and his grandfather. For aunts Evelyn, Patricia, and Brenda, he bought perfume and gift cards to Macy's, and for his uncles he bought season tickets for the Yankees. In the spirit of the holiday, he bought Kim, Aunt Ruth, and Ms. Hattie a day at a spa, and he laughed at his attempt to scandalize Aunt Ruth. On the evening of his birthday, he went out with Gary and Sean to have drinks and watch a fight. They didn't ask what was going on with Lisa, and he didn't tell them.

Lisa was approaching seven months and was glad for the few holidays she had so she could rest. Kim wanted her to come to her house on Christmas Eve, but Lisa assured her that she really didn't want to come. She told Kim that she would see her on Christmas Day. She didn't bother with a tree, and she had decided to go to bed early so she would be ready for the next day. If she knew her cousin, Kim would be over to get her if she didn't show at a reasonable time. Taking the stairs slowly, she headed to her bedroom to watch TV until she fell asleep, but when she got to the top of the stairs, her doorbell rang.

She trekked back down the stairs just as slowly as she went up and headed for the door. It had to be Kim, she thought, who would be worried about her and refuse to take no for an answer. At the bottom of the stairs, it occurred to her that Kim had her own key, but she dismissed the thought, reasoning that she must have forgotten it. Opening the door, she said, "Kim, I'm not coming over. I'm going to bed."

The words died on her lips as she came face to face with Seven. He stood in the doorway dressed in a black leather bomber, jeans, and timberland boots that matched his coat. On his head, he wore a black skullcap, which made him look rough. Looking him in the eye, Lisa pushed down her feelings and asked, "What are you doing here?"

"I bought some gifts for you and the baby," he said, his voice laced with deep emotion.

They continued to stand in the doorway staring at each other. Lisa was overwhelmed by his presence and looked away. She couldn't invite him in, and she wasn't dressed to step out. What should she say? He was the child's father, and it was just stupid to think that he wouldn't bring anything for his own child for Christmas. It was a stalemate, as they stood saying nothing. For Lisa, the burden was on him—after all, he had come to her house. Building some resistance against him, she remained quiet, and although she was moved by the situation, the silence allowed her to project a sense of aloofness that she wasn't feeling.

"Can I come in?" he asked, even though he was clear on what her answer would be.

"Bring the packages for the baby and I'll put them under the tree." She took a deep breath, as if getting up the nerve, and said, "No, you can't come in."

He could see that she was starting to shiver from the cold. "I just want to talk to you. You can't deny that we have things we need to discuss."

He could see that she was in conflict with herself on whether she should let him in or not. Turmoil showed in her eyes, and he felt ashamed that he could put her in the position to have to contemplate letting him in. She was about to deny him again, when he cut her off. "Please, baby, don't turn me away."

He could see from the streetlight that her eyes were glistening with tears, but she didn't respond. She stepped back, opening the door to let him in, and he felt relief, having thought that she was going to close the door in his face. He followed her through the porch into the living room, and she stopped at the door. It was apparent that he was getting no farther. She didn't even bother to ask him to sit, but he decided that he would take what he could get for now.

There were no Christmas decorations at all around the living room, and when he studied her face she looked a little tired. He couldn't stop staring at her; she was radiant. She wore a robe, and at the top, where it opened a little, he could see the lace of her nightgown. On her feet, she wore mismatched socks. The roundness of her belly was prevalent, and he could see that she was nearing the end of her pregnancy. Her body had changed so much in the time that he had seen her last that he felt regret. Her hair hung around her shoulders, and he could see that it had grown.

He wanted to touch her, but he was afraid that she would pull away, and he didn't think that he could handle that. He was desperate to place his hand on her stomach and feel the life they had created together from love. "Can I touch your belly?" he asked, but before she could respond, he had leaned down and placed his large hands on her.

She tensed at his touch and asked again, "What do you want?" As she spoke, the baby kicked, and the tears that she had been holding back burst forward. "What do you want, damn you?" she said, stepping back out of his reach.

"I want to give you my love and have yours in return," he said, and to her surprise, he sounded close to tears. "I'm lonely, Lisa."

Shaking her head she said, "I'm afraid..."

"I know, and that's my fault. Sometimes you can get so hung up in your own problems that you don't see that other people have problems too. I felt dirty in your company when I found out what my father did to my mother. I couldn't shake the feeling of unworthiness, and I needed to feel worthy of you and the baby. I didn't handle things well, and I let my anger get in the way, but I would never hit you. I'm opening up, baby, and it's not easy. I need you."

It was unfair that the love she had for him responded to his words, leaving her weak in her resolve to stay away. To gain strength, she turned and awkwardly started running toward the kitchen. When she heard him behind her, she tried to open the back door, but he caught her. "No!" she yelled and roughly tried to get away from him.

He pinned her against the door and leaned in, pressing himself against her, feeling his child move between them. Touching her face with his hands, he whispered, "I'm begging you, Lisa. I'm begging you."

She stopped struggling against him and looked him in the eye. "I still love you, but I don't want to." She cried, releasing the pain caused by doubt and fear.

He held her, kissing her face all over while repeating just above a whisper, "I'm begging you, baby. I am begging you, don't turn me away."

She turned her face up to his and he kissed her lips, tasting her. He looked thin in the face, as if he hadn't been eating. "What are we going to do now?"

They left the kitchen holding hands, and when they got to the steps leading up to her room, he stopped, unsure of himself. He was giving her the right to choose him again. Taking him by the hand, she led him up to her room, where they both removed their clothing. She stood before him wearing nothing but motherhood, and he was moved. As he looked at her body, he felt honored that she would give him a child. She was radiant as she stood for him to see all of her, her nipples a deep chocolate and larger now with the advancement of her pregnancy, her belly also larger and the skin smooth and tight. The only lighting in the room was a slice of light from the hallway where the door was slightly opened.

As he stood before her naked, she could see that he had lost weight, and she knew it was from the stress of their situation along with other issues. The weight loss wasn't significant, but she noticed because she loved him. She stepped forward to touch him, but he grabbed her hand to stop her, and instead he bent down on his knees in front of her, placing his lips to her belly. She held him close to her, and he leaned his forehead to her belly and spoke. "I'm whole with you, baby."

As a man, he had cried in his life but always alone, viewing it as a sign of weakness even in his own company. It was ironic that at his weakest moment, he felt his strongest, and there on his knees, while she held him, he cried. The strength within her called to him, telling him that she was there for him. He heard her murmuring words of comfort to his soul, as he felt the burden of yesterday lift from his shoulders. This intimacy was the binding of man, woman, and child.

Rising to his feet, he led her to the bed. They made love slow and easy with him entering her from behind. He was careful with her, giving her enough of himself to achieve oneness but not enough to hurt her. It was not a sexual encounter but the coming together of two halves to make a whole. Seven stroked her, but she was so tight that the friction was unbearable, and because of that, coupled with the fact that he missed her, it ended sooner than he would have wanted it to. Their climax was so intense that it produced a burst of white light that bled over into hues of red, orange, and purple.

They lay in the afterglow of their lovemaking, with him spooning her, and she could hear his harsh breathing slowing and returning to normal. Thinking that he was falling asleep, she started to doze. It was then that she heard him say, "Will you marry me?"

There was nothing to think about. She knew that she couldn't live without him.

"Yes."

He kissed the back of her neck but made no comment about her answer. They would marry before their child was born. He was content and said nothing more. Snuggling warmly against her, he felt her relax and he knew that she was falling asleep. He wanted to be a man that Lisa and his child could depend on for more than just financial support. Clarence popped into his mind, and he considered his eyes when they saw each other for the first time. His father's eyes were empty, indicating a lack of appreciation for what was important in life. They lacked the understanding of what it took to be a man.

When he looked at Lisa in total womanhood, he was moved, and it was then that he knew he was not his father's son. His child would not know the heartache of being a stranger to him. Lisa, unlike his mother, would know the meaning of being cherished, for sharing her body, for bearing his child, and for being his woman. He would see to it. He learned a tough lesson about love: when you truly love someone, it hurts you when you hurt them.

As for his mother, her interest in his child made him understand her love for him, and for the first time in his life, he saw himself as his mother's son. He identified with her and her family, and he was adding to the history of it as well. Betty had not held against him the cards she had been dealt, and he wanted to experience that kind of parenting with his child. He thought about her telling him that she wanted him, and he felt no more doubt about his relationship with his mother. Smiling, he thought this child would have a good grandmother, just as he had a good mother. It was his last thought before he fell into a dreamless sleep, holding Lisa close to his heart.

At 5:00 on Christmas morning, she woke with a start, thinking that she had dreamed being with Seven the previous night. When she felt his warm body against her, she knew that she had not dreamed it—he was here with her. She lay there not moving, thinking about him and their child. There were no regrets about taking him back, and like him, she felt whole again. Her heart belonged to him, and she knew that it would never belong to another.

Nature called and she could wait no longer. She climbed out of the bed and headed for the bathroom. When she came back, he was sitting up in the bed waiting for her.

"Merry Christmas," he said.

"Merry Christmas to you," she replied.

"Come."

Taking off her robe, she climbed back into the warmth of his arms, and once she was settled, he said, "I bought some things for you and the baby. They're in the backseat. I'll go get them."

When he was about to get up she said, "Not yet."

Sitting back in the bed, he looked at her before saying, "You want to talk?"

She shook her head. "We have to."

"I'm ready," he said, staring into her eyes, showing his honesty and his true self. "Lisa, I'm ready."

"I'm lost when you say my name. For that reason alone, I need to make sure that this is right. I love you, Seven, but I need to know that you will trust me. I need to know that you will not think my love shallow when you're in trouble. Will you allow me to be there for you? Will you accept my love?"

He wanted her to feel confidence in him, so he didn't hesitate when he answered. "It was never you that I didn't trust—it was me—and, yes, I will accept your love. I know that I don't deserve it, but trust me, and know that I will never lift my hand to hurt you or our child."

She read the truth in his eyes and she knew that everything was going to be all right. Leaning up, she kissed him, and they held each other for a time before she said, "You lost weight. Are you all right?"

"I'm fine, baby. Mary always goes away from Thanksgiving until after New Year's, and I have to fend for myself. This year, I thought you would take care of me, and when you left, I stopped eating."

She looked so serious that he stopped teasing and whispered to her, "I was sick without you, and that's the truth."

"I didn't get you anything for Christmas."

"Yes, you did. You agreed to be my wife. Stay where you are. I'll be right back."

He didn't have to talk her into staying in the bed; it was cold, and all she wanted to do these days was sleep and snuggle and watch a good show. Seven threw on his clothes and ran outside. It was a few moments before she could hear him struggling up the steps with some packages. Kicking the door open, he walked back into her room, dumping everything on the bed. He smiled at her and handed her the first gift. Watching her tear the wrapping paper off, he got excited too.

It was a car seat, and she was happy. Some green and yellow baby outfits came next. (He would buy pink or blue later). A stroller was in the next box, and there was also a tub and bassinet. She just stared at all he had bought, thinking he was wonderful. He stood and left the room for a second and came back with his coat. Reaching into his pocket, he handed her two boxes. She opened the first box, and she cried when she saw that it was her ring.

He took it from the box for her, removing the ring from the velvet bed and placing it back on her finger, where it belonged. He pulled her up to stand on the bed and she placed her arms around his neck. She kissed him, biting and suckling his bottom lip.

"Open the second box," he said anxiously.

Doing as he asked, she opened the box, and keys fell out on the bed. She stared at them for a moment before it registered, and she jumped down and ran to the window. "It's the champagne-colored Acura Legend sedan. Get dressed. Let's check it out."

Turning, she looked at him speechless for a moment. "I want you to be able to get around easier when the baby gets here. Say that you're happy. I also want to spoil you. I miss you."

"I'm happy about the car. I love you."

They went down to check it out, and Lisa, at 7:00 A.M., started the alarm and couldn't figure out how to stop it. Seven thought it was funny. Thinking back on his life, he couldn't remember a better Christmas. They drove around in her new car for a while and came back to the house to eat and shower. They made love again, and he knew that if she weren't pregnant already, she would be now. The couple didn't leave the bed other than for the mother to tinkle. Seven, having been restless for weeks, fell into a deep sleep. Lisa called Kim to tell her that Seven was there and that they needed time to work things out. After her call to Kim, they closed the world out and enjoyed each other.

# CHAPTER 22

Lisa stood in the back room of the small church with Kim fussing over her, and finally, when she deemed that Lisa was ready to face the mirror, she said, "Oh, Lisa, look at you."

She turned slowly to look in the mirror, and she was taken aback by the image before her. In her eyes she saw contentment and the glow of love. Seven had insisted that she wear white regardless of her advanced pregnancy. Kim had helped her search high and low until they stumbled onto the perfect dress. It was off the shoulders, accentuating her now very full breasts, but tastefully so. The dress flared out around her, not to conceal her condition but to enhance the beauty of motherhood.

There was a knock on the door and Kim stepped up behind her, saying, "Sweetie, it's time."

There was nothing to say, so she just nodded her acknowledgement. Then Kim stepped up behind her and pushed the veil down over her face. "You're gorgeous, and I'm happy for my little cousin."

"I love you, Kim," Lisa said, and they hugged. "Don't make me cry and ruin my eyes."

"I won't," Kim said but she was crying.

The knock came again and Kim opened the door and held it for Lisa. They walked through the corridor until they came upon a set of double doors.

"It's time; everyone is waiting for you," Kim said.

The two women stood in the vestibule awaiting the commencement of the ceremony. Kim was the first person in line, and the bride was at the back. The double doors were pulled open by two ushers, and the organist started playing the bridal march. Kim stepped into the sanctuary first and then, on a count of ten, Lisa followed. The altar boys fell into step behind her, picking up her train.

As Lisa stepped in line behind Kim, she took in the scenery. The church was small and quaint, a romantic setting. When Seven had taken her for a drive and they ended up here, she was shocked that he had put so much thought into this day. The parson was an old man of African descent who had been with the church for more than twenty years. He welcomed them, and it was agreed that they would marry here on January 20, 2001. When Lisa looked into his eyes, she saw no judgment with regard to her condition, and that made the decision for them to marry here easy.

The late afternoon, sun danced through the stained-glass windows, adding beauty to the meticulously polished wood in the church. On the left side of the aisle sat Lisa's family, with Aunt Ruth in the front seat wiping tears from her eyes. On the right side of the church sat Seven's family, with his grandfather grinning proudly from ear to ear. Kim had taken her place and was now standing facing the families and watching the bride approach. She was dressed in a beautiful lavender dress that brought out her dark brown hair and her radiant complexion.

Finally, when she couldn't avoid looking at him any longer, she focused on her reason for being there, Seven. He stood tall with his hands behind his back, wearing a black tux and a white shirt with a white flower in his lapel. Seven was a picture of masculinity, and Lisa felt privileged that he was her man. He appeared calm and sure of himself, exuding confidence in her and their love, and she was comforted. Next to him stood his best man, Betty, and she, like Seven, was dressed in a black tux (with a skirt instead of pants) and a white shirt with a flower in her lapel.

As she approached the front of the church and her husband to be, her uncle William stood and gave her away, as was tradition. Seven, anxious to make her his, reached for her hand, bringing her to stand next to him. Instead of turning to face the parson, he stared at her in awe, struck by her gracefulness, her beauty, and his love for her. He didn't release her hand, as he should have, but held it to maintain a physical connection with her and his child. She smiled at him through the veil, and he was ready. Turning, they faced the parson and the beginning of a new life.

The ceremony happened in a blur as they exchanged vows. They were not words of eloquence but simple clumsy words spoken from the heart. Betty stepped forward with the rings, the final declarations were made, and they were pronounced husband and wife. Facing Lisa, Seven removed her veil and kissed her thoroughly, causing both families, which had become one, to cheer. Turning, they ran down the aisle while their families threw rose petals at them. They climbed into an awaiting limo and sped off in pursuit of the rest of their lives.

# *Epilogue*

They had not gone on a honeymoon because Lisa was too far along for Seven to feel safe taking her out of the country. After the wedding, they traveled back to Betty's house for a family celebration. It was decided that the reception would take place at Betty's house so that when her father got tired he could retire to one of the bedrooms and still be in the bosom of his family. Seven and Lisa, along with their family and friends, partied into the wee hours.

As Lisa neared her due date, Seven stayed close to home, conducting all his meetings by phone. He pushed her to take leave from work and encouraged her to quit when she told him that she wanted to stay home for a while with the baby. The nursery was finished before New Year's Day in anticipation of the new arrival. The only thing left to do was to wait for their baby and enjoy each other's company until it was time.

At night, they slept naked, and although they were not having sex, they were enjoying the feel of each other. On the morning of March 20, 2001, at 3 A.M., Lisa got out of bed and headed to the bathroom. As she approached the door, she bent over clutching her stomach. Seven was at her side immediately.

"Baby, are you all right?" he asked, and she could see that he was racked with fear.

"This is it. I think I'm ready to go."

He rushed around getting her belongings, which had been laid out in preparation for this moment. She had insisted on staying at his house, which was farther from the hospital, and he was worried. He helped her dress then dressed himself. She instructed him to call the doctor and then Betty, which he did. They left the condo and waited for the elevator. On the ride down, he told that her that he would get the car. She was to stay put.

As they rode to Jamaica Hospital, he checked regularly on her condition. Once at the hospital, she was admitted into a private room. What he saw from that point on scared the hell out of him. He was her coach, but when her pain grew, so did his guilt at having gotten her pregnant. Trying to help, he asked if they could give her something for the pain, but he was informed that they couldn't because the baby's head was in the canal. Lifting the sheet, the doctor showed him the top of the baby's head and explained that this was called "crowning." "Giving her medicine now could cause her and the baby to sleep," he explained.

Lisa screamed his name and he was back at her side, but unable to stay focused. Every time the minute hand went around twice, she would start screaming. He felt helpless, and when she grabbed his hand to bear down, he thought she broke his fingers.

Looking down in between her legs, he saw that the baby's head was out. The room started to recede as he concentrated on what he was seeing. Lisa pushed again and the shoulders were out. From there, the rest of the body came out quickly. He didn't know what he was expecting, but it wasn't what he had just seen.

As the sound came back to his picture he was handed his child, and he could hear the doctor saying, "It's a girl."

When his daughter was handed to him, his love for her was so great that he felt it physically. She was beautiful, with a head full of curly black hair. Her skin was dark, like his, but her facial features were like Lisa's. They had come together, mixing the best parts of themselves to create this wonderful gift from God. He thought of what his mother had said and now he understood, because his daughter was his one perfection.

After the baby and Lisa were cleaned up, Seven just sat and watched them, feeling yet another layer of intimacy unfold. His heart burst with love for Lisa and his child, and when Lisa smiled at him after all that she had been through, he felt a deep devotion to her and their family.

In his few short months with Lisa, he had experienced an introduction to love and self that would be with him for the rest of his life.

Angel Thomas was born on March 20, 2001
Weight 7 pounds, 7 ounces
Time 7:00 AM

978-0-595-39338-1
0-595-39338-1

Printed in the United States
64790LVS00010B/157-168

9 780595 393381